EAGLE FALLS

A HOWARD MOON DEER MYSTERY

Books by Robert Westbrook

Howard Moon Deer Mysteries
Ghost Dancer
Warrior Circle
Red Moon
Ancient Enemy
Turquoise Lady
Blue Moon
Hungry Ghost
Walking Rain
Eagle Falls

Coming Soon!
Yellow Moon
A Howard Moon Deer Mystery

The Torch Singer *series*
An Overnight Sensation
An Almost Perfect Ending

Left-Handed Policeman *series*
The Left-Handed Policeman
Nostalgia Kills
Lady Left

Other Books
Intimate Lies:
F. Scott Fitzgerald and Sheilah Graham – Her Son's Story
Journey Behind the Iron Curtain
The Magic Garden of Stanley Sweetheart
Rich Kids

EAGLE FALLS

A HOWARD MOON DEER MYSTERY

Robert Westbrook

SPEAKING VOLUMES, LLC
NAPLES, FLORIDA
2023

Eagle Falls

ISBN 978-1-64540-957-1

For my grandchildren:

Marlon, Wilder, Mays and Quinn in the U.S.
Zarin, Kade, and Taya in South Africa

Chapter One

Zia McFadden, seventeen years old, stood on the edge of a high cliff above Eagle Falls fighting an overwhelming urge to jump. The temptation terrified her, yet it was the most seductive call she had ever known.

The ledge was barely three feet wide. From here, inches away, the cliff plunged straight down for five hundred feet to the deep pool below. The sound of the water crashing over the rocks was overwhelming, making it hard to think. Zia was pretty, she was smart, she appeared to be the perfect girl. But her life was troubled.

It was an August day, midweek, and rain was threatening. The sky alternated with blue skies and dark clouds that rushed past the sun. Eagle Falls was in a narrow box canyon in a remote part of the National Forest nearly an hour east of the closest town. Locals knew about the falls but you had to be hardy to reach it. The trail was six miles round trip and had rough stretches that were barely wide enough for a goat. This kept out the casual tourists. Today there was no one else around.

Standing at the top of the waterfall, amid the mountains and valleys of northern New Mexico, Zia McFadden peered over the edge of her known world into the void and felt the lure of death. She dared herself to look down. It amazed her that all she needed to do was walk forward a single step—one step!—and she would tumble hundreds of feet onto the rocks below. Her life would be over. It would be the end of all problems, all pain, all struggles. She would be free.

How simple that would be!

The wind blew hard, the rushing water chilled the air. Zia's life stood balanced like a boulder that could roll either way. It was such a big thing, really: your life. Yet it was nothing. It could be over, just like that. One small step . . .

She felt a shadow in the sky and looked up.

There was a large bird flying over the canyon. A hawk, she thought. Definitely a bird of prey. The bird glided on the thermal currents without moving its wings. As it circled closer, Zia could see its white body and brown wings.

It wasn't a hawk. It was an eagle.

An eagle at Eagle Falls!

Shading her eyes with the palm of her hand, she followed the eagle as it flew off into the mountainous distance. At the last moment, it appeared to tip its wings at her, a salute from his world to hers.

Zia threw back her head and laughed for no reason except she suddenly felt wonderfully alive.

"Oh beautiful eagle!" she called. "Fly, fly away home!"

She stepped away from the edge. The shadow of death had passed her by.

She heard a footstep behind her and turned around. She expected to see a friendly face. So she was surprised to find two eyes glaring at her with implacable hatred. She had never seen such hatred. A mouth frozen in cruelty, palms raised, anger that burned.

A cloud passed over the sun. The day turned dark. At the final moment, Zia understood the calamity of her innocence.

Chapter Two

It was Claire who found the body.

"Howie! Look down there! Is that . . ." She hesitated. "Is that a person?"

They were on a trail a hundred feet above the river on the side of a steep slope. Eagle Falls was close enough to hear the rush and crash of water.

Howard Moon Deer looked down and saw what appeared at first to be colored material floating in the shallows of the river by the shore. But it wasn't material. It was a body bobbing on the current. A woman.

"Hello!" he called loudly. "Are you okay?"

There was no answer. Which was no surprise. Even from this distance he saw that she was dead.

Claire was looking at him with concern. "Howie?"

"It's a woman, Claire. I'm afraid she's . . ."

He didn't finish the sentence. Claire's blue eyes opened wider.

"Good God!"

Claire had arrived only two days ago from Amsterdam. She had been there as a guest soloist with the Royal Concertgebouw Orchestra, living in an expensive hotel, a cosmopolitan life. She hadn't yet adjusted to the wilds of New Mexico.

Howie was taking time off work in order to hike and picnic and spend the day with her. He had visualized skinny dipping in the pool at the foot of the falls and sneaking off into the woods. A dead body hadn't been in the plans.

Claire had her phone out and was poking her index finger at 911.

"There's no service, Howie!"

"There wouldn't be. Not out here, Claire. Look, I'm going to climb down to the river and see if there's anything I can do for her. Wait for me here, okay?"

"Howie—"

"It'll just take me a few minutes. There's a chance she's alive. I don't think so but it's important to check."

He left Claire on the trail and made his way carefully down the bank to the river. There was a short stretch where he needed to clutch onto a small tree to keep from falling. He slid the last few feet but made it down in one piece.

As he came closer, he saw that the body was a teenage girl. She was half floating on her back. It looked as though she'd been carried down-river until she had been caught in the shallow reeds. She was dressed in khaki cargo pants, a dark brown T-shirt, and a light yellow shell. She wore expensive hiking boots. Her hair was long, a dark golden color, and it waved gently around her head. In life, she had been pretty; in death, she was oddly beautiful, pale as ivory. Her arms were out-stretched, her eyes were the enigmatic eyes of the dead.

Ophelia! he thought.

"Howie, tell me!" Claire called from above.

"She's . . . she's not alive," he called back, keeping his voice steady. The sight of the dead girl had shaken him. "I'll be up in a minute!"

Howie saw that there was a fisherman's path a few dozen feet away that climbed back to the main trail in an easier fashion than how he had come down. He took one last look at the dead girl then began the hike back to Claire.

As he was climbing, he saw someone on the main trail fifty yards downriver from where Claire was standing. Howie couldn't tell if it was a man or woman, or where the person had come from. The figure was dressed in grey sweatpants and sweatshirt and was hiking away from the falls in the direction of the parking area.

"Hey!" Howie called. "Hello! There's been an accident . . ."

He had been hoping to catch the hiker before he or she was out of earshot, but by the time Howie climbed back onto the trail, the figure was only a hint of grey in the distance.

"Who were you calling to?" Claire asked.

"Didn't you see? There was someone there. I was going to ask whoever it was to call 911 when they found a signal. But he's gone. Or she."

"I'll go," she told him. "You probably want to stay with the body."

"I think one of us should stay until the rangers arrive. But I can hike back to the car, Claire. You can stay."

She smiled. "No, I'll do it. I'll be quicker."

Howie knew she was right. Claire was a jogger. She could run the three miles back to the parking area and hardly be out of breath. As for Howie, he was in reasonable shape but he needed to go on a diet.

Claire left him with the backpack that had the sandwiches and bottle of wine for the picnic they would never have. She took off running in search of a cell phone signal. In the huge empty spaces of New Mexico that could be a challenge.

Left alone, Howie knew that he had at least an hour to kill. He turned toward the waterfall and decided it might be a good idea to take a look around.

***

The box canyon narrowed into a V until it came to an end at the waterfall. It was a harsh, lonely, wild place. The high canyon walls kept the river below in shadow. The rush of water pouring down from the falls blended with the wind into a white noise that was forever present.

Howie stood on the trail and tried to imagine how the girl had died, and where it had happened. The trail was steep and dangerous. There were many places where a person could fall, and if the heights didn't get you, there was always a chance that a rattlesnake would. It was hard to imagine that a young woman would hike to such a remote spot alone.

He didn't want to leave the body unattended, but he knew that within an hour this area would be thick with the technicians of death. If he was going to do any exploring, he needed to do it now.

He left his daypack by the side of the trail with its gourmet picnic packed inside—smoked salmon, an assortment of good cheeses, crackers, wine, fruit. The sound of cascading water grew louder as he continued along the trail toward the falls. The mist in the air was cool.

The trail split in two just before the falls. One fork climbed down a dozen feet to the pool beneath the waterfall, the other ascended upward through a natural stairway in the rock to the cliffs above. Howie had to strain his head to look up. He had been to Eagle Falls before, years ago, and knew that there was a flat rock, a natural ledge with a great view at the top of the falls. The climb there wasn't easy.

If the girl had made her way to the top, she might have easily gotten too close to the edge and fallen to her death. Perhaps she had been taking a selfie and had leaned over too far. Maybe she had simply stumbled. He could imagine her terror as she fell through the void, bouncing over the sides of the cliff into the pool below, where she would have been swept downstream to where Claire had found her.

Howie didn't like heights. They made him queasy. But he knew he was going to have to climb up the chimney rock to the top of the falls to take a better look.

Howie followed the upper trail until he came to a tunnel in the rock, a natural staircase. The climb wasn't bad, once you got into the rhythm and didn't worry too much about what would happen if you slipped. If you were looking for outdoor adventure, this was supposed to be fun.

Up he went. It took him no more than ten minutes but he was panting at the end, out of breath. Going down, he knew, was going to be more difficult.

He came out onto the flat plateau of rock. The ledge was crescent shaped, only wide enough for two or three people. On one side, it backed against a cliff, which rose another thirty feet to a jagged point. On the open side, it looked out on a grand view: the mountains, the valleys, the river approaching the top of the falls, the waterfall itself, the pool at the bottom, and a portion of the river as it continued its relentless journey below. This was a Beethoven version of nature, powerful and grand. There were no guard rails.

Howie got as close to the edge as his stomach dared. Looking down—a long way down—he could see the pool, the rocky beach, and a hundred yards of river. The girl had possibly fallen from here. A tragic accident.

But when Howie turned, he saw that this had not been an accidental death.

On the cliff wall, etched into the sandstone with the point of a sharp rock, she had written a final message:

DAD I'M SORRY BUT IT'S THE ONLY WAY.

Howie shook his head. Suicide! What a waste of a young life!

In a dark mood, he made his way down the rock staircase and returned on the trail to the body, where he sat and kept watch over the dead girl as he waited for the authorities to arrive.

Chapter Three

In the days that followed, the dead girl was identified and a trickle of information about her death was released to the media.

Zia McFadden was a recent graduate of the San Geronimo Valley School, a small progressive private high school that had made the news several years ago when teachers and students had been found together skinny dipping in the Rio Grande. The tuition at the SGV School was more than $40,000 a year. The editor of *The San Geronimo Post* had made a special note of this, as though attending a school for the privileged somehow contributed to her suicide.

There had been no identification on her body but her car, a Honda Civic registered in her name, had been found in the gravel parking area at the head of the trail. For locals, the most interesting fact about Zia was that she was the granddaughter of San Geronimo's most famous writer, Charles McFadden. No one could say why she had been hiking alone in such a wild place.

The death occurred in the San Geronimo National Forest. This meant the head ranger, Brad Lawson, responded to Claire's 911 call, along with two SUVs from the San Geronimo Sheriff's Department. Howie and Claire had spent the rest of the afternoon and well into the evening telling various officials what they knew.

In fact, there hadn't been much to tell. They had gone for a summer picnic but had found a body in the river instead. Howie had climbed to the top of the falls to find the suicide note scratched into the cliff. Claire had run off (literally) to call the authorities. And that was it.

After Claire and Howie gave their statements, they returned home in a dejected mood. This wasn't a great start to Claire's month-long visit. She had come to New Mexico to recuperate from her stressful career as a classical musician—to find silence, as she put it, so that she could hear music again. Death had not been on the agenda.

"I'm sorry, Claire. I'm really, really, sorry. Somehow I always end up getting you into . . . predicaments." It took Howie a moment to find the right word for the messy situations he often encountered as a private investigator.

"Howie, this wasn't your fault! That poor girl. There she was . . ."

Claire turned a whiter shade of pale as she remembered finding the body in the river. She was a pale person at the best of times, of Norwegian descent, fragile. With her long blond hair, she looked like a princess from a medieval tapestry, the kind of princess who had to keep an eye peeled for passing unicorns. Howie always felt a need to protect her.

"Anyway, it's over," he said. "And we have the rest of the month ahead of us."

"Yes, it's over, it's over!" Claire said delightedly, as though saying it twice made it more over still. A smile came to her lips. "Let's go upstairs, why don't we?"

For a sensitive creature, Claire had a remarkable appetite for sex.

Upstairs in Howie's eco-pod meant the sleeping loft that was reached by a narrow ladder. They needed to disrupt Howie's large cat, Orange, who had taken over the center of the bed. There were a few angry meows, but Howie and Claire were soon in each others arms, putting the death of Zia McFadden out of mind.

It was good for Howie that Claire was here. He missed her when she was gone. But that night he couldn't sleep remembering Zia floating in the reeds, how oddly beautiful she had looked, like something from a Pre-Raphaelite painting. It was an image that was hard to forget. Death and the Maiden.

Nor could he forget the figure he'd seen on the path minutes after he had climbed down to Zia's body. He had mentioned this figure to both the Sheriffs and the head ranger, but they had seemed only mildly interested. The Eagle Falls trail was popular and there were always a few hikers around. Unfortunately, hardly anyone signed the register at the head of the trail, and no one was ever found except Howie and Claire who knew anything about the body.

On Thursday, the Wilder & Associate Private Investigations agency received a call from the girl's grandfather, Charles McFadden, the author. He wanted an appointment on Friday morning to talk about the death of his granddaughter.

"Of course," said Howie. He was curious himself to learn more about Zia's death, and having a client would give him a reason to investigate.

Howie had met McFadden several times over the years at book signings and art openings, though he doubted if the author remembered him. By mainstream publishing standards, Charles McFadden was no longer important. He'd had a bestseller fifty years ago that had been made into a movie, but his career had faded after that and his later books barely sold a copy.

Nevertheless, in the small arty town of San Geronimo, Charlie—as he was known to locals—remained a celebrity. At least for the portion of the community who still read books.

***

The author arrived twenty minutes late, which wasn't a good start.

Howie watched impatiently through the office window as Charles McFadden pulled into the vacant space in the alley at the rear of the building. It took several minutes for him to free himself of the seat belt, gather himself and get out of his car—a battered Toyota Corolla whose taillights were held in place by silver duct tape.

McFadden looked as battered as his car, an old man in baggy clothes. He had long white hair that was pulled back tightly in a pony-tail. His face was intellectual and gaunt. Howie opened the back door and ushered him into his office.

"Hey, how's tricks?" McFadden asked without much enthusiasm.

It seemed an odd greeting under the circumstances.

"Please come in, Mr. McFadden," Howie said, guiding him toward one of the client chairs.

"Call me Charlie, for chrissake. *Mister* McFadden sounds like an old fart I wouldn't want to know. Nice old adobe, by the way. The real thing," he decided, looking around. "But how can you stand to be in town with all the tourists?"

"They don't really bother me," Howie answered. "As long as they don't try to steal one of my parking spots."

Charlie had a pleased-with-himself sort of smile. Despite his ragged appearance, it was the smile of a man who assumed, as a matter of course, that he was the smartest person in any room.

Howie arranged himself behind the huge wooden desk that had once belonged to Jack Wilder, his boss. Jack was officially retired, con-fined to a wheelchair at home, so this was now Howie's desk, though he still felt like an imposter.

He hadn't changed the decor in Jack's old office, except for a new computer system. The building was a traditional New Mexico adobe, two hundred years old, with thick mud walls and vigas and latillas hold-ing up the ceiling, natural wood stripped of bark arranged in a herring-bone pattern. Unfortunately, the ceiling was where the current problem lay. It had begun to leak in heavy thunderstorms and Howie was afraid the entire roof would fall in. He only hoped it didn't happen when there was a client in one of the two Amish rocking chairs that were for clients.

"So, Charlie, what can I do for you?"

"You were the guy who found Zia?" He said this almost accusingly, as though Howie was responsible for his granddaughter's death.

"Yes, I was hiking with my partner at Eagle Falls. We found her in the water floating close to the bank. She looked very peaceful, actually."

"What do you mean, hiking with your partner? You're talking about Jack Wilder?"

"My girlfriend," Howie told him. "Jack's retired."

"Then *say* girlfriend, for chrissake! Not this partner crap! God, I hate what they're doing to the English language!"

Howie smiled. "All right, my girlfriend," he said for Charlie's benefit, though Charlie was starting to annoy him, and Claire didn't much like being referred to as a girl. "I'm so sorry about your granddaughter. It was a shock for both of us to find her. Can I get you something to drink? Coffee, tea, water?"

"How about tequila?"

Howie raised an eyebrow but didn't blanche. "I have that, too. How would you like it?"

"Hey, man, just give me shot, okay? There's no need to put an umbrella on it. That's the problem with America, you know. Everybody wants an umbrella in their reality!"

Howie walked to the trastero that Jack had turned into a liquor cabinet. Everybody drank more in Jack's time than they did today. The bottle of tequila didn't have much left, only an inch of Cuervo Gold. He poured Charles McFadden a shot.

"So what is it you want from a private investigator?" he asked as he handed over the glass.

"Moon Deer, I want to know how Zia died," he said angrily. "If she killed herself, I want to know why. And if someone killed her, I want to know that, too. I want to know who the fuck he was!"

"You think Zia was murdered?"

"I don't know. That's what I'm saying. Talking to the cops, I know they're going to call it suicide because that'll make life easy for them. These cops are underfunded, their budgets are stretched. I understand, Moon Deer. I know everything there is to know about this town. If they call it suicide, they won't have to spend time and money on an investigation."

"Zia left a suicide note."

"Come on, man! What kind of note was that? *I'm sorry, dad, it's the only way!* You saw the note, didn't you, Moon Deer?"

"I did. It was etched into the side of the cliff where she fell."

"Well?"

"Okay, sure," said Howie. "Anybody could have scratched that message onto the cliff. It's true. But the Sheriffs are looking at this as we speak and I'd suggest you wait to see what they conclude. If it's murder, they'll need to find a motive or a witness or some physical evidence. If not, you're right—they'll probably go with suicide. My guess is we'll have more of an idea within a week."

McFadden shook his head emphatically. "What cosmic bullshit!" he declared. "Man, this planet if full of people running around with their heads up their ass!"

Howie's smile was starting to fray.

"Did you have any warning that Zia was in danger?"

"Moon Deer, we're *all* in danger! Every one of us! We could die any moment! We're so damn fragile! We're broken hearts walking around on skinny little legs!"

"I see what you mean," said Howie patiently. "Look, Charlie, I'll take the case. I'll try to find out how Zia died. I don't guarantee anything. She might have simply slipped from the path, that happens. I'm willing to look into it. But first, I need to get some background information from you. I need to know about Zia's life."

"Her life?" Charlie said wistfully. He was clearly having profound Goethe-like thoughts.

"You're her grandfather, I got that. Now tell me about Zia's mother and father and her family situation."

Charlie McFadden sighed heavily. "You want the whole David Copperfield shit, huh?"

"Exactly. To get started, I need to know everything you can tell me about her."

"How about another shot of that Cuervo?" Charlie asked.

Howie handed him the bottle.

***

Listening to McFadden, Howie recalled the famous Tolstoy line: Happy families are all alike; every unhappy family is unhappy in its own way.

It seemed to him that the McFadden family was unhappy due to the fact that Charlie had only ever cared about his writing. Whether his wife and daughter went mad with hunger and neglect wasn't as important to him as getting a good review in *The New York Times*.

Charlie wrote his first novel in his early twenties when he was an English teacher at Deerfield Academy in Massachusetts. It was a coming of age novel, like many first novels, and it did well enough so that he was able to quit his job, move to New York City, and call himself a novelist.

For the next hour, Howie heard about the ups and downs of being a novelist, his three marriages, Hollywood, New Mexico, three divorces, and always alimony to pay. Charlie put special emphasis on the alimony, how he had been stripped bare by angry women so that he—with all his many books and screenplays!—was reduced to driving a 20 year old Toyota held together with duct tape.

Charlie enjoyed talking about himself. He had made a career of it. It was more of a challenge to get him to talk about Zia, but with a bit of guiding, Howie managed to learn something about her as well.

"So where do we go from here, Moon Deer?" Charlie asked, almost belligerently, when he came to a pause.

"As I told you, I'm willing to take the case. But I'm expensive, Charlie. And to tell the truth, family investigations can turn nasty. Zia most likely had her secrets. Are you sure you want to know about them?"

"I'm sure," said Charlie. "I'm very sure. Maybe she was pregnant, maybe she was taking drugs. But I want to know, Moon Deer. I want the truth."

Howie nodded. "Okay, I'll need for you to sign a contract. I charge $500 a day plus expenses and normally I ask for a thousand dollar retainer in advance. Can you manage that?"

"No problem." Charlie stood up from the rocking chair with some difficulty. "But look, I'm in the middle of Chapter 10 right now, my new book, and I got to get back to it. It's calling me. It's burning a hole in my soul, man. So just send me your bill, okay? I'll put a check in the mail."

Howie walked McFadden out the back door to his ancient Corolla and watched as he attempted to start his car. The engine coughed and sputtered and Howie was afraid he was going to need to call a tow truck to get the wreck hauled away. But after a few tries the engine caught with a gush of white smoke from the rear end.

Charlie rolled down his window and stuck his head out.

"Hey, Moon Deer, I forgot to tell you. I'm giving a reading next Saturday night at the Owl. I'll put you on the guest list. Be there, or be square!"

Howie shook his head as McFadden drove off in a cloud of smoke. Aging hipsters were a sad breed and he suspected he was never going to be paid for this job. But he had decided to take the case anyway. He was intrigued with Zia McFadden and wanted to find out for himself why she had died.

He shook off the shadows that Charlie had left behind and walked through the agency building to the front office.

"Georgie," he said to his daughter, who was at the reception desk getting the agency's books in order. "Why don't we go have ourselves an early lunch at Ernestina's. I'll tell you all about our new client, Charlie McFadden."

Chapter Four

"So, Da, the new case," Georgie said. "I know the name Charles McFadden but I've never read any of his books."

"You're not alone. Not many people read him any more. But he's still a big deal in San Geronimo."

"A big fish in a small pond?"

"I'd say he's floundered."

"Da, that's a terrible pun!"

Howie smiled fiendishly. He loved bad puns. His Scottish daughter called him Da, which gave him a warm glow.

They were sitting across from each other under a yellow sun umbrella at Ernestina's food cart, *Burritos y Mas*, by the side of the four-lane highway south of town. Cars and trucks zipped by in both directions leaving behind occasional whiffs of gasoline fumes.

Georgie had arrived in New Mexico in early June after finishing her final exams at Cambridge, swearing she couldn't get out of the U.K. fast enough, an island full of despicable men. Apparently she was recovering from a broken heart. Howie was curious but he didn't enquire too closely.

San Geronimo was the perfect escape for someone who needed time off to reconsider her life and he was glad to have her. Georgie wanted to earn her keep so he had put her to work in the office. Ruth, the agency's previous secretary, had retired six months earlier and moved to Florida, so the agency was in need of help. Fortunately, Georgie was competent beyond her years and she had the office organized in no time. It was barely two months since she had arrived, and already Howie couldn't imagine how he had managed without her.

At the age of 21, Georgie was spectacular. She was poised and self-contained. She had long black hair tied back with a simple tortoise shell clip. She was Native American without any doubt, but with a hint in her face of her Anglo mother, the beautiful Grace Stanton, Howie's first love.

She wore almost no make-up, only an occasional hint of lipstick, and no jewelry except a small silver bracelet with a turquoise stone that Howie had bought for her. Howie was aware—sometimes uncomfortably—of the attention his daughter received when they walked into restaurants together. She was lovely.

"McFadden's big opus was a novel called *Blood Red Mountains*," he continued. "It's an interesting story about the traditional Spanish culture of northern New Mexico, and the stress of change when the outside world starts moving in. It's a good, serious novel. But to be honest, it's kind of slow and boring."

Georgie gave him a penetrating look. For a girl who had just graduated with honors from Cambridge, slow and boring didn't enter into the equation. She probably read Thomas Aquinas in bed at night. In Latin.

"That was my feeling, anyway," Howie continued. "But then I'm tired after working all day, and when I pick up a book, I want to be entertained. In any case, I admire McFadden's talent, but I've never warmed to him."

"It must be hard to watch your reputation decline."

"I'm sure it is," said Howie. "And I'd feel for him except he's arrogant and not very likable. Some people just become more full of themselves with failure. It's the fault of the big bad New York publishing establishment, you see. They're crass capitalists who don't understand genius. Meanwhile, Charlie's broke. Three ex-wives have done him in. So I'm afraid we're not going to see any money on this case."

"You're going to take the case for free?"

"Most likely. He says he's going to put a check in the mail, but I can't imagine him getting around to it."

Ernestina called Howie's name from inside the food cart and Howie brought the food to the table. Being a vegetarian, Georgie had the chile rellenos plate. Howie, an omnivore, had a pork mole burrito.

As they ate, Howie gave Georgie an overview of the McFadden family and where Zia fit in.

"Let's start with the three wives," he told her. "Wife number one was an associate editor at Random House, Sophia Berger, recently graduated from Vassar. The way Charlie put it, he was the hippest thing going and women were attracted to him in hordes. In reality he was a shy young man who spent nearly all his time tethered to his typewriter. Sophia was a wild young woman, a free spirit with flaming red hair who brought him out of his shell."

"How do you know that, Da?"

"I was coming to this. When I first arrived in San Geronimo, I had a brief relationship with Charlie's ex-wife number three, Danielle. This was long before I met Claire. Danielle liked to tell stories about Charlie, usually not very flattering ones. In fact, as far as I was concerned she talked about him too much. Of course, she hated Charlie by the time I met her so I take her tales with a grain of salt."

"Did you have a lot of girlfriends before you met Claire? I bet you did!"

"Not really, Georgie. I was too poor to be much of a Casanova."

"Oh, you shouldn't be so modest, Da. Women are drawn to you. I've seen the way they look at you!"

"Anyway," said Howie, changing the subject. "Charlie and Sophia moved to New Mexico where they took lots of peyote and wandered ecstatically into the desert and did the whole free spirit thing. The money was flowing at that point which greased things along. They had one child together, Mikaela, but it wasn't too long after Mikaela's birth that Sophia began to show signs of instability. At first it seemed like only eccentric behavior, maybe too many drugs. But there were a number of crazy episodes, each one worse than the last—getting arrested for shoplifting something she didn't need, another arrest for driving 97 miles per hour on a country road with Mikaela, four years old, unbuckled in the front seat.

"From the perspective of their bohemian crowd, none of these episodes seemed particularly out of the ordinary. Free spirits did wild things. They didn't worry about boring stuff like responsibility. But then when Mikaela was eight, Sophia set fire to their house while Charlie and Mikaela were inside sleeping. To make a long story short, Sophia was arrested, found insane, and sent to an institution. Such was the end of marriage number one. Mikaela remained with her father, who never took much interest in her. It wasn't a great situation for a child.

"Two more marriages followed in quick succession, the longest of which lasted three years, the shortest six months—that was Danielle, who I knew. Wives number two and three were both vivid, unconventional women, much like Sophia had been. But they weren't crazy, and being of more practical stuff, when the marriages were over they took what remained of Charlie's money. There were no more children, which probably was fortunate since Charlie wasn't much of a dad.

"Which brings us to Mikaela, Zia's mother. She was a problem from the start. A little monster—that's how Danielle described her. She was an unhappy kid who grew up getting into trouble of one kind or another. She even got kicked out of her pre-school. Like many of the children around here—at least, the kids whose parents can afford it— she was a skier. If you're the right age, there's a lot of partying up on San Geronimo Peak and at the age of 17 she got pregnant from a casual fling with a ski patroller, a guy by the name of Keir Aaronson. As it happens, I know Keir, though not well. He's one of those bearded mountain men who can pass for a Hell's Angel. In the off-season, he's a woodworker. When you get near him, he smells of woodsmoke and goat. But I suppose he had some sex appeal to an unhappy girl. Maybe he felt sorry for her."

"Maybe he was horny," Georgie said less charitably.

"Whatever it was between them, it was brief. The surprising part is that Mikaela decided to have the child and raise it on her own."

"And this is Zia we're talking about?"

"Yes. There's a lot here I don't know yet, but it appears that getting pregnant and having Zia caused Mikaela to turn her life around. She moved to Albuquerque with Zia, went back to school, and managed to graduate from UNM. Today she's the CEO of a television station down there, KABB."

"Good for her!"

"I agree. But here's something a little strange. Zia grew up in Albuquerque—I don't know anything about her childhood. But for some reason during her junior year in high school, she decided to leave her school, leave her mother, and come up here to San Geronimo to live with her father."

"The ski patroller?"

"Right. I don't know how well Keir and Zia knew each other up to this point, but she came north to be with him. Mikaela paid Zia's tuition at the San Geronimo Valley School, so I guess she didn't have a complete break with her mother. But still, it's a big thing when you're a junior in high school to quit in the middle of the school year and go live with a different parent. Something must have driven her away."

"I can understand it, Da," Georgie said, giving Howie a look. "She wanted to get to know her father. That's a good thing."

21

"Well, yes," he told Georgie with a smile. "But it's something we'll need to look into."

"*We* will need to look into it? You're saying you're going to let me do more than keep your books and answer the phone?"

"If you'd like to, Georgie. If you're interested."

Her smile turned into a grin. "Of course I'm interested! Where do we start?"

"We'll begin tomorrow morning with Keir. We'll make a visit to his workshop and see where that leads us. Hopefully he'll be able to fill in some blanks. But look, Georgie. I've kept you in the office up to now because this sort of work can be dangerous. Even a simple thing like going to see a ski patroller whose daughter has been killed. You never know when an interview like that will explode."

"Da, I am very fit. I can handle myself. Believe me, growing up in Glasgow wasn't always so bonny. I learned to fight, I played rugby and football—soccer to you. I'm tougher than I look. And besides, with Jack retired and Ruth gone, you can't do everything by yourself!"

Howie felt a flush of happiness.

"Look, let's surprise Claire with a good bottle of champagne!" he said impulsively. "We'll go home and celebrate!"

She laughed and to Howie she looked so perfect in the shade of the yellow umbrella by the food cart at the side of the New Mexico highway that he was afraid to breathe.

My daughter! He had only learned of her existence when she was 15 years old, and it was a miracle to him that she was here.

***

Howie remembered that day as the last good time before all hell broke loose.

The summer evening was golden. The sunset went on forever.

They closed the office at 5 and drove home with all the windows of Howie's dusty old Outback open, singing along to Elton John's Greatest Hits on the Bluetooth audio. They really let loose on "Goodbye Yellow Brick Road." Elton John was a rare meeting point between Georgie's generation and his.

Howie parked in the gravel parking area at the edge of his land and they walked single file along the winding forest trail to the small complex of buildings that he called home. As they walked, they could hear the sound of a cello floating through the trees, a Bach suite that started and stopped, repeating a passage several times. Claire had set up her cello in the shade near the vegetable garden and she was playing with her eyes closed, her face raised slightly to the sky.

The path crossed a stream on a wooden bridge and came out onto a clearing. Howie's house sat at the far side—the Egg, as Claire called it, a high tech eco-pod Howie had bought as a kit from two avant-garde German architects.

The Egg was a metal shell propped up by four legs that looked as though it had just landed from Mars. A satellite dish, a solar panel, and a number of antennae bristled on the top. After buying ten acres of land in the foothills, Howie hadn't had enough money left over to put up a real house and the kit had appealed to him. Small as it was, it was cleverly designed and contained everything he needed. He had a sleeping loft, a tiny kitchen, a bathroom only slightly larger than a telephone booth, even a small office with a computer nook. The electronics were sophisticated and gave him a satellite connection to the internet.

Unfortunately, the Egg was very small. There was enough room inside for Howie, his cat, and for Claire when she was here. Four years ago when Georgie was preparing to make her first visit to New Mexico, Howie saw he was going to need more room, and with the help of his hippie neighbors he put up a cabin on the opposite side of the clearing.

It was astonishing to him and wonderful that he had both Claire and Georgie with him, the two people he loved most. They had both come wounded from their battles with the world—Claire, because she believed she had lost music somewhere in her busy life. And Georgie . . . Howie wished he knew more about what went on beneath her watchful exterior, but he knew she was troubled and looking for what she was going to do with her life.

He would do what he could for them, though he didn't have any particular answers to life's problems—not his, not theirs. He simply loved them both, and was painfully aware that once they were put back together again, they would be gone.

Claire made a vegetarian lasagna and they ate dinner outside around the fire that Howie had made in the clearing. The moon rose. The forest was full of the rustlings of small animals. The stars were a billion diamonds sparkling in the black sky.

They talked about a hundred things and laughed and Howie went along with the pretense that time could stop here.

It was a perfect August night that he hoped would never end. Though a voice inside Howie whispered that perfect summer nights were brief, impossible to hold, and quickly gone.

***

Ever since she had arrived in New Mexico, Georgie had taken to sleeping by the tepee her father had set up on a plywood platform overlooking the creek. The tepee was very old. It had belonged to Howie's great-grandfather. She put her sleeping bag on the platform outside so she could listen to the sound of the creek and look up through a clearing in the trees to the stars.

The two nights it rained, she slept inside the tepee itself, trying to imagine Howie's Lakota great-grandfather who had once lived here— feeling his spirit watching, and wondering what he thought. Probably he had never imagined a person like herself, a half-Lakota girl who had grown up in Scotland, unaware of her heritage until six years ago when Howie had found her.

To Georgie, her life seemed an amazing tale.

Growing up in Glasgow, people had taken her for Pakistani because of her olive complexion. Pakis weren't popular with thuggish Weegie boys, so she had learned to be tough, and she wasn't sorry for that. She had always known that she was adopted. Carol and Ray, her adoptive parents, never lied to her. But they themselves didn't know the story of her birth. It was only when she was fifteen, when Howie discovered her existence, that he spent a year hunting for her and found her. Incredibly, she learned that she was half Lakota—and she loved it! It released her somehow. She knew now why she was different from other people.

The night was so still and velvety that Georgie could hear the rustling sounds of all the forest creatures—owls, deer, bobcats, skunks, all sorts of rodents, maybe even mountain lions, foxes, and bears. An owl in a tree not far from the tepee swooped down through the branches and swept up a rodent that screamed in terror.

This was a wild land, the Rocky Mountains that went up and down the spine of the North American West like giant vertebrae. It still wasn't tamed.

Lying on her back, her head on two pillows, Georgie could just barely make out the muted grunts of Howie and Claire having sex. It was obvious they thought the sound wouldn't carry from the Egg. It made her smile.

She was very glad for Howie and Claire. They were a great couple, and she had come to love them. But listening to Claire's stifled cries made her think of Ashton Woolridge the Third, her elegant, wealthy Cambridge lover whom she had found in bed with her best friend.

The bastard!

She had to admit that sex had been good with Ashton, and liberating. To someone coming from a modest family in Glasgow, he had seemed the most charming, handsome, smart man she could imagine. With his Cambridge education, he was obviously headed for great things.

How she had loved him!

How he had broken her heart!

And now . . .

Lying on her back, gazing up at the stars, Georgie breathed in the mountains and felt a savage joy welling up within her. She was free here in the American West, unencumbered in this wild, open land. She had found a part of herself that she had never suspected was there.

As for Ashton Woolridge III, he could take his good looks and money, his clever conversation and infidelity and go to hell!

I'm an Indian! Georgie said to herself fiercely. *And I've found my way home!*

Chapter Five

On Saturday morning, Howie and Georgie drove to see Keir Aaronson who lived nearly an hour away, leaving Claire alone to do her practice. In September she was scheduled to perform the fiendishly difficult Shostakovich cello concerto and there was a great deal of work she needed to do in order to make the performance appear effortless.

Howie had vowed to take weekends off work for the month of August while Claire and Georgie were here, but he wanted to question Zia's father as soon as possible. He was hoping Keir would be able to give him a clearer picture of the last days of his daughter's life. He found Keir's address in the local weekly paper where for the past twenty years he had kept a small boxed ad in the classified section to sell his woodwork: KEIR AARONSON CUSTOM FURNITURE 47 Mesa Blanca Road (575) 555-2997. This was the only advertising Keir did. He didn't have a website.

Georgie was quiet as they drove through the wooded foothills down into the desert. But as the two-lane highway came around a bend and the huge vista of high desert opened into view, Georgie burst into speech.

"I love this land!" she said passionately. "It's so open and empty! What a relief after Cambridge! It was so claustrophobic there! All those snooty, uppity, oh-so-educated people! I just wanted to break out and be free of it forever!"

Howie didn't know what to say. "Really?"

"It's the British sense of privilege. It makes me want to throw-up! The men especially. They think they're so superior and smart, but they're smug and awful!"

"I see," said Howie. "Was there one British man in particular who caused you to feel this way?"

Georgie sighed. "I don't want to talk about it, Da. If that's okay."

"Of course it's okay, Georgie."

They drove another few miles in silence.

"In any case," Howie said at last. "I'd like you to have a pen and notebook when I talk with Keir. I'm hoping to get as much information as he'll tell us about Zia, especially what he knows about why she left Albuquerque. If you write down the details—dates, names, all the things that are easy to forget—it'll leave me free to have a more natural conversation with him."

"This must be very difficult for him, the death of his daughter. Perhaps he won't want to talk."

"I can barely imagine what he's going through!" Howie said, giving Georgie an involuntary look. "But we have a kind of history together. There was an avalanche a few years ago on the Peak in which a 19-year-old boy died. I was at the top of the mountain when the avalanche broke, so I got involved in the rescue. Keir and I were the ones who found the body under the snow. I don't know him well. I've never been to his house and I know nothing about his personal life—I didn't even know he had a daughter. But when you share an experience like that, it leaves a bond."

"You didn't tell me you have avalanches up at the ski resort."

"They're rare. And honestly, they don't happen on the lower parts of the mountain on the slopes where you'll be learning."

Howie had promised to teach her to ski this coming winter . . . if she was still here. Georgie had agreed to give it a try, but she was dubious.

Keir's cabin and workshop were a few miles southwest of town in an area of canyons and sagebrush. They passed through a mixed neighborhood of expensive faux-adobe homes, run-down trailers, and some experimental architecture that made you feel you had wandered into the Twilight Zone—straw bale homes, Earthships, inflatable domes, even a pyramid.

The road ambled through the sage brush, came over the top of a hill, then descended into a green belt that followed the course of the Rio San Geronimo, the local river that ambled through the county before it emptied out into the Rio Grande.

A sign for 47 Mesa Blanca Road stood at the head of a long dirt driveway that descended through a copse of Siberian elms and cottonwoods to the river—a creek, by Howie's reckoning, hardly more than a dozen feet across with a few inches of water trickling over shallow rocks. The river flooded occasionally in monsoon rains and the workshop and cabin were both raised several feet from the ground on posts made from railroad ties. The two buildings looked as though they had been built by hand, starting with the felling of trees for lumber.

The property covered at least three or four acres and it was unusually green for the high desert. Someone had planted this stretch of the river decades ago. The cabin was a one-story rectangular structure, very simple, surrounded by wild rose bushes and flowering shrubs. Howie and Georgie stopped at the cabin first where they found a sign on the front door: I'M IN THE SHOP.

Howie hadn't phoned ahead to tell Keir they were coming, so he couldn't be certain he was home. It was one of Jack's rules to show up unannounced, if that was possible. Don't let them know you're coming. Don't give them a chance to say no. People are usually more willing to answer questions when you meet face to face. However, running around the countryside without an appointment meant you could waste a lot of time.

They continued on a gravel path to the workshop, a low, barn-like building with a pitched roof. A wide wooden door on rollers was pulled open to let in the morning air.

"Hello!" Howie called.

There's no answer, nor any sign of Keir.

"It's Howie Moon Deer!" he called again. "From the Peak. I'm here with my daughter . . . ."

Stepping inside, Howie saw the shop was well-equipped with table saws and band saws and jig saws and tables full of tools and clamps. It was a large, comfortable place to work that smelled of sawdust. Half-finished tables and chairs were pushed against the walls. Drills and screwdrivers and hooks with different tools on them were arranged on the far side of the building.

Though the door was open, there didn't appear to be anybody here.

"Da, there's a note," Georgie said, coming up behind him. She pointed to a sheet of yellow legal-sized paper on a half-finished table.

Howie leaned closer. Written in pencil, in a large neat hand, were the words: *I'm so sorry.*

Howie felt the first tickle of worry that something was wrong. These words were too similar to what Zia had sketched on the cliff at Eagle Falls.

"Georgie, let's go. I'll try to phone Keir from the car. I should have done that at the start. And, uh, look, don't touch anything, okay? Just to be on the safe side."

"The safe side of what? Da, what's wrong?"

"Probably nothing," he assured her. "But let's go anyway."

Howie left the note on the table and followed Georgie out of the workshop into the green shaded parking area outside.

Georgie stopped abruptly. "Da!" she cried. "Look up!"

Howie looked up.

Two legs dangled in the air a dozen feet above the ground. The legs wore brown corduroy pants and battered work boots. The body of a man was hanging by a rope from one of the sturdy lower branches of a cottonwood tree. A stepladder lay nearby on the ground. It looked as though it had been kicked away.

Howie recognized Keir. His gray face lolled sadly to one side, his empty eyes looked down into nothing.

Georgie said aloud what Howie was thinking.

"A second suicide! . . . that seems unlikely, don't you think? In one family?"

Howie admired her calm. Personally, dead bodies in trees raised his blood pressure and caused his breath to quicken. He already had his phone to his ear and was calling 911.

***

Howie would have preferred to call the State Police than 911. He had friends at the State Police. Unfortunately, 911 dispatch would send the Sheriff's Department where there was a new chief, a woman, who had made it plain she didn't like private investigators. But 911 was the only option in this situation. Among other concerns, the Fire Department would need to be involved to get the body down from the tree.

Howie studied his old-fashioned wristwatch, a Timex. It was cheap but it kept time. He figured he had fifteen to twenty minutes before the Sheriffs arrived. Perhaps longer. In San Geronimo, law enforcement moved at its own unhurried pace. From past experience, Howie knew that a wise P.I. followed the rules when death was involved. But he had time on his hands, and those who seek occasionally find.

"Uh, look, Georgie, the cops aren't going to be here for a few minutes so I'm going to take a quick look around. What I'd like for you

31

to do is to stay outside by the car and let me know the second you hear a siren or see any sign of them. Okay?"

Georgie gave him a discerning look. "You're going inside the house? Isn't that against the law?"

"It's a gray area," he said. "It depends on a number of things."

"Such as?"

"Such as whether the Sheriffs decide this is a crime scene. Probably they will. However, if we split hairs, this isn't a crime scene *yet*."

"Da, you would have done well in the philosophy course I took third year. Total gibberish! Well, you'd better be quick about it, hadn't you? I'll stand guard."

Howie jogged quickly down a flagstone path to the cabin. The front door was locked, but when he moved around the building to the back, the rear door opened. People were casual about locking up in rural New Mexico. He used his shirt sleeve as a glove to pull the handle, knowing how useless this was if a good forensic team gave the cabin a looking over.

He came in through the kitchen/living room area. It was a rustic kitchen, snug and warm, well-cared for. There were counters made of thick old planks that had been sanded and sealed. The cabinets were darkened teak. The shelves were crowded with bulk foods, beans, flour, rice, and spices.

The kitchen opened onto an all-purpose common room. There was a dinner table that was covered with stacks of mail and old newspapers. Closer to the front windows were two well-worn sofas and several rocking chairs. There was no TV.

The bookshelves were crammed with books. Howie was always curious to see what people read—it was almost as telling as seeing what they put in grocery carts. Keir's library leaned heavily toward history and natural sciences. There were several books about utopian communes.

Knowing time was short, Howie continued through the living area and down a hallway in search of Zia's bedroom, hoping that nothing had been touched in the three days since her death. The first bedroom on the left was very Spartan and it appeared to be where Keir slept. There was a single bed, a battered chest of drawers, and one wood chair.

At the end of the hall, a door on the right stood open to what was clearly a girl's bedroom. It was the larger of the two bedrooms. Keir had given her the best room, with the smaller one for himself. Howie found this touching.

He stepped inside for a quick look around, knowing not to touch anything.

There was a poster on the wall for a band he had never heard of. The room was sparsely furnished with an oak dresser and a double bed covered by a white bedspread. For a teenager, she had kept a neat room. Everything was put away. A desk by the window looked out onto a shaded patch of weedy grass. There was an empty place on the desk where a laptop had been. Howie could see the top of the power cord on the left of the desk, and a Mac mouse on the right, but there was nothing in between. Zia's computer was gone.

Howie wished he had gloves. He was able to use his long-sleeve flannel shirt to open the closet doors but it was awkward. The closets had shirts and pants and two casual dresses hung neatly on hangers. Zia had not been a girl obsessed with clothes.

Moving on, Howie found nothing interesting. The room had a feeling of emptiness and loss. Whoever Zia McFadden had been, there wasn't much of her here. The bedroom left few clues.

Howie glanced at his watch. He figured he had six minutes left.

He had one last idea, to look under the bed to see if Zia had hidden anything there. As hiding places went, this was a cliché, yet it was surprising how many people believed they were the first person to think of it.

He wasn't expecting much. It was almost a humorous gesture to futility. With some difficulty, he lowered himself to the hardwood floor, stretched out on his back and slid headfirst beneath the bed. The mattress was held up by a wooden frame. He saw the book immediately, propped between the bottom of the mattress and the wood slats. It was an oversized notebook, cloth-bound, with stars and planets on the cover.

Howie pulled it out from the slats and wiggled his way out from under the bed.

He opened the notebook and saw immediately that he had struck gold. It was Zia's diary. He flipped through the pages, all of them written in the same neat cursive hand.

On the first page, Howie read: *I wish I could kill her!!!*

Howie was torn. This journal, hopefully, would reveal what he had been hired to discover. With this book, he would be able to peek inside Zia's intimate life. But he could already hear the faint whine of police sirens on the desert air.

His phone vibrated in the front pocket of his jeans.

"Da, they're here!" Georgie said when he was able to answer.

"I'm coming."

Howie knew he should leave the diary for the police. Of course, he should . . .

Meanwhile, finders, keepers. He jogged down the hall with the diary, ducked through the kitchen and out the back door. Georgie was waiting by the car with an unhappy look on her face.

"They're coming up the driveway, Da!"

"One second," he told her.

There was a decent hiding place in his Outback in the side panel of the rear driver's side door. He had created this space a year ago when he needed to carry sensitive papers to a courtroom in Wyoming. Howie fiddled with the latch quickly, stuffed the journal inside, and was stepping around from the side of his car as the first of two patrol cars was coming down the driveway to the cabin, its red and blue lights flashing.

Howie and Georgie stood together, models of civic helpfulness, as law enforcement spilled into the driveway.

Chapter Six

Sheriff Sharon Kincaid, the top cop, stepped out of the lead car. A second Sheriff's car, lights twinkling, came up behind her and two deputies got out and joined her.

In San Geronimo County, the Sheriff was an elected position and Sharon Kincaid was the first woman ever to win. She had ridden in on an anti-corruption platform, promising openness and competence, after the last Sheriff, a man, had been found with his hand in the cookie jar. In San Geronimo politics, this didn't automatically rule a person out from office, but he had cheated too many of the town's power elite, too many times.

Sheriff Kincaid was a hefty middle-aged blonde woman, barrel shaped. She wore a tan shirt with a star on it, dark brown trousers, and a gun on her hip which added several inches to her already considerable waist.

"What goes on here?" she demanded.

"I don't really know," said Howie. He didn't like to lie, but he had been getting better at it since he had taken over the running of Wilder & Associate.

"I only stopped by to see about a chair," he continued. "We didn't see anyone so we walked back to the wood shop and found a man hanging from the big cottonwood. I assume it's Keir Aaronson, but I don't know that for certain. Would you like me to take you—"

"What do you mean, you came about a chair?" she demanded.

Howie was taken aback. With a dead man hanging from a tree, he would have thought there would be more pressing questions than one about a chair.

"A rocking chair," he said without hesitation. "I came to see if he could design a rocking chair for me. Something custom made that would fit into the very small space I live in. You see, I live in an eco-pod that was designed by two German—"

Sheriff Kincaid wasn't interested in his eco-pod. "Did you have an appointment to see him?" she interrupted.

"Well, no. I thought I'd just stop by."

The Sheriff wore aviator sunglasses, which made her hard to read.

"Who are you?" she asked, turning to Georgie.

"I am Georgie," she answered firmly. "Howie is my father."

"You don't sound American."

"I grew up in Scotland, but I have a U.S. passport. I don't carry it with me, but I can certainly bring it into your office if you'd like."

"You found the body with your father?"

"I did. It all happened just as he told you."

Howie was glad he had persisted through two years of government hurdles to prove he was Georgie's father and get her a U.S. passport. A situation like this made the effort worthwhile. Unlike Lieutenant Ruben of the State Police, Sheriff Kincaid enjoyed arresting illegal immigrants. The heartland of America—land of immigrants—could be heartlessly anti-immigrant.

The Sheriff turned back to Howie. "Okay, show us the body," she said gruffly.

"Sure enough," said Howie deferentially.

But there was something in his tone she didn't like. "Don't you be a smart-ass Indian with me, sonny!"

"I wouldn't dream of it," he told her.

Howie led the way along the shaded path to the wood shop, with the Sheriff and her deputies close behind.

Ten minutes later, an ambulance arrived, and after that a fire truck with a long ladder.

Howie and Georgie were happy to fade into the background.

***

"I can't believe you took that diary!" Jack Wilder said in his deepest voice, shaking his head gloomily as he and Howie sat in the garden at the rear of the Wilder home.

It was later that afternoon and they each had a glass of good Argentine malbec from Jack's wine cellar, a closet off his bedroom. A jar at the end of the day, as Jack called it, had once been a ritual part of Wilder and Associate Private Investigations.

Howie thought the wine was pretty good. But not good enough to pay what Jack had probably paid for it. For a man who was blind and confined to a wheelchair, Jack liked to live grandly.

"This time you're going to lose your license for sure, damn it!" he said to Howie in a voice that was almost too low to hear. A growl. "You took an important piece of evidence from a crime scene!"

"But it wasn't a crime scene when I took it," Howie attempted, knowing it was a weak argument. "It still isn't, as far as I know. I was only doing my job. I was hired to investigate Zia McFadden's death, and that's what I was doing. I had no idea the cops might want it."

"Yeah, yeah. You think Santo's going to fall for a bunch of baloney like that? And if you lose your license, where will I be?"

"Where will *you* be? What about me, Jack?"

"I own half that business, Howie. If you lose your license, we'll have to close down. Have you thought of that?"

Howie sighed.

"So tell me this," said Jack patiently. "Did you know this guy, this hippie woodworker who hung himself?"

"Jack, *hanged* is the correct past tense of hang when it refers to death by suicide or external circumstances," Howie informed him. "You use hung only when it means to suspend something. As in, justice hung in the balance. And of course, when a guy is—"

"Howie, for God's sake!"

"Plus Keir wasn't a hippie. He was one of those silent mountain men, there's a difference. Hippies tend to blab their mouths off, especially when they're high. Mountain men keep their mouth shut. I knew Keir from Ski Patrol. Furniture was his off-season employment."

"Hung himself, hanged himself—for chrissake, Howie, you're going to drive me nuts! You shouldn't have found that body! And you sure as hell shouldn't have taken that diary!"

"I think I can weather this, Jack. And look, I didn't intend to find a body. I was just following the most logical lead to Zia's father. The body found me."

"No, Howie—*you* found the body! Don't blame a dead guy. Bodies don't find people. People find bodies!"

Jack wasn't in good shape. Six months ago his beloved guide dog, Katya, had died. She was nineteen, the death hadn't come as a surprise. But Jack had been devastated. He had fallen into a deep melancholy and wouldn't hear of finding a new seeing-eye dog.

Then a month after Katya's death, Jack had a stroke which had left him partially paralyzed and confined to a wheelchair. Now not only was he blind, he couldn't stand by himself. He needed a day nurse while Emma was at work.

Howie made a point of visiting at least three times a week, usually late in the day after the office was closed. Georgie had been visiting also. She and Jack got on surprisingly well. She had been badgering him to write his memoir so not only did she bring a breath of youth into his life, she was a new person to listen to his stories. He adored her.

The late summer afternoon in Jack's shaded backyard was lulling. The red wine made Howie realize he was tired. He needed to make an effort to stay awake. The two men didn't speak for several minutes, each lost in their own thoughts.

"Where is the diary now?" Jack asked, breaking the silence.

"It's about to go into the safe. Georgie is working on it, making a copy on the office machine. We've been doing this together. It's slow going because we're using surgical gloves and taking precautions not to leave fingerprints on the original. I'm going to sneak back to the cabin tonight and return the original under the bed where I found it. My guess is the Sheriffs are still thinking suicide and they haven't turned the cabin into a crime scene."

"Bullshit! Cops are smarter than they look. They figure these things out."

"Yes, but they're short staffed. There aren't enough deputies to guard a place that's so far out of town. Not at night, certainly. I'll be in and out and they'll never even know the diary was gone."

"And what about the copy? What are you doing with that?"

"I've asked Georgie to read it. She's closer to Zia's age than I am, so I'm hoping she'll see things I don't. I'll read it myself later and then I'll destroy it."

Jack shook his head. "Okay, Howie. I don't like any of this, but I guess you'll have to do it. Just be careful you don't get caught. I sure wish you hadn't gotten into this mess!"

"Jack, Claire found that girl in the river. I'm in this, like it or not."

"Okay, okay," Jack said with a sigh. "What's done is done. So let's go over this again. Two suicides from the same family, wham bam one right after another—I'm not buying it! There's some bullshit going on here and obviously you're going to need help—"

"Jack, I have it under—"

"No, you don't. I'm still your boss, Howie. So start from the beginning. What's the damn book this McFadden guy wrote?"

"*Blood Red Mountains*. It was made into a movie."

"Yeah? What's it about? Tell me the plot."

"You want to know the plot of a book written fifty years ago?"

"Fifty years doesn't matter! What have I taught you, Howie? Death casts a long shadow!"

***

Howie left the Wilder house in a melancholy mood.

It was painful to see Jack getting old. He had lost too much: his eyesight, his beloved Katya, his mobility, his life as a detective. Not to mention the old days when he had been a law enforcement big shot, Commander Jack Wilder of the San Francisco Police Department, virtually the Deputy Chief of Police.

Oddly, among these losses, he seemed to miss Katya the most. There were still signs of her about the house, a gnawed bone lost in the grass, a metal water dish upside down near the compost pile.

At least he had Emma. Jack and Emma had been together now for more than fifty years.

From Jack's house, Howie drove to the office where he took the photocopy of Zia's diary from the safe where Georgie had left it. The safe was from Jack's time and it was a very good one, cleverly concealed beneath a floorboard. As for Georgie, she was at her regular Saturday afternoon yoga class. The plan was for Howie to wait for her and they would drive home together.

Half an hour later, as he was in the back office examining the photocopy, he heard Georgie and another girl coming in the front of the building, from the Calle Dos Flores entrance.

He nearly left the copy of the diary on his desk in order to go to the front room when he thought better of it. The diary was too important to leave his sight. He took it with him to the reception area where he found Georgie at her desk talking to a young woman.

"Let's make it 6 o'clock," Georgie was saying to her friend. "It'll give me time to change and get there . . . Da, hi," she said when she saw him. "This is Elke, my yoga teacher. We're going to hear some music tonight. She says she can drive me back home afterwards."

"I can come and pick you up," Howie offered.

"It is no problem," said Elke, who had a pronounced Scandinavian accent. She had short blonde hair and rosy cheeks and looked like she climbed mountains and sang folk songs to sheep.

Howie smiled graciously. He always tried to be on his best behavior with his daughter's friends. But he couldn't help looking Elke over a bit, wondering if she was old enough to drive. She looked awfully young. He hoped drinking wasn't part of the evening's entertainment.

Georgie didn't drive. Growing up in Glasgow, she had never felt the need to get a driver's license. The U.K., once a socialist country, still retained widespread public transportation, though it was deteriorating fast under privatization. In San Geronimo, Georgie got around on one of Claire's old mountain bikes, which didn't add to the carbon footprint and she said she much preferred the bike anyway.

"We're going to hear CMO!" Elke said enthusiastically. "It's sold out but the owner of the Loft is a friend of mine."

"Wonderful. What is CMO?" Howie asked.

"The Cosmic Mushroom Orchestra," said Georgie. "They're from Boulder," she added, as though this explained a great deal. "It's a non-alcoholic event, by the way—I see that concerned look on your face, Da. We'll be drinking fruit punch."

"Just so you're safe on the road," he told them benignly. Hopefully the fruit punch wouldn't be spiked with ecstasy.

Howie hadn't ever imagined he would become so middle-aged.

With an effort, he wished Georgie a fun time, then he left the two young women to their own devices and drove home with the photocopy.

"You look tired," Claire said when he walked up the path to the Egg.

"It's been a long day. And it's not over, I'm afraid. I'm going to need to go out later to return something. Zia's father is dead," he added, doing his best to make light of it so Claire wouldn't worry. "It's looking like suicide. Georgie and I found him hanging from a tree outside his workshop."

"That's awful!"

Claire lived in a better world than he did, a world of classical music and civilized people . . . with the exception of the occasional mad maestro. She was sensitive when it came to blood and gore and bodies in trees.

"Well, suicide is for each person to decide. To be or not to be, sort of thing," he told her. "In Japan, it's considered an honorable way to make an exit."

"This isn't Japan, Howie."

"No. And I suspect Keir's death may not have been suicide."

"You mean, it's . . ."

Claire couldn't say the m-word. Howie didn't say it either.

"I stopped off to see Jack on the way home," he told her. "He's amazing, he really is. The old guy's blind, half-paralyzed from his stroke, confined to a wheelchair, but he's still as bossy as ever. I told him about the McFadden case and he's decided that he needs to be in charge."

"Then you should pretend to let him. Humor him, Howie. Jack's bored, he needs something to do with himself. And it's so sad that Katya died!"

It was all sad, as far as Howie was concerned. It was sad that Jack had gotten old, sad that Zia McFadden had fallen to her death. It was sad that a person couldn't live on burritos and bear claws and never get fat. Life was a challenge. But Howie didn't let any of that ruin his evening alone with Claire.

He changed into his at-home clothes—sweatpants and a T-shirt. For Claire's sake, he put on one of his "good T-shirts," one from the Standing Rock oil pipeline protest. Howie had joined the gathering briefly, and it wasn't something he would ever forget—the many tribes who showed up to do what they could to protect the earth and water from bulldozers.

Howie had only gone for 10 days, fitting the time in between cases, so he knew he hadn't done much. He had volunteered in an open air kitchen, making huge vats of beans and tortillas, cutting up onions and potatoes. It was rough living, with very nasty State Troopers lurking. But it felt good to make an effort, put himself into the fight, and he got a T-shirt out of it. The cotton was getting old and he only wore it on special occasions, trying to make it last. Claire had once told him that he looked sexy in it, so he was preserving it as long as possible.

He poured her a glass of wine—none for himself since he was going out later—and he put the tragedies of life behind him. He barbecued salmon steaks, Claire made a large salad with greens and tomatoes from the garden, and they watched the sky fade slowly to night. Howie had coffee after dinner in order to stay awake for his outing tonight and he settled down to read Zia's diary with Claire beside him reading her own book in bed. Orange settled between them, happy for the valley of two warm bodies, purring from time to time.

It would have been a peaceful evening if it hadn't been for the diary.

"Oh, hell!" Howie cried aloud after reading for ten minutes. He woke Claire who had nearly been asleep. "Zia was being sexually abused by her mother's boyfriend!"

Chapter Seven

Zia's journal was written on good quality art paper, unlined. She wrote in a small, neat cursive. It was what Howie thought of as Good Girl Handwriting, very prim. But though her handwriting was prim, her entries were the opposite. The first entry had been made nearly two years ago.

Thursday, July 11. Okay, here it is, my journal. My thoughts, my feelings, blah, blah, blah. So boring, really, but what else do I have? A mother who hates me, a father I don't know, friends I don't really like, a school that sometimes I fantasize setting fire to. Frankly my life in Albuquerque sucks.

I wish I lived in Paris! I'd be the mistress of a famous artist. We would go to cafés on the Left Bank and have deep conversations. We would faire l'amour!

Why am I writing this nonsense. I'm trying to understand my empty boring life.

Sunday, July 14.

Julia had a party at her house last night while her parents were skiing in San Geronimo. There was the usual bad music. Sean's older brother bought us 2 cases of beer and we all got drunk. Yuck! I hate beer but I drank it anyway! Doesn't anyone drink wine around here?

I made out with Billy Tomasito who's on the football team. He stuck his tongue in my mouth which was disgusting. I let him take off my bra and feel my breasts but I stopped him when he tried to put his hands between my legs. I'm sure he'll

tell his friends I'm a tease but I don't care. I'm saving myself
for Paris!

The journal continued in this fashion, the life and thoughts of a
smart, privileged American teenage girl. She had everything, all the
advantages, yet it made sad reading. When Zia turned sixteen, her
mother gave her a new car, a Honda Civic. She enjoyed zipping around
Albuquerque for a month or two, but that soon got old and she was
bored.

In the spring of the following year, her entries became suddenly
more combative. Something had changed in Zia's life.

Thursday, March 11. I am free!! I will not bend!! I know
who I am! I will fight! I will not let CB win!!!

Howie wasn't sure at first who CB was, a person who
needed three exclamation points. But several entries later CB
was clarified:

Saturday, July 13. Cow Bitch made me stay home tonight.
The Dweeb will be here.

Now Howie was left to wonder who the Dweeb was.

Monday, July 15. CB won't be home tonight. Has something at the station. Fabulous to have house to myself!

With Cow Bitch gone

I sing my song!

Howie got it. Cow Bitch was Zia's mother. Mikaela McFadden,
CEO of KABB TV. His client's unloved daughter. Throughout the
journal, Zia used CB and Cow Bitch interchangeably. Zia had seriously
disliked her mother.

Howie skimmed days where Zia hadn't had much to say. It was getting late, Orange had settled onto his stomach, and Claire had begun (very softly) to snore. He knew he needed to keep moving before he fell asleep himself. He continued reading quickly, hoping at least to get an overview.

A page later, Zia's life became unfortunately clear.

> Monday April 15
> Big fight with CB this afternoon after she told me I needed to be nicer to the Dweeb. I told her to fuck off and she slapped me.

On April 29 there was the first mention that the Dweeb was abusing her. He wandered into her bedroom late at night when she was sleeping. Her bedroom door didn't lock. Cow Bitch didn't believe children had the right to lock parents out. Zia's bedroom was in the basement of a split-level suburban ranch house on the slopes in the Northeast Heights, on a different floor from where her mother slept, so it wasn't difficult for the Dweeb to slip into her room. The first time it happened, she woke to find him touching her breasts and masturbating. It was disgusting!

Zia described the night in detail.

> I had to take a bath after he left! In the morning I told CB what happened, but you'll never guess!—she didn't believe me! She said I was making it up because I didn't want her to have a boyfriend! When I laughed she slapped me again.

Howie cheered when Zia decided to leave home and finish high school up north with her father.

January 1st! Happy New Year!

I made the decision! I'm getting out of here to go live with my dad. I've only met him twice. CB says he's in San Geronimo in some shitty little cabin. My mother hasn't had anything to do with him since even before I was born. But she's always talking about him, how boring and silent he was. All bottled up—her version. I get the sense from snickers and the look on her face that he was really good in bed. That's about as deep as CB goes. Haha deep penetration! The Dweeb's penis, by the way, is pink and tiny, a laugh!

Howie only had time to scan a few of the San Geronimo entries, her new life in the far north of the state. She seemed to like her father, who she described as "a good guy." She also liked her new school, the San Geronimo Valley School, though it wasn't easy being a new student in a small town where most of the others had known one another since kindergarten. She made friends with a girl named Uma. Beyond that, Howie would need to read the rest of the diary later.

He turned quickly to the last page to see how much was left in the manuscript, and was startled to see Zia's final entry. It wasn't dated:

> penis remus cum cunt and bum
> what kind of girl am I to have such fun?
> How do I love thee?
> Let me count the ways,
> I spread my legs and crave your cock
> until all is lost and you take a walk.

This was certainly a very different Zia McFadden than he had visualized up to this moment. An interesting girl, but unhappy, he decided.

He liked her so far, though he was worried about her. Reading her diary, he had found himself cheering her on.

But her story hadn't ended well. He came back to the image he would always have of her, floating in the shallow water at Eagle Falls.

Howie climbed down from the loft in a thoughtful mood, unresolved, leaving Claire asleep in bed. Orange immediately took his place on the pillow. He turned off the reading light, leaving them both in the dark.

Downstairs, he took the photocopy to the hiding place he had created in the interior wall of the pod beneath the desk in his computer nook. It had a hidden spring lock that had to be touched in a certain pattern or it wouldn't open. Howie was quite proud of it—he'd found plans for the safe on the Internet, but it had required some delicate carpentry to install it.

He retrieved the original of Zia's diary from the hiding hole and replaced it with the photocopy. The original was inside a see-through plastic ziplock which he would get rid of after he returned the diary to the slats beneath Zia's mattress.

If all went well.

Chapter Eight

Midnight was a lonely hour on the high desert south of San Geronimo. All was still, except for the rustling breeze and the occasional howl of a coyote. A half moon sat fat in the sky.

Howie came over a hill and down a long grade toward the marshy woodlands where Keir had built his workshop and cabin by the river. He continued a dozen yards past Keir's driveway, turned off his headlights, and glided into the shadows beneath the trees at the side of the road. When he turned off the engine he could hear the pulsating orchestra of cicadas having their nightly party in the trees. There was the porch light of a house in the distance, but otherwise there was no sign of human existence.

Howie wanted to get this over with as quickly as possible. He locked the Subaru and hiked back to the head of the driveway, guided by the light of the moon that lit the land like a black and white negative. The original of Zia's diary was in his daypack along with a strong flashlight. He had an additional flashlight on his phone, should he need it.

The long driveway took him beneath the canopy of trees. The night air was cool. Howie kept to the night shadows and made as little noise as possible. The darkness beneath the trees was velvety, spooky with hidden things, but he resisted the temptation to use his flashlight.

He wasn't expecting to find anybody home. Keir had been a solitary person and if he had any relatives beside Zia, they would only just now be finding out about his death. There wouldn't be cops here either. He hoped.

He came out from the tunnel of trees to find the cabin was dark. The only vehicle in the driveway was Keir's Toyota pickup. Howie knew it was Keir's because it had a San Geronimo Peak Staff Parking sticker on the front window.

He approached the cabin warily, listening for danger. The front door was locked but when he went around to the back, the kitchen door opened as it did before. Howie didn't waste any time. He moved through the house quickly to Zia's bedroom, careful not to touch anything.

The bedroom was as he'd last seen it, as though Zia might return at any moment. There was always something terrible about everyday objects the dead leave behind.

He got busy. He crawled under her bed, took the diary from the plastic bag, held it in his gloved hand, and wiggled the book back between the mattress and the wood slats.

This had gone easier than he'd feared. Mission accomplished, Howie was walking back to the kitchen door when he froze. Through the window above the sink, he saw a dark figure in the driveway, a person walking silently toward the cabin from about a hundred feet away. The figure was so indistinct that Howie had to look hard to make certain it was real.

It was a man, he believed, though he couldn't be sure. Howie didn't think it was a cop, but was uncertain about that also. It seemed to him that a cop would have driven up the driveway in his car, lights blazing. The Sheriff's Department wasn't known for its subtlety. The figure, whoever he was, was walking silently toward the front door.

Howie realized he needed to get out of the cabin fast. He didn't want to be trapped here. He backed away from the window and made his way to the kitchen door. The door opened with an unfortunate screech. He lowered himself into a crouch and scampered across a strip of backyard toward the trees.

His impulse was to continue through the woods, circle back to the driveway, and escape to where he had left his car. But he was curious to know what the intruder was up to. There should only be one stealthy figure in these woods tonight, himself.

He backtracked a dozen feet, returned to the edge of the trees, and lay prone on his stomach, hoping to make himself as invisible as possible. From here he had a view of the front door and one side of the cabin. At first, he couldn't see anything. The figure had disappeared.

But there it was again, moving toward the door.

He still wasn't sure whether it was a man or a woman. The figure was slight, somehow feline, dressed in black clothing. He/she crouched by the door and fiddled with the lock. Howie saw the flash of a metal tool reflected in the moonlight. The door was quickly opened and the figure disappeared inside.

Howie waited, lying on his stomach, propped up on his elbows. Through the windows, he saw the beam of a flashlight come on inside the house. The beam swept about the common room and moved toward the bedrooms in the rear, searching through the house. At last the light came to Zia's bedroom.

Several long minutes passed as the beam explored the bedroom. The flashlight flickered off abruptly leaving the house in darkness.

Howie waited. A minute later, the front door opened and the intruder emerged and continued walking quickly up the driveway toward the road. In the darkness, the black form almost seemed to be floating through the trees.

Howie waited until he heard the distant sound of a car starting up on the road. He listened as the car drove off in the direction of town.

He stood up, brushed himself off, and tried to make sense of what he had seen. Curious, he decided to take another look inside the house.

Everything was as neat and orderly as he had left it. Like Howie, the intruder had been careful not to disturb anything.

He made his way to Zia's bedroom and turned on his phone flashlight to get a better look.

Everything appeared to be as he had left it. But Howie knew the intruder had come for a reason. He got down on his back and slid back beneath the bed.

Zia's diary was gone.

Chapter Nine

Georgie wasn't having a great night in town. In fact, it was awful.

For starters, the Cosmic Mushroom Orchestra was possibly the worst band she had ever heard. As far as she was concerned, they weren't so much fungi as mulch. Nor was she much in a mood for the trendy San Geronimo youth scene.

The new crop of young bohemia had enough money to afford expensive climbing equipment, skis and kayaks, and expensive beer at local pubs. They were attractive. They were hip. They were almost frighteningly healthy. But as a group, Georgie found them shallow and privileged. Boring, really.

The Loft, the venue for the performance, had been open for less than six months. It was the newest place to go, according to Elke, on a side street in an industrial building that had once been an auto glass repair shop.

The music was trance tribal. Or tribal trance. She wasn't sure what to call it. It was hypnotic, endless, no beginning, no end. There were two sitars, a cello, four hand drums, plus a lone flugelhorn. The strings created a wheezing junkyard of sound while the flugelhorn soared and the four hand drums went crazy, creating enough sound to keep the crowd dancing. They played tribal instruments. Their flyer described them as "world tribal reggae soul."

The dance floor, not very large, had been taken over by several women who were doing inspirational leaps and bounds.

The $15 admission included psychedelic mushrooms that were distributed discreetly in the back room. Georgie had politely declined. All the others, including Elke, were dancing in an ecstatic haze.

The big problem for Georgie was a guy in yoga pants and a gypsy vest over his bare chest who wouldn't leave her alone. He seemed to think they might get into the spirit of world tribal reggae soul by him and her getting it on. Georgie wasn't interested. After Ashton Woolridge III, she wanted only to be left alone. She wasn't ready for anyone. Certainly not the idiot who was gyrating in front of her in yoga pants.

By ten o'clock, she was ready to leave. The bad mood she was in was about more than the Cosmic Mushroom Orchestra. She had found Zia's diary deeply disturbing. She'd had only a few hours with the manuscript, but she had read the diary from start to finish. Sexual abuse of young girls made her almost sick with anger. Frankly, she would have liked to find the Dweeb, whoever he was, and beat the shit out of him. She could do it, too. Georgie had grown up on the streets of working class Glasgow, a tough town.

She found Elke in the crowd to say she wasn't feeling well and would find her own way home. Elke was doing a kind of whirling dervish dance with several people and barely noticed her departure. Georgie didn't mind.

It was a relief to be under the night sky away from the loud music. She could breathe again. She found summer nights in New Mexico gorgeous, cool after the heat of the day. The breeze was full of dry mountain smells, sage and desert and pine all mixed together. At 7000 feet, the thin atmosphere sparkled with a clarity that could only be fantasized from soggy Britain.

She walked quickly with her head down, knowing the back streets of America could be dangerous. Everybody had guns here. Coming from Scotland, that seemed insane. In Scotland, possessing an unregistered gun meant a long prison term. Georgie was relieved when she reached the tourist district where there were still crowds of people coming and going from restaurants and bars.

She entered the agency building through the rear door, turning off the alarm system as she walked inside. She was glad to shut the door behind her and be alone. She knew she was becoming anti-social, but she didn't care.

She kicked off her shoes and put a kettle on for tea in the small kitchen alcove. Waiting for the water to boil, she texted Howie and Claire so they wouldn't worry about her:

Hey H & C! Music was terrible so I split thinking I'd have a quiet night on the futon at the office. Elke wanted to stay but it's not a problem. The office is snug and comfortable and I'm enjoying the night alone. See you both tomorrow!

She ended the text with an emoji of a heart.

There were two folded futons in the utility closet by the kitchen. Georgie took one of the futons and set it on the floor of Jack's old office—Howie's office now, the largest room in the building. There were sheets and pillows and she made herself a really comfortable bed where she could lean up against Jack's old liquor cabinet. When she was ready, she turned off all the lights except one, a desk lamp near her head, took off her outer clothes and slipped into bed in her underwear.

She was glad to be alone with a good book and a cup of tea within reach on the floor. Her book was on Kindle, on her phone, written by an astrophysicist, Brian Greene. It explored such things as the beginning and the end of the universe, and what it all meant—if anything at all (probably not). Georgie tended to be attracted to books like this recently. Ones that attempted to look at the Big Picture.

The book absorbed her and it was well after midnight when Georgie turned off the light. It was strange sleeping in town. Over the last few months, she had become accustomed to nighttime forest sounds—wind through the trees, coyotes, sometimes desperate struggles between beasts and birds.

Sleeping in town was very different. She closed her eyes, snuggled into the pillow, and heard something rustling in the alley at the rear of the building. Probably a cat getting into a garbage can. Or a homeless person. In the distance, a siren rose and fell on its way to some emergency. From the front of the building, she heard three young people walking noisily down Calle Dos Flores, laughing loudly, not very sober.

Georgie fell asleep thinking about the different creatures of the earth, coyotes and people, and how strange it was to be alive. She had been asleep for several hours when she woke with a start. Her heart was beating rapidly.

She didn't know what had woken her. She'd had panic attacks before. She was prone to them: unreasonable moments of fear. Here, lying in the dark—in a strange town, in a strange part of the world—she felt particularly vulnerable. But this was silly.

I'm safe as houses! she said to herself. Safe as houses was an expression her Glasgow parents, Ray and Carol, used. Just to say it was comforting. There was nothing to be afraid of here.

But just as she was thinking this, she heard the sound of the back door rattle.

Come on! I'm imagining it! she said to herself with a laugh.

But the back door rattled again.

Somebody definitely was trying to get in.

***

Georgie listened hard, which wasn't easy over the beating of her heart. She could hear nothing beyond the loud thumping in her chest.

The office was dark. All the lights were off in the building. Only a single beam from a lone street lamp a hundred feet down the alley came though the curtained windows at the rear of the office.

Georgie sat up on the futon. She didn't like being in her underwear. The blue numerals of a digital clock glowed from the bookshelf across the room. As she watched, 3:28 AM became 3:29.

The back door rattled again. There was a scraping sound against the lock.

Had she set the security alarm when she came in? She was almost certain she had, but not completely so. Jack, with Buzzy's help, had set up the security system more than ten years ago and at that time it had been theoretically state of the art. Buzzy was a cyber genius who had once been Howie's little brother.

So she was safe. Probably.

The scraping stopped. Georgie relaxed just a little, imagining that whoever it was outside had been stymied by the security. She used the opportunity to find her jeans and sweatshirt and get up from the floor. She found her phone on the office desk and held it guarded in the palm of her hand, a lifeline to help, should she need it.

But she didn't want to call the police if it wasn't necessary. Most likely the noise outside was only a homeless person looking for refuge for the night. Georgie was sympathetic to the homeless. If this was a homeless person, she wanted to give him a chance to get away.

She looked across the room at the digital clock to see the time. It was 3:41 AM. But as she was looking, the blue digits went dark. The clock itself disappeared into the shadows of the room. There was a new silence in the building.

It took Georgie a moment to figure out what sound was missing. It was the fan for the humidifier that was in the alcove off the reception area, a constant hum Georgie had always found irritating, going day and night. The fan was necessary in a two-hundred year old building to fight against the tendency of adobe to return to dust. Georgie had become so accustomed to the sound that its absence was startling.

The electricity was off.

Georgie had 911 ready on the screen of her phone. She pressed the green button and walked barefoot across the room and picked up the iron poker by the kiva fireplace.

A female voice said, "911. What is your emergency?"

Georgie spoke quickly and softly. "I'm at 29 Calle Dos Flores, just off the Plaza. It's the Wilder private detective building. Someone is trying to break in from the wynd at the rear. Please come quickly!"

"Would you say that more slowly, please?"

The operator was having trouble with her accent, which suddenly—in panic—had reverted to hardcore Glaswegian. Wynd was Scottish for alley.

There was a new sound at the back door, a sonic hum. The door itself was vibrating. Whoever was breaking in the back door had good electronics.

Georgie was determined to stand her ground. She held the iron poker in one hand and her phone in the other. With some fast thumb work, she brought up the camera.

The back door opened slowly. Georgie could make out the silhouette of a tall thin man. He stood very still in the doorway surveying the inside. He hadn't seen Georgie yet.

"Ah-uuu!" she cried, like a crazed coyote, as she launched herself at him.

In a single motion, she raised the phone, snapped a photograph, and slashed down with the poker. The flash of the camera blinded him. The poker came down hard on his right shoulder near his neck.

"Yee-ahh!" he cried.

He still wasn't down. Fortunately, Georgie had taken a women's self-defense class in Glasgow. She knew what to do.

Balanced on her left foot, she raised her right foot in a kung-fu move she had practiced for an entire summer. She kicked him hard in the balls.

"Yee-ahh!" he cried again, an octave higher.

The intruder didn't stand a chance. He staggered backward into the alley, howling in pain. He fell onto his back on the gravel, picked himself up, and scampered off like a wounded bug down the alley.

"I've called the coppers!" she shouted after him. "Fucking bampot!"

Georgie couldn't say what Scottish part of her brain that came from. But it did the trick. The bampot—ugly sleaze, loosely translated from Weegie—ran as though all the demons of hell were after him.

Georgie slammed the door behind her, made sure it was locked, then collapsed in the chair behind the oversized desk and sobbed.

Chapter Ten

Sunday morning Howie woke up groggy after two hours of sleep. "How's the bear?" Claire called from the foot of the ladder.

"Coffee?" he grunted.

"It's made."

Claire climbed half way up the ladder to the loft to hand a mug of strong coffee to Howie, who leaned over the edge of the platform to accept it. He didn't move too quickly. He slipped back into bed with a groan. The caffeine brought him slowly to life. Very slowly.

The memory of last night left him with an uneasy feeling. What an irony!—to return Zia's diary only to see it stolen again. And by who? *Whom*? A ghost-like figure who had drifted through the trees. Whoever he was, he had come for Zia's diary.

Howie cast a bleary glance at the screen of his phone, which told him it was 8:43 AM.

The screen also said there was a text from Georgie that had been sent last night at 11:41. He brought it up:

Hi, H & C. Music was terrible so I split thinking I'd have a quiet night on the futon at the office. Elke wanted to stay but it's not a problem. There's coffee and breakfast in the fridge so don't worry about me. The office is snug and comfortable and I'm enjoying the night alone. See you both tomorrow!

At the time Georgie had sent this, Howie had been on the road driving. He had turned off his phone a few minutes later as he parked near the top of Keir's driveway, but he should have heard a text come in at 11:41. This was a problem for Howie. He and his phone did not live in harmony. The phone had issues and as a result he often missed texts and calls.

He had some misgivings about Georgie spending the night in town, but decided to keep them to himself. He knew an independent young woman in the bloom of youth should get about among people her own age. But he worried about her just the same. There were such odd things going on.

He wondered if it was too early to phone her. It was Sunday morning, people were supposed to sleep in. Howie decided to call anyway. He was her father, which gave you some leeway when it came to being intrusive with your children. He poked her number on speed dial.

"Da, good morning," she answered on the second ring. "I was just thinking to call you but I didn't want to wake you. How did last night go?"

"Good and bad," he said. "I did what I needed to do but then a strange thing happened. I'll tell you about it when I see you. So you decided to stay in town?"

"I did. I hated the music and Elke wanted to stay. So the office seemed a good choice. The futon was totally comfortable, I didn't mind at all."

"So everything's okay?" Howie had heard something in Georgie's voice that seemed off.

"Well, just like you said about your night. There was both good and bad."

"Georgie, what's the bad part?"

She knew that Howie was going to be upset when she told him about the intruder. She tried to be as calm and undramatic as possible.

"Da, there was a break-in."

"A *what?*"

"At the office. Somebody tried to break in through the back door. But I stopped him."

"Didn't the alarm go off?"

"You see, he neutralized it, Da. He seemed to know his electronics. The electricity went off also."

"Are you saying he got in?"

"Da, calm down. I told you, I stopped the bugger. I was standing by the back door and I whacked him with one of those iron pokers. You should have seen him scamper off down the alley!"

Howie lay back on the pillows with a groan.

"I got a photograph of him, though. I used the flash to disorient him. Unfortunately, he was wearing a mask so you can't see who it is."

The thought of the danger Georgie had been in made Howie feel awful. He tried to think this through. Was any of it his fault? Had he gotten his daughter in danger?

"What time did this happen?"

"3:43, Da. I was keeping an eye on the digital clock on the bookshelf just before the electricity went off."

The timing made it possible that the intruder at the office was the same person Howie had seen earlier taking the diary from Zia's bedroom.

But if this was true, the thief had possession of the diary, so why break into the office? Was it the photocopy he was looking for? Could he have known there *was* a photocopy? A lucky guess?

Howie had many unanswered questions. Meanwhile, he was glad the photocopy was in his hiding hole at home. But now he had Claire to worry about, as well as Georgie.

"Did the cops come?" he asked.

"Aye, eventually. I called 911 but the coppers took forever getting here. To be honest, I played it down. Once the danger was over, I didn't see a reason to make a fuss. So they took a report and I doubt if we'll ever hear from them again. Da, it will be easier to tell you about all this when you get here. Why don't you and Claire come in for brunch and we'll go home together. Okay?"

Howie said they were on their way.

***

Claire decided to stay at home, saying she wanted to weed the vegetable garden before it got too hot. Plus there was cleaning she needed to do.

Howie knew it was solitude she craved above all. He had seen Claire in action, on concert hall stages in London, Edinburgh, Berlin, Tokyo, Paris—playing for thousands, dealing with a stressful world. If anybody needed decompression from a high-wire act, it was Claire. She had her leased SUV so she had mobility if she needed to get to town. But all she really wanted was time to spend in nature—Howie's forest on a summer day. After a month, he knew, she would be longing for the bustle of London and Berlin.

"Go," she told him, giving him a kiss. "I'll be fine!"

Howie drove to town in a troubled mood. He had an itchy feeling of badness hovering nearby. He needed to figure out what was happening before the badness came any closer.

His plan today was to find a man he knew, Shawn Basset, the head of ski patrol. Shawn had worked with Keir for more than 20 years. Ski patrol was a dangerous business and patrollers tended to get close. He was hoping Shawn would be able to tell him about Keir's life with Zia, how they managed together, any problems that may have come up.

Howie's phone rang as he was coming out of the foothills into the high desert. The screen said it was Lieutenant Santo Ruben, head of the

San Geronimo substation of the State Police. Santo. Howie debated whether to answer. Santo was Jack's good friend, but this didn't automatically extend to Howie. When it came to police work, he could be a hard ass.

Howie decided he might as well get it over with.

"Morning, Santo," he said with as much cheer as he could summon.

"Don't good morning me, Moon Deer. We need to talk! What were you doing at Keir Aaronson's house when the body was found?"

"It's the case I'm on, Santo. I'll be honest with you—I'm looking into the death of Zia McFadden. She's the teen whose body was found at Eagle Falls. Keir was Zia's father. I was hoping he'd be able to tell me what was going on in his daughter's life."

"And you just happened to find him hanging in a tree?"

"Yes, I know that sounds . . ." He struggled for the right word. "Serendipitous. But that's exactly how it happened."

"Who's your client?"

"You know I can't tell you that. Anyway, what's your interest? I thought the Sheriffs were working the case."

"They were. They handed it over to us last night."

"So it's a murder investigation, then?"

Santo paused.

"Santo," said Howie, "I know the Sheriff's wouldn't hand you the case unless it was a homicide. So you might as well tell me."

"Okay. As long as you're honest with me, Moon Deer, I'll be honest with you. The ME says Keir was dead before he was put up into the tree. I'll let you figure it from there. Did you know Keir?"

"Only a little. From skiing up on the Peak."

"Here's my last question. Do you know who killed him?"

"I do not, Santo."

"Hmm," said Santo ponderously. "Okay, look, I'm in the car right now. I'm on my way to Santa Fe for a meeting I need to attend. I don't know how long I'll be, but I want to see you in my office when I get back. From here on out, I want to know exactly what you're up to. I don't want there to be any secrets between us. Is that clear?"

"Absolutely," Howie promised.

Santo didn't seem convinced. "This is serious, Howie. I don't want you to be finding any more bodies in trees!"

In this, he was in complete agreement. He didn't want to find any more bodies in trees either.

***

Howie felt bad about concealing evidence from Santo. Zia's diary was something he should know about. He liked Santo but he was in a bind. He probably shouldn't have searched Keir's cabin, and he definitely shouldn't have taken the diary for a day.

But he had.

He had borrowed Zia's diary.

Howie memorized "borrowed" as a word he might need. Unfortunately, he would not be able to prove he had returned it since it had now gone missing again . . .

His phone rang as he was pondering these matters. This was a nuisance. Ordinarily, he didn't like to talk on the phone while he was driving. He was about to let the call go to voicemail when he saw it was from Emma Wilder. Emma didn't phone often and he had a horrible thought that Jack had had another stroke.

"Yes, hi, Emma," Howie said, grabbing the phone from the passenger seat. "I'm driving into town. Is everything all right?"

"Everything's okay, Howie. I just want to invite you and Claire and Georgie for dinner tonight, a barbecue in the backyard. I thought it would be nice to get together. I know Jack will welcome the company."

Howie understood immediately that this was about Jack. "How *is* Jack?" he asked.

Emma paused. "Well, I'm not entirely sure," she admitted. "He's been very quiet the last few days so I worry a little. I'm thinking maybe you can tell him about the case you're working. Make him feel included. Remind him that he's a detective emeritus, so to speak."

"Emma, Jack will always be my mentor. Of course, I'll fill him in on what's happening at the office."

There were several things unspoken here: Jack still owned half the business, and it was Emma's money (inherited) that had set up the agency in the first place. The summons to a Sunday barbecue was part business, part social.

"So you can come? I'm thinking 6 o'clock?"

He told her that was perfect. Six o'clock. He looked forward to it.

In fact, he wasn't looking forward to it, not a bit. He had been hoping for a night with Georgie and Claire at home. But Emma was obviously babysitting Jack and hoping for help from Howie. This felt like an obligation.

When he arrived at the office, he found Georgie on the phone in the front room in the midst of a conversation. She raised her hand as she continued talking to let Howie know she'd be a second.

"No, it's okay, Elke, honestly. I didn't mind at all. I went to the office and crashed on a futon," Georgie was saying. "And that guy you met sounds terrific . . . you went home with him?"

Howie sat in one of the two canvas directors chairs they kept in the reception area for clients and walk-in inquiries. He listened as Georgie assured Elke once again that she'd been fine spending the night at the

68

agency. She made no mention of the break-in. Georgie shook her head in frustration as she disconnected.

"I don't know why Elke needed to apologize," she complained. "Like I kept telling her, I was great here last night! I thought I'd go batty if I had to listen to the Cosmic Mushroom Orchestra another second more!"

"Georgie, you weren't great here last night," Howie said gently. "Somebody with some skill bypassed the security to break in and attack you."

"Da, I was the one who attacked him. He didn't stand a chance. I hit the wanker with a poker and kicked him in the balls. He will not be coming back any time soon."

"We can't assume that," Howie said. "This case has gotten nasty. Let me see the photograph you took. Maybe it'll give me some idea what's going on."

Georgie brought up the photograph on her phone. She had told Howie about the mask the intruder wore, but it still came as a shock. It was white, quite thin fabric, with two round holes for eyes and a mouth hole to breathe. Everything about the mask was evil. The white material, with the vague outline of a human face beneath, gave it a hellish look. It reminded Howie of Edvard Munch's, "The Scream." The camera had caught a monster by surprise.

Howie wasn't sure what to say. He was horrified that Georgie had been in danger. But she didn't seem a bit worried. She appeared to enjoy getting the better of the scuffle.

"You're all right, that's the main thing," he said.

"Yes, Da, I'm all right."

Howie sighed. "Did you read the diary?"

"I did, yesterday while you were off at Jack's. I read it all the way through. I'd like to read it again more closely, but I got the idea of what was going on."

"So what did you think of Zia?"

"I liked her. From her diary, she seemed a very thoughtful, honest person. It sure made me angry reading about the Dweeb! Imagine sneaking off to Zia's bedroom like that! What's really awful is the mother didn't believe Zia when she told her what happened!"

"Do you think Zia was telling the truth?"

"Of course, I do, Da! Don't you?"

"Yes, I do. I'm angry just like you are. But we have to look at all the possibilities. What do you think about her last entry?"

"That strange little poem? *Penis remus cum cunt and bum . . . what kind of girl am I to have such fun?* I'm not sure. It wasn't like anything else in the diary. My guess is she was bored and was just being kind of dark and sarcastic."

"Perhaps something happened to put her in a dark mood."

"A man? Do you think she was having sex?"

"I don't know, Georgie. There's a lot to find out. Obviously, we need to find the identity of the Dweeb and look at what happened to Zia in Albuquerque. But first I want to find out more about what was going on in San Geronimo. She was here for nearly a year, and this is where she died. I'm going to try to see a ski patroller today who was a friend of Keir's. I'm hoping he'll be able to fill in some blanks. But I have something for you to do, Georgie, if you're interested."

"Of course, I'm interested, Da!"

"Good. Do you remember the girl Zia mentioned here in San Geronimo? The one friend she made at school?"

"Yes. Her name is Uma. I don't believe Zia gives her last name."

"Exactly. Uma. I'd like you to try to see if you can discover her last name and who she is. The paper might have a list of the graduating class at San Geronimo Valley School. I'd like you to see if you can find any information about friends she might have made here. Anyone who knew her at all."

"Aye, I can do that," Georgie told him. "If Uma was on a sports team, it should be especially easy to find her last name."

"It's a private school, expensive, heavy on the arts. The sort of place where privileged kids get to discover their creative potential."

"You sound like you don't approve."

"No, it's not the kids' fault. Or the parents, really. They just want the best for their children. It's that all kids should have these opportunities, not only a few."

Howie and Georgie ended up skipping brunch. They were both preoccupied and wanted to get to work.

Howie retreated into his office where he busied himself on the phone tracking down Shawn, the head of ski patrol. Forty-five minutes later he rejoined Georgie in the reception room.

"Okay, I'm off," he told her. "Shawn is working up on the Peak today even though it's Sunday. There's a special project they're doing on one of the lifts, but he says he can take some time to talk. By the way, we're all invited to a barbecue tonight at Jack and Emma's. I've accepted on our behalf, so get ready for a ton of food. And Jack's stories of the Old Days on the force in San Francisco."

Georgie merely nodded. She was on a Internet quest to find Zia's friend, Uma, and she had just struck gold.

Chapter Eleven

Georgie found the last name of Zia's friend, Uma, by searching through the late May and early June editions of *The San Geronimo Post*. She looked for stories about high school graduations, sports teams, high school drama clubs, anything. Local newspapers were big on school events.

The June 3rd edition had a photograph of the graduating class at the San Geronimo Valley School that showed twenty-five boys and girls who were being launched into what passed today as adulthood. Uma Rothenstein was in the top row, a tall, heavy-boned girl.

Georgie's eyes widened slightly as she learned that Uma was the daughter of Edward Rothenstein, the famous New York artist. Georgie knew his work. She had seen several of Rothenstein's paintings at the Tate Modern in London. He was what she thought of as a Rothko clone. It wasn't necessarily a complaint. She liked Rothko.

Rothenstein had made his reputation with moody seascapes where the ocean met the sky in gradually changing bands of color. They were impressionistic, not entirely abstract. If you looked hard, you could make out the seashore, the cliffs, the ocean, the muted sun, the sky. Georgie had seen the exhibit at the Tate with Ashton. They were on a sexy weekend in London at a small hotel in Knightsbridge.

"I'm sorry, but Rothenstein doesn't pass muster!" Ashton declared as they walked through the museum with serious Cambridge-bred expressions on their faces. "If you're going to be an Abstract Expressionist, go for it, I say. But don't mix styles. Don't throw Realism into the Abstract Expressionist pot!"

"Why not?" Georgie had asked naively. She wasn't sure she had understood a word Ashton said.

"You just don't," he lectured. "Mixing styles muddies the waters. Myself, I'm sticking with Gainsborough."

Ashton had been taking Georgie in hand, culture-wise, ever since they met. As far as he was concerned, she was a wild Scottish lass. His family had several Gainsboroughs in the grand hallway of their country manor. Scenes of tranquil English life from long ago.

What an asshole! Georgie said to herself as she remembered Ashton.

There were dozens of articles about Rothenstein online, as well as reviews of shows he'd had in such places as SoHo, Ft. Worth, and Rio de Janeiro. He was successful enough to have apartments in New York and Paris, as well as a house in San Geronimo—his New Mexico escape, as he put it. In a *New York Times* article, Rothenstein claimed "the light in New Mexico is sheer illumination." Whatever that meant. Georgie didn't like pretentious art talk.

Rothenstein was married to a Dutch woman, Catherine Van Gieson, who had been his model in the early years of his career. He had done several paintings of Catherine in the nude in which she looked very dishy, to use an Ashton expression. Catherine was also an artist in her own right, though not nearly as famous as her husband. She exhibited in Santa Fe, not Paris.

The most interesting article Georgie found online was a New Yorker profile of Rothenstein from 15 years ago which portrayed the artist as an unrepentant womanizer. The article described how Rothenstein had shown up at the Cannes Film Festival with the French actress Michele LeFebre, both of them in outrageous attire, nearly naked, and drunk.

"The rock star painter," the New Yorker dubbed him. "A throwback to the macho days of Jackson Pollock and Norman Mailer. A time when to be an artist was to be male, drink too much, and treat women badly."

The writer of the article was a woman and she didn't approve. Georgie didn't either. The article mentioned Rothenstein's wife, Catherine, back home in New Mexico.

It took Georgie nearly an hour to find the address of Rothenstein's San Geronimo home. She found it eventually under the name of Catherine Van Gieson. It was fifteen miles south of town in the foothills, in the opposite direction of Howie's land. Georgie had ridden her bike there. It was a beautiful part of the county and one of her favorite rides. Georgie didn't ponder the question long. She decided to give in to her curiosity and go for a ride. She had no idea what she would find. For all she knew, Uma and her family might be gone for the summer. But it wouldn't hurt to take a look. Besides, she was dying for outdoor exercise. Georgie didn't like to be cooped up in an office.

At a few minutes before 2 o'clock, she rolled her mountain bike out the back door, locked the office, and set the alarm behind her. Mid-afternoon was the hottest part of the day, and Georgie was soon sweating as she peddled through town toward the four-lane highway that led south toward Santa Fe. She was glad to let herself loose on the open highway, feeling her legs and body in motion.

Five miles south, she turned onto the two-lane county road that climbed into the foothills. The Rothenstein estate sat in an open area of piñon and juniper on the knoll of a gently rounded hill. Georgie was out of breath by the time she reached the top. The complex of buildings that comprised the Rothenstein estate were at the top of a long paved driveway. There was a main house, a large adobe hacienda, and three smaller adobe buildings that wrapped around three sides of a meadow.

The view from here was breathtaking and Georgie took a few moments to enjoy it. You could see for at least a hundred miles, maybe more, the world spread at your feet, mountain range after mountain range and brown/red mesas and desert. It was a view that stretched your mind and opened your heart. Georgie felt herself expanding in the expansiveness. She felt at home in this land.

Her breathing had almost returned to normal when a man's voice startled her.

"Tell me what you're thinking?" the man asked.

Georgie jumped. She hadn't heard anyone approach. She turned and looked, but she couldn't see anybody anywhere. She was mystified.

"Up here," said the voice.

Georgie looked upward and was surprised to see a camera and a small speaker on a metal pole at the side of the driveway.

"What are you thinking?" he asked again.

She laughed because this was so ridiculous.

"If you must know, I was thinking the view from here makes all the mess and hustle of humanity disappear. I feel I could stand here forever and breathe it in!"

"I see. Now here's what you're going to do. You're going to peddle your way up to the studio and I'm going to draw you."

"*What?*"

"Please," said the man, "I'm going to immortalize you."

"Oh, really?" said Georgie. "And just who are you exactly?"

"Edward Rothenstein. Who else should I be? Now be a good girl and hop back on that bike of yours. I'm in my studio, the first building on the right."

***

Georgie stood at the head of Edward Rothenstein's driveway for a full thirty seconds with her bike leaning against her leg, debating the invitation.

Should she? Should she not?

75

Edward Rothenstein was a notorious womanizer, a man to avoid. Georgie didn't approve of him in the least.

But she had a job to do. She wanted to question Uma and possibly the mother as well. The invitation to come onto the property made everything easier. Plus she was starting to feel foolish, standing indecisively at the edge of the property, knowing that he was watching her on his screen.

Okay, she was going to do it. She got back on her bike and pedaled up the long driveway. He stood watching her from the shade of a porch outside one of the adobe outbuildings. The studio was modern, a new take on traditional New Mexico architecture. There were much larger windows, more air and light than the original. Probably the roof didn't leak, unlike the Wilder & Associate office building in town.

Edward Rothenstein was in his early sixties, tall, lean, dressed in tan slacks and a faded Hawaiian shirt that had palm trees on it. There were slashes of paint on his pants, and his clothes looked old and comfortable. He had a paintbrush in his right hand.

Georgie had seen photographs of Rothenstein online, so she was prepared for the fact that he was handsome. His hair was silvery and curly, slightly wild. His face had sharp angles, as though etched in stone. He looked more like a pirate than an artist.

She felt self-conscious getting off her bike in front of his steady gaze.

"Hmm," he said, as she leaned her bike against an apple tree and walked his way. "Now, tell me again? Who are you?"

"My name is Georgina Hadley. We've never met, Mr. Rothenstein. I've come to see Uma. Is she here?"

"My daughter? She's not here right now. You're not American, are you? What are you, Irish?"

"Scottish," she answered with irritation.

"Really? And I could have sworn you were an Indian."

"I'm that also," Georgie told him. "Where I come from, one does not need to be monodimensional."

"Monodimensional? Is that an actual term?"

Georgie was embarrassed. The phrase had come to her without much thought. It did sound a bit poofy. She was nervous.

"When will Uma be back?"

"Soon. She went shopping with her mother in town. You can come inside and have a glass of plonk with me while you're waiting."

Georgie could see past him inside the open door to the studio. There was an easel with a painting on it, and a stack of more canvases against the wall. There was also a bed.

"Why don't we have a glass of plonk out here?" she suggested. "Outside."

He shrugged with good humor.

"Have a seat," he said, offering her the choice of a deck chair or a hanging swing for two. Georgie chose the chair.

He went inside and came out a moment later with a bottle of white wine in a silver ice bucket. He brought two square stubby glasses that looked like they'd be better suited to whiskey. He put them on a round wrought iron table then ducked back inside his studio.

This time he came out with a drawing pad and a tray of pencils.

"No, no!" Georgie told him. "I don't want you to draw me!"

"Why not?"

Because it was much too intimate, and she wasn't going to open that door.

She told him, more mildly, "I would feel too self-conscious. Besides, I'm not here for that. I'm here to see Uma."

He set down the pad and pencils on the table and poured them each a glass. It was an expensive French wine that Georgie had drunk before at posh parties at Cambridge. Pouilly-fumè. Ashton had liked it.

"Chin-chin," he said, clinking glasses. He sat down on the swing and pushed it gently with one foot. "Tell me your name again."

"Georgina Hadley," she said sternly.

"And why are you here to see Uma? I can't believe you're one of her friends."

"Do you know her friends?"

"I do not. But you are of another cut entirely. Uma is still a little girl. You, my dear, are a woman."

Georgie shook her head. Horny old men with big egos were all the same.

"Why are you shaking your head?"

"Because you're so obvious, Mr. Rothenstein."

"Perhaps. But you, you're a mystery, Georgina Hadley. What do you want with my daughter?"

Georgie debated several choices of lies.

"I'm looking into the death of Uma's school friend, Zia McFadden. I'm a journalist," she said. "I'm writing an article about suicide deaths of teenage girls in America."

"Are you?" he asked, studying her intently.

"For *The Guardian*," she added.

"You're a staff writer there?"

"I write for them only occasionally. I just graduated from Cambridge." She blushed, knowing that she had added her university credentials in order to impress him.

"How old are you, Georgina?"

"I'm twenty-one," she answered firmly.

"Good! I'm going to draw you!" he announced, standing up from the table. "Then I'm going to paint you. You're going to be my model."

"No, I'm not, Mr. Rothenstein! I've told you I'm not interested!"

He came closer. "What? You think I want to fuck you? Of course I want to fuck you! Who wouldn't? But this has nothing to do with that. This is about your eyes."

"My eyes?" she managed.

"Mmm," he said gravely. "Your eyes are touched with untamed poetry. They make me think of the Irish Sea."

"Oh, puh-lease!" she cried. She had no intention of becoming his latest conquest. "And for God's sake, I am *Scottish!*"

He was about to reach for her. Georgie felt it coming. But fortunately, at this moment, they heard a car coming up the driveway. It was his wife, Catherine, arriving with their daughter, Uma.

***

Uma Rothenstein was as large and gawky as she had appeared in the graduation photograph. She had short dye-blonde hair, painted blue fingernails, and a weary expression on her face.

There was a small gold ring in her left nostril. She was barefoot. Each of her ten toenails were painted a different color. She was dressed in expensive designer jeans that were torn at the knees and a T-shirt from a concert of a band that called itself Purple Piss.

Georgie had only a brief sighting of Uma's mother, Catherine, as they got out of their dusty Mercedes station wagon. Catherine was a large blonde woman, clearly of northern European descent. Uma had inherited the hefty build but not the beauty.

Without a word, the mother set off at a brisk pace toward the large hacienda at the edge of the meadow, while Uma walked in a separate direction toward the smallest of the two adobe outbuildings.

"Hi," said Georgie, catching up with her. "I'm Georgie. I was wondering if I can talk with you for a moment."

"What for?" Uma asked without stopping. She broadcast a faint scent of marijuana.

"I'm a graduate student at Cambridge University," Georgie answered, changing occupations without a blink. "I'm on a research assignment into teenage suicide in America. It's a terribly important subject. I'm hoping you can tell me something about Zia McFadden."

This time Uma did stop. She gave Georgie a better looking over.

"How old are you?" she asked unexpectedly.

"I'm twenty-one."

"I'm fucking seventeen," said Uma. She didn't seem enthusiastic about the age. She was no dancing queen. "I can't do anything. I don't have a life!"

"I'm sorry," said Georgie.

"Yeah, I am too. So what do you want to know about Zia?"

"Anything you can tell me. Was she depressed? What was she like?"

Uma sighed and shook her head. She turned and continued on the path alongside the meadow to the smallest of the casitas.

"Is this your little house?"

"I guess," said Uma. "It's where I sleep."

"You live in your own casita? By yourself? That's genius! I would have done anything to have my own space when I was your age!"

"I guess," she said again, even more dispiritedly.

Uma didn't invite her inside the casita. They spoke outside sitting on the grass in the shade of a huge blue spruce that must have been planted decades ago, not a native tree.

"I really can't tell you much about Zia," Uma said as she lit a cigarette. "We were friends for a while, but then we sort of had a falling out."

"Why was that?"

"I don't know!" said Uma profoundly. "It just was."

"Well, okay. So what was she like?"

"Zia? She was different. I don't know. It's hard to describe her."

Try! Georgie wanted to scream. She nodded patiently.

"I'm trying to understand why she killed herself," Georgie urged. "Was she unhappy?"

Uma shrugged. "You know what I think? I think maybe she stood at the edge of that cliff and just wondered what it would be like to jump. Maybe it was only curiosity."

Georgie considered this. "Curiosity?"

"Sure. We're all going to die anyway, so why not? I mean, you wouldn't have to go through all the muck, would you? You could give the whole show a miss!"

Georgie didn't know what to say. It took a moment to think of an answer.

"But then you'd miss the good parts. Falling in love. Having children. Traveling in the Himalayas. Sex."

Uma shook her head. "Come, on, none of those things turn out to be any good! Sex is sure overrated! Gimme a break!"

Sex hadn't been overrated in Georgie's experience, not with Ashton Woolridge III. That part of the relationship had been great. It was the other parts that were problematical.

"Did you and Zia talk about relationships?" she asked.

"Sometimes."

"Did Zia have a boyfriend?"

"You know, you have a funny accent," Uma said, changing the subject. "Where are you from?"

"I grew up in Scotland."

"But you're an Indian."

"That's a long story," Georgie told her. "And mostly it's my parents story, not mine. My story is just getting started."

Uma looked at Georgie with new interest.

"Huh!" she said thoughtfully. "That's an interesting way to look at it."

Uma had gradually relaxed as they were talking until she almost seemed a different person. Her eyes had life in them. Not a lot, but a little.

"Do you have a boyfriend?" she asked.

"I did," Georgie replied. "But not now."

"Where did you go to college?"

"Cambridge University. Do you know where that is?"

"In New York somewhere?"

"England. But tell me about *your* school. I've heard it's very progressive."

"Yeah, I guess." After a brief flare of interest, Uma had gone sullen again. "It's okay. The teachers leave you alone, pretty much. Most of them are off smoking weed."

"And that's where you met Zia? At school?"

"She was new and we all sort of avoided her at first. I mean, the rest of us had known each another forever. But Zia and I were on the same volleyball team and somehow we started joking about the teachers and things. I liked her. She was funny. And God, she was . . . beautiful! She could have been the most popular girl anywhere but she didn't even try. She was kind of odd that way. But I guess I'm odd too. That's what drew us together."

Uma gave Georgie a steady look. "I'm not gay," she added. "But if I was gay, Zia would be the girl I'd be hot for."

"I understand," Georgie said. She knew how intense relations could be between teenage girls.

"And Zia, was she . . ."

"Naw. She was nothing. She wasn't interested in anything like that. Boys, girls, nobody . . . at first, I thought she was kind of a nun."

"At first?"

Uma shook her head and didn't answer.

"Did she ever talk about boys?" Georgie asked.

"*Nada*. All the boys were after her. But she just pretended they weren't there."

"So what did you two talk about?"

"I don't know. Movies, music, stuff like that. She talked about her mother a lot. She really hated her. She called her the Cow Bitch."

"And that's why she moved up here to San Geronimo, was it? To get away from her mother?"

"Yeah. She liked living with her dad. And she liked the school here better."

"Did she ever mention somebody she called the Dweeb?"

"Sure, the Dweeb was her mother's boyfriend. She hated him, too."

"Did she say why she hated him?"

"Naw."

"What was the Dweeb's real name? Did she say that?"

"No, she was totally into these names she made up. The Cow Bitch, the Dweeb. It's like she was too angry to call them by their real names. Like that would make them more real."

"What was she angry about?"

Georgie, of course, knew why Zia was angry. It was the Dweeb coming to her bedroom at night, and her mother who didn't stop it. But she pressed anyway hoping Uma might tell her more.

But Uma only continued to shake her head. "I never understood her, I really didn't. I'm sorry she's dead. None of the other girls at school liked her except me. She was sort of strange, you know. And mysterious about stuff. I stuck by her as long as I could."

"You said you had a falling out?" Georgie said, hoping for more.

Uma sat quietly regarding her fingernails. Georgie thought she wasn't going to answer. But then she began to speak.

"My mother didn't like her. She told me she didn't want Zia coming around anymore."

"Really? Your mother? Why was that?"

Uma shrugged. "I don't know. Why does anyone do anything?"

"I don't understand. Did Zia come here often?"

"Not really. Once or twice, I guess."

"And your mother—"

Look, I don't want to talk about this," Uma interrupted. "I mean, Zia's dead, so what does it matter? I just want to forget about her, okay?"

Georgie continued trying to win Uma's confidence. But Uma had shut down. She shook her head with a sullen pout and refused to say another word.

***

Georgie walked her bike along the path past the main house toward the driveway wondering why Uma had stopped talking.

What an unhappy girl! But of course high school was an unhappy time for a lot of girls. Georgie wasn't particularly bubbling with joy herself back then. But it seemed odd that out of her classmates at school Zia had chosen to befriend Uma Rothenstein. And why had Uma's mother turned against Zia?

Georgie wondered if Uma was gay despite her protestations to the contrary. Georgie didn't care in the least one way or the other. She'd had a number of friends in her life who were gay, and many more who had gone through a gay period in adolescence. Apparently the sex question had become a problem between Zia and Uma—Uma lusting, Zia saying no. But maybe their falling out was about something very different. Georgie had many unanswered questions. She suspected that Uma knew more about Zia than she was willing to say.

As Georgie walked her bike past Edward Rothenstein's studio, he waved at her from the front porch.

She had to admit there was something enticing about an internationally famous artist taking an interest in you. But of course, there was nothing special about that. Rothenstein had the hots for all the young females.

Georgie laughed. She suddenly had a very good idea why Uma's mother didn't want Zia coming around!

She didn't return Edward Rothenstein's wave. Without glancing in his direction, she climbed on her bike and rode swiftly away.

Dirty old man!

Chapter Twelve

Howie liked getting up into the high country. It was a different world at 9000 feet, a slice of Switzerland. It was hard to believe the desert was only a forty minute drive down a treacherous two-lane highway.

It was a fine summer day on San Geronimo Peak, the temperature in the high sixties, the sky blue, the ski trails green with grass, bright with wild flowers.

Howie found Shawn Basset at the base of the Coyote Lift, one of the three chairlifts that climbed the front side of the mountain. In summer, Shawn ran the crew that worked on the trails, getting rid of stumps and clearing out trees for the winter ahead. Sean had been required to work on a Sunday to meet with the head of lift ops and two people from management, a man and a woman, new faces who Howie didn't know.

They were discussing the bolts that connected the chairs to the cable overhead. Shawn was saying the bolts needed to be replaced. The man and woman from management were skeptical. Replacing the bolts would be an expensive operation. Maybe they could just tighten the existing ones. The woman believed this would satisfy the yearly inspection.

Howie stayed back respectfully until there was a break in the conversation. The safety of ski lifts was a matter of prime importance. Two seasons ago, one of the bolts on the Porcupine Lift came loose and a chair with three people on it slid backwards on the cable, hitting the chair behind it and sending two skiers tumbling onto the snow. The incident was hushed up tighter than plutonium at Los Alamos.

Shawn was a mild, elfish looking man who looked more like an accountant than the head of ski patrol. This was deceptive. He was tough and smart, an ER medic with a master's degree in forest management. In the summer, he also ran workshops on wilderness survival. Howie knew him from a rescue operation on a New Year's Day several years ago. A teenage skier had ducked a rope to go off-piste and was now missing on the mountain. Joining a team of thirty volunteers, Howie had helped find the 19 year-old fool who had come close to freezing to death.

"Howie!" Shawn said, coming his way. "How's your summer going?"

"Good. And thanks so much for seeing me. I see how busy you are."

Shawn lowered his voice. "Howie, you don't know! These assholes know nothing. They're real estate agents, that's all they care about. Building condos. They know nothing about running a mountain!"

There was a new owner at San Geronimo Peak. It had been a family operation for fifty years. But a year ago the family sold out to a billionaire from New York, Leonardo Hamm, and Howie had been hearing rumblings for months. Ski Patrol was unhappy that the sport itself—skiing, snowboarding—was being neglected for an orgy of development. Patrol, who kept the mountain safe, was still paid very little.

"I have just a few questions about Keir Aaronson," Howie said. "I'm looking into his death."

"Are you? I was sorry to hear about his passing." Shawn walked with Howie from the lift onto a flat grassy area where in winter people got in and out of their skis and snowboards. "I liked Keir. We worked together for, what?—twenty years. But I'm not sure I knew him well. Man, it was a shock to hear he hanged himself."

"Well, that's not quite true. The medical examiner is saying Keir was dead before somebody put him up in that tree."

Shawn gave Howie an intense look. "You're saying he was killed?"

"That's what it looks like."

Shawn sighed deeply. He shook his head.

"Oh, man! Well, that sure is fucked! What do you want to know?"

"I'm interested in his daughter, Zia. She came up here from Albuquerque to live with Keir last year while she finished high school. Did he talk about that to you?"

"Yeah, a little. Keir was the kind of guy who kept his private life to himself. But he needed to change his work schedule sometimes because of Zia—dentist appointments, school stuff. He was trying to be a good dad, he really was. The logistics weren't always easy for him, taking care of a teenage daughter while working up here, needing to be on the mountain sometimes at five in the morning after a storm."

"How did he and Zia get along?"

"Just fine, the way he described it. Here's the thing. His romp with Mikaela was eighteen years ago and it wasn't anything serious. It was party time back then. He never meant to get her pregnant, that's for sure. They were only together for a month or so. But when Mikaela got pregnant, he did his best to take on the responsibility. He was a good guy, Howie. A very good guy."

"You knew Mikaela?"

"We all did. Like I was saying, Ski Patrol was party central back then once the mountain closed for the day. We were the dudes and Mikaela was just one of the girls who came and went. I remember she always wore this really cute ski outfit that showed off her butt. I think a lot of guys slept with her that winter. Zia's father could have been any of them."

"Really?"

"Listen, Howie, this was a girl who only wanted to boogie. My guess is Mikaela decided to name Keir as the father because he was a pushover. She knew he wouldn't make a fuss."

"That's harsh."

"Well, like I say, she was a party girl. Keir was a pretty simple guy, really, and she left him high and dry. After that winter, she moved to New York, then Europe for a while. I heard she's in Albuquerque now running a TV station."

"So did Keir see anything of Zia while she was growing up?"

"There were a few times, sure. Mikaela would call from wherever she was at the moment to say she needed him to babysit Zia for a week or two while she went off to do other things. I believe Zia spent a summer with Keir when she was nine or ten, but that's pretty much it."

"Did you ever meet Zia?"

"Last winter, sure, but not before then. She was a good skier and Keir used to bring her into the Patrol shack. She was a sweet girl, we all liked her. Like I say, Keir tried to be a real father to her. He didn't have to, but he gave it his best shot. I was shocked when I read in the paper that she killed herself."

"It's strange, isn't it? From what I've heard, Zia was happy here in San Geronimo. She liked her school, things were going well for her."

Shawn's mouth fell open. "Oh, man! You don't think Zia's death was suicide, do you?"

"I don't know, Shawn. That's what I'm trying to find out. It's just too coincidental to have two deaths in the same family."

Shawn shook his head. "I never liked Mikaela. She drank too much and she was loud. But I'm damned sorry Zia is dead!"

Shawn glanced over to the group by the chairlift who were waiting for him. Howie saw his time was up.

"Look, I see you're busy, Shawn. But is there anything else you can tell me about Zia?"

"Not really. Except for that incident last winter with the ski instructor. You heard about that, didn't you?"

"No, tell me."

89

"Well, Zia was in a race clinic and one of the instructors put his hand on her butt. The stupid shit felt her up! She totally went ballistic. She exploded. She went to management and got the guy fired."

"Which instructor was that?"

"Dwayne Richards. A hotshot guy in his twenties. He was only here for one season."

"Was he angry when Zia got him fired?"

"That's hard to say. He smiled it off, like he was this big Casanova who couldn't help himself where women were concerned. I have no idea where he went after here, but I don't think he's in San Geronimo anymore. . . . Howie, look, I got to get back to work." Shawn had to pat Howie on the arm to get his attention.

"She exploded?" Howie repeated, returning from his thoughts. "I can imagine that . . . Zia exploding . . . interesting!"

"Howie, you can't get away with that sort of behavior anymore. Sexual harassment, my God! You should have seen how fast management made it go away! Look, give me a call if you need anything . . ."

Shawn was already hurrying back toward the lift where the head of Lift Ops and several worried faces from management were waiting for him.

Before he got to the lift, he turned briefly back to Howie.

"Look, man, I'm totally onboard. I want to know what happened to Kier and Zia. Whatever you need, whenever you need it—I'm there."

***

Howie had skied so often on San Geronimo Peak that the many curves of the highway down to the desert were almost automatic. This was helpful now when his attention wasn't on driving but the dysfunctional history of three generations of McFaddens:

Charles McFadden, his client. Mikaela McFadden, the daughter. Keir Aaronson, Mikaela's lover (briefly). And finally, Zia McFadden, the 17 year-old granddaughter floating in the reeds below Eagle Falls.

Three generations. An unhappy family, Howie concluded—but in *what* unique way? Why had everything gone wrong?

Howie pulled over into a turn-around and phoned Charlie McFadden. It was time they had another talk.

***

Charlie lived in a run down barn-like building on a one acre lot in a neighborhood of old adobes and box-like FHA houses. There were junk cars and pickups in most of the front yards.

Poor as it was, the neighborhood was abundantly green and shady. You only had to drill a dozen feet to find water. It was mostly old Spanish families who lived here, families whose ancestors had been in this valley for hundreds of years. The newcomers were the ones who would need to dig deep wells out in the sagebrush.

McFadden's home was a one-story wooden structure in an advanced state of decay. Essentially it was a shed with a number of small rooms that had been added on over the years. The yard was chest high in weeds. The porch roof sagged. Even the wood fence between the house and the road was falling down.

Howie parked behind Charlie's battered Corolla. There was another car in the driveway, a gleaming Mercedes station wagon, a recent model. McFadden had an upscale visitor.

Howie met the owner of the Mercedes on the overgrown path to the front door. It was Martha Davis Birdsong, the inspirational writer, who was nearly as famous as McFadden had once been. She was a tall grey-haired woman with ecstatic eyes. Howie had met her several times at art openings. She wrote How-To-Be-Happy books, which was why she had a Mercedes while McFadden, a better writer, drove a heap held together with duct tape.

She took Howie firmly by the arm.

"Oh, good, I'm so glad you're here! How *are* you, Moon Deer?"

Martha managed to turn a simple greeting into a probing question of utmost importance. She peered intently into his eyes, one soul seeking another.

How was he? "I'm . . . well, I'm okay, I guess. You've been visiting Charlie?"

"We're old friends. And I mean old, old friends . . . past lives, you know. He's exhausted, Moon Deer, so be kind. He's broken by his granddaughter's death. And as always he's been writing too hard. I keep telling him, you can't write like that! You have to relax your way into the Creative Spirit! You can't fight the river! You need to let go!"

"Yes, I see what you mean," said Howie. He would have gladly bypassed Martha Davis Birdsong, but the path was narrow and she stood between him and the front door.

"I made him a cup of linden and oak milk tea," she confided. "Please, don't let him get near any alcohol. And speak in a gentle voice! He needs our help, so allow me to say it a second time—be kind!"

Howie got past Martha with difficulty, after assuring her that he would be gentle, he would speak in a soft voice . . . though speak, he would, because there were things they needed to talk about.

He found McFadden in a stained overstuffed armchair next to a wood burning stove that was in its summer mode, with a potted cactus on top. The room had a low ceiling and it was a mess, full of papers and books stacked up on every surface. McFadden was a mess also. He sat slumped in the armchair with a mug of foul-looking tea on the floor by his feet.

"Hello, Charlie," Howie said. Gently, he hoped.

McFadden looked up as though waking from a dream. "Is she gone?"

"I think so. I passed her on the path."

"Thank God! Let me dump this damn tea and I'll break out the Jack Daniels."

"Not for me, thanks," Howie told him. "It's a little early."

"Oh, come on, Moon Deer—don't be such a plebe!"

Charlie rose from the armchair with some effort. He picked up the mug from the floor, walked across the room, and dumped the tea down the drain in the kitchen sink.

"I used to fuck her, you know."

"I'm sorry?"

"Birdsong, for chrissake! I gave her the name. She was Krakenberg, or something. Martha Krakenberg from Brooklyn. I told her, babe, with a name like that, you're going nowhere. Try Birdsong! Didn't mean it as a compliment. Bird shit, more likely! But she was hot! Lord, did she go at it! Forty years ago."

"Right," Howie said vaguely, hoping to cut McFadden off. "Charlie, we need to talk."

Charlie found the bottle of Jack Daniels and brought it with him back to the armchair along with a glass. He sat down heavily.

"Sure I can't tempt you?"

Howie shook his head. "Charlie, you need to listen. There's been another death—Zia's father, Keir. The cops are going to be here asking questions, maybe today, tomorrow at the latest."

"Keir's dead? What was it, a ski accident? Ran into a tree, did he?"

"Charlie, it's August," Howie said patiently. "There's no skiing this time of year. Generally, we wait for snow. Keir was found hanging from a tree in his yard. It was set up to look like suicide, but the police

93

are saying he was dead before somebody strung him up. This is murder, and a murder is going to cause a storm in this little town. You're going to be drawn into this whether you like it or not."

McFadden threw his head back and groaned.

"What a drag!" he cried. "I don't have time for this!"

"Keir probably didn't have time for it either," said Howie.

Death brought a moment's pause from both men as they each thought about Keir Aaronson in their own way.

"You know, I liked Keir," Charlie said after a moment. "Not the brightest star in the sky, but a decent dude."

Howie made room for himself on a chair near the wood stove. "Did you know that your granddaughter was being sexually molested?"

"What? I don't believe it! Where did you hear that?"

"I can't reveal my source," Howie said primly. "But it's true."

"Well, that sucks!" said Charlie. "Who would do something like that?"

"Your daughter's boyfriend."

A blank look came over McFadden's face.

"*My* daughter? Mikaela?"

"Right, Mikaela. Unless you have another daughter stashed somewhere."

"No, she's the only one. I haven't seen her for years."

"You didn't know she had a boyfriend who was molesting Zia?"

"Of course not!"

"Well, that's why Zia came up here to live with Keir. She told her mother about the abuse, but Mikaela didn't believe her. Didn't Zia tell you about any of this?"

"No, she didn't. Not a thing."

"How much did you see of her this last year?"

"This last year?" he repeated vaguely. "Yeah, I saw her a few times. I took her to dinner once at the San Geronimo Inn. But it was awkward. I mean, what was there to talk about? Her mother? Believe me, we left *that* subject alone! We're such different generations, you see. That was the main problem. And I was working really hard just then on my new book . . ."

Howie felt the numbing sadness of the room. Howie wanted to say to hell with your new book, you should have taken the time to get to know your granddaughter.

"Did you see her much when she was growing up?" he asked. He feared he knew the answer already.

"Zia? No, not much, Moon Deer. I bet that looks bad to you, from your bourgeois point of view. But that's the thing about being an artist. You have to make a decision. Are you going to be an artist, or are you going to be a family man? Do you want to know what I decided?"

"I believe I know the answer to that, Charlie."

"I hope you're not judging me, Moon Deer!"

Howie had to pause a moment. In fact, he had been judging like crazy.

"I'm trying not to," he answered. "You're saying you ignored you family for your writing?"

"That's what it boils down to, I guess. Is there something wrong with a choice like that?"

Howie could only shake his head. "I don't know. I'm trying to understand your family."

"Take Gauguin, for example," said Charlie. "He blew off all his responsibilities and sailed to Tahiti. That's what you have to do for art! You start by telling the world to fuck off!"

"I get it," said Howie. "It's the greatest bullshit excuse I've ever heard for being irresponsible, but I get it."

"Robert Louis Stevenson . . . 'to travel hopefully is better than to arrive!' Now, that's genius! That's how I want to write. And he went to Tahiti, too."

"Samoa," said Howie. "Now forget Robert Louis Stevenson and let's talk about your daughter. Why were you and Mikaela estranged?"

"Oh, Moon Deer, it's a long story! Can't you spare me? You want me to relive all that?"

"Charlie, two people have died and I need to understand what's happening. Now, tell me about Mikaela."

Charlie sighed. He poured himself another shot.

"You want the truth? The truth is Mikaela was a nasty child. She wasn't cute. She wasn't appealing. She always had snot on her face and you didn't want to pick her up and cuddle her. She cried all the time and she had temper tantrums when she didn't get what she wanted. Sophia and I got saddled with a monster."

"Whose fault do you think that was?" Howie asked.

"My wife, of course! She was nuts. She didn't give Mikaela any discipline. Sometimes she forgot to feed the kid, it was that bad. Don't get me wrong, Sophia was a real beauty when I met her, a free spirit. It was the Sixties! Christ, we had a great time! It was only later that I realized she was crazy."

"So you had her committed?"

"I see you've heard the stories. Everyone has who lives here long enough. Sophia tried to set fire to our house while Mikaela and I and Dorothea were sleeping. She tried to murder us. I didn't have any choice."

"Who is Dorothea?"

"The woman I was seeing. Dorothea became my second wife. I had to dump Sophia, I just couldn't take it anymore. When she set the fire, that was the last straw. I had to sign the papers to commit her. Mikaela was eight at the time and she's never forgiven me for it. After that, Dorothea and I tried to raise Mikaela the best we could, but she grew up wild. She dropped out of high school, didn't go to college—she liked bad music, she didn't read books. I tried, I honestly did. But in the end I washed my hands of her, Moon Deer."

Howie took a deep breath. "Did you know that Mikaela and Zia were in Albuquerque?" he asked.

"I heard they were there," McFadden answered. "But I didn't try to see them. Mikaela hated me, what could I do?"

"And in the entire year Zia was here in San Geronimo, you only saw her a few times?"

"Like I told you, we didn't really connect. My guess is Zia grew up hearing all the bad stories Mikaela told about me."

"When you took her to dinner, did she talk about her life here?"

"No, not really. I tried to get her to talk, but she just gave short answers. 'How's school?' 'Okay.' 'You making any friends here?' 'A few.' It was like trying to milk a stone!"

"I'm going to need to go down to Albuquerque and talk with Mikaela," Howie said. "Could you give her a call and explain who I am?"

McFadden shook his head emphatically.

"She'd hang up before I could get a word in!"

"With Zia dead, you couldn't convince her to let bygones be bygones?"

"No way! Absolutely no way! Now, look—you've stirred up some memories, so if you don't mind, I'm going to sit here and wallow in nostalgia and regret for a little while. Maybe get myself good and drunk. You're welcome to join me, Moon Deer. But if you're not drinking, I'd say we're done."

Howie stood, smiled, and said he preferred to give nostalgia and regret a pass.

Chapter Thirteen

"The good part of old age," Jack Wilder said to Georgie, "is that it doesn't last forever!"

Jack delivered this pronouncement from his wheelchair in the backyard while Emma was tending the barbecue. In his ruby colored workout clothes and dark glasses, he looked like a cross between a Roman emperor and a street bum.

Georgie smiled but didn't laugh. As jokes went, this was a sad one. She had just arrived at the Wilder's house, glowing from her bike ride, feeling very much alive and young.

"How's the memoir coming?" she asked.

"It's going well, Georgie. Very well, indeed. I'm up to how I enrolled in the police academy. This was in the early 1970s. My God, it was a different world back then! San Francisco in its hippie heyday. Riots and rock and roll! Striptease up and down Broadway. Lots of sin, Georgie. Plenty of crime. Being a cop in North Beach in those days was something to remember!"

With Georgie's encouragement, Jack was dictating his memoir to his computer, Nancy. He was calling it *Chronicles of a Cop*. Everyone was amazed at how well Georgie got on with the grouchy old curmudgeon. He was certain *Chronicles* would be an international bestseller. It had been a shrewd move on Georgie's part to get Jack talking about what he enjoyed talking about most. Himself. He was already thinking about who would play him in the movie. Brad Pitt would be the obvious choice, but he wanted someone more subtly *noir*. It was a shame Marlon Brando was dead.

Howie arrived a few minutes later with a cherry pie he had picked up at the Dos Flores Bakery. Claire arrived ten minutes after that with two bottles of white wine she had bought on her way through town.

The Wilder backyard was an oasis of green shade and flowering plants, a refuge at the end of a hot summer day. The barbecue sizzled, drifting smoke up past the trees to the evening sunset.

Emma was preparing to grill half a dozen trout that had been caught in the mountains only hours earlier. The fish were spread out cleaned on a large chopping board along with half a dozen lemons and herbs from Emma's garden. The trout had been given to her by a very literate fisherman who was grateful Emma was fighting against banning books in libraries.

Howie accepted a glass of white wine from Emma and took it to the back deck where Georgie was sitting next to Jack.

He said hi to Jack and sat on the creaky garden lounge chair next to Georgie.

"How was your afternoon?"

"Fine, Da. But that family's pretty weird!"

"Which weird family is that?"

"The family of Zia's friend from school, Uma Rothenstein. I found her last name and address online, so I rode my bike over to see her."

Jack, in his wheelchair, was straining to hear. "Hold on, Georgie. Let me get this straight. Who is Uma Rothenstein?"

"She's a school friend of Zia McFadden, the girl who supposedly committed suicide."

Georgie looked to Howie wondering if she should continue.

"It's okay," said Howie. "Jack knows about the diary."

"I still can't believe you took that diary!" said Jack in his end-of-the-world voice. "Goddamnit, Howie—you're going to lose your license for sure one of these days!"

"We only borrowed the diary," Howie said, trying out his new approach. "I returned it."

"And how did that go?"

"Well, it was a little strange. I got to the cabin after midnight. I returned the diary to Zia's bedroom and then just as I was leaving, somebody else showed up at the cabin. No car, he—maybe it was a she—just appeared walking onto the property. I didn't get a good look. I waited outside in the dark and watched the guy go through the house. When he was gone, I checked the bedroom and the diary was gone again."

"*What*? That's not good! Santo needs to get his hands on that journal."

"I think I understand what's happening," said Howie. "It's what Zia wrote in her diary, that she was being sexually abused by her mother's boyfriend. The guy who did that to her wouldn't want it to get out."

"Sure, Howie. Sexual abuse is terrible, but it doesn't often lead to murder. Do you know who this guy is?"

"I only know the nickname Zia gave him in the diary. The Dweeb. But I'm going to keep at this and find out who he is. In any case, this is a starting point. The low hanging fruit. I'm going to see where it leads."

Jack turned to Georgie. He knew just where she was, despite his blindness.

"So today you visited Uma—you say she has a weird family."

"Her father's the artist Edward Rothenstein. He's the one who's awful. There's something odd going on with those people."

"Okay," Jack said, in his most imperial manner. "I want to hear about everything you've both been doing. Everything you've seen, every thought you've had. Don't skip anything. We'll start with you, Georgie—tell us what happened at the Rothenstein house. Then I want to hear from you, Howie, all your midnight adventures—and I have to tell you, I'm not sure I'm liking what I've heard so far!"

***

Jack was exhausted by the time Howie, Claire, and Georgie left for the night.

They had talked for hours. They had eaten trout, a tabouli salad, spinach from the garden, corn on the cob (also from the garden), and the cherry pie Howie had brought from the bakery on Calle Dos Flores.

Several bottles of white wine had also been consumed. The evening darkened into night.

After the guests left, Jack remained in the kitchen to keep Emma company while she did the dishes. The screen door was open to the backyard, letting in a summer chorus of cricket and bug sounds. Social occasions exhausted Jack more and more these days, and he sat in silence as Emma washed. She had the radio on, the public station from Albuquerque, and Jack was grateful for being able to be with Emma with no need for conversation. They understood each other without words. Jack had waited impatiently for the guests to leave, but once they were gone, he felt a wave of depression.

Emma turned off the radio. "How are you doing, Jack?" she asked from the sink.

"Okay," he told her.

"Really?"

"Emma, it's not great being a blind old man recovering from a stroke in a wheelchair. I won't lie to you, it's not something I hoped for. But I accept life as it is. I make an effort to make the best of it."

"Your new caregiver is coming tomorrow morning," she told him.

"I'll try to behave myself," he promised.

"Please do try, Jack. I'd appreciate it."

Jack knew he was at fault. His behavior had already driven away two previous caregivers. He hated the fact that he could no longer take care of himself without the help of a day nurse, and had taken out his frustration by being as difficult as possible. Looking back, he knew this wasn't fair. Certainly not to Emma who couldn't leave him alone in the house to go to her library job without someone at home to take care of him. For Emma's sake, he had resolved to be more compliant, a better patient. He didn't want to be a burden for her.

"So, let me tell you about your new caregiver," Emma continued. "I think you're going to like him."

Him? Jack knew he wasn't going to like him. He was going to hate him. But he nodded and did his best to appear interested.

"First, I got to tell you, Jack, it hasn't been easy to find somebody. Both agencies in town told me that they didn't have anyone available. They were firm about it. To be honest, you've scared them all off. But then, just as I was getting discouraged, I got a name. I met him yesterday and, well . . . I think he'll be fine."

Jack sensed a note of caution in Emma's tone.

"He's African-American, a big man. Hefty. He looks like an ex-linebacker. But he's really a gentle giant. And here's what you're going to like most of all. He used to be a cop!"

For Emma's sake, Jack managed a tortured smile. "No kidding. Where?"

"Reno. He was on the force there for six years."

Jack remembered Reno, the way it was thirty years ago. He had often gone there as a San Francisco detective. The Bay Area and Reno were joined together at the hip—Interstate 80—a highway of vice and crime.

"Reno!" Jack shook his head at the memories. "There's a lot of grift in that town! Believe me, those people play rough. So, why did he quit?"

"Well, they let him go, Jack. After he changed sex. He's a she now. Transgender."

Jack shrugged. This part of having a day nurse didn't bother him. What was it to him what the sex life of his caregiver was? He tried to remember the Reno police chief's name from thirty years ago but he couldn't come up with it. Names had become increasingly lost in his memory banks. *That* worried him more than his caregiver's gender.

"Her name is Shayna," Emma continued, undaunted by Jack's apparent lack of interest. "I have to warn you, she's a tad outrageous. She wears fiery red lipstick and long red fingernails and tight dresses."

Jack nodded. "Okay," he said cautiously.

"I wanted you to know that she attracts attention, just in case you go anywhere with her. She has huge hands, so there's no question she's a man. Or *was* a man—I'm not sure how you're supposed to put these things anymore. She's very nice, Jack. And she's strong enough to move your wheelchair around. You're going to like her."

Jack tried to picture a beefy black linebacker with red lipstick and tight dresses. For the first time tonight he smiled.

"I see," he said.

He stayed with Emma in the kitchen until she finished cleaning up, then they kissed goodnight and went their separate ways. Emma to her upstairs bedroom, Jack to his bedroom and adjoining office, his suite of rooms on the ground floor.

He didn't sleep well. Insomnia for Jack was a nightly battle. Tonight he fell asleep almost immediately, but he was awake an hour later, his mind racing. In these late hours, in a silent house—only the refrigerator coming on and off—he felt like a brain trapped in a room within a room. Blind, confined to a wheelchair, only his memories were free, alive in Technicolor. And his dreams.

He had been dreaming he was on a police boat in the rough blue waters beneath the Golden Gate Bridge, looking for a body. The fog was rolling in. That was all he could remember. The dream faded from memory almost instantly on waking, but it left an anxious, unfinished feeling.

What was worrying him? he wondered.

Everything!

The planet was going through a bad time, and he was too. How could any sane person *not* worry?

As he lay thinking, he realized there was a specific worry that was bothering him. The McFadden case. It seemed to him that Howie had put his nose into a viper's nest.

Jack hoped Howie was up to a case like this, but he wasn't sure. Two people dead—one murdered for certain, the other—the girl—a possible homicide. Jack had warned Howie countless times, don't take family investigations, they're the worst. Dark secrets, old hatreds, old resentments, you don't want to get involved. But Howie was still learning the trade.

In the beginning, before the Wilder & Associate Private Investigations Agency was dreamed of, Jack had hired Howie simply to do yard work and drive him around. Medically retired from the San Francisco Police Department, Jack needed the help of someone who could see. Howie, for his part, had been an impoverished graduate student staying in a small cabin on friends' land while he was working on his PhD. He was glad to earn some extra money to stretch the small grant he received for his living expenses.

The arrangement had worked for both Jack and Howie, and within six months Jack proposed that they start a detective agency together.

Jack would be the brains and Howie the eyes. That was the original idea. He would teach Howie the ropes, and Howie in return would make the agency possible with his ability to navigate the seeing world.

This was years ago now and much had changed. Jack was in a wheelchair and Howie was running the business. But Jack still carried an idea of Howie as the kid who had mowed his lawn and needed his help.

"Nancy, wake up," Jack said to the ceiling.

"What can I do for you, Jack?" his computer answered obediently.

"Let's start at the beginning. I always told Howie that, but I'm not sure he ever listened."

"The beginning of what?" Nancy inquired.

"The *beginning!*" Jack said with irritation. "The client, Charles McFadden. The guy who walked in the door and gave Howie the case. His family sounds like a daytime soap and I don't like it. So do a search on Charles McFadden, author, and tell me everything you find."

"Got it," said Nancy without missing a millisecond. "There are 4023 entries on Charles McFadden, author. Some of them are short so I can read them to you in 13 hours, 32 minutes, and 41 seconds."

Jack turned his head to the ceiling where Nancy's bedroom audio was attached. "God help me, Nancy! I'm going to take a sledge hammer to you one day!"

"Would you like me to give you a twenty minute summary of what I've found?"

"Yes," said Jack. "I'd like that very much."

"However, it's 2:23 AM. Shouldn't you try to sleep? I can play you some Brahms that will really put you out."

"I'll sleep when I'm dead, thank you," said Jack. "Now get to it!"

Chapter Fourteen

Nancy's twenty minute synopsis of Charles McFadden's life wasn't especially interesting, and Jack had known much of it already.

The author was 72 years old. Back in his early twenties, he had written two coming-of-age novels that had set his career in motion. He had been one of the youthful voices of the time, at a time when youth was in vogue. His writing career culminated with one of his novels being made into a movie. Unfortunately, the movie hadn't been a box office success and it didn't leave much of a mark. All this was decades ago. McFadden's recent work was published by small local presses and sold very few copies. He was broke.

Nancy discovered McFadden's financial information from a program that Buzzy Hurston had installed on Nancy. The software allowed Jack to look into private bank accounts, which was useful but far from legal. Buzzy, who was once Jack's badly paid driver, was a cyber-genius who had grown up on a commune outside of San Geronimo. Eventually the CIA scooped him up and at the moment he was working in some geeky department at Langley that had a number rather than a name.

According to Nancy, Charles McFadden had a total of $1,374.36 in a local checking account. He also owned a house and property in San Geronimo which was worth some money—the land, not the house. McFadden had bought the property over forty years ago and it had appreciated in value. However, if he sold it, the author would be homeless. Meanwhile, social security provided barely enough money for booze and groceries. Jack scowled, certain that Wilder & Associate was going to get stiffed.

"Howie, Howie!" Jack chided aloud in the solitude of his bedroom. "You shouldn't have taken this case!"

The three wives, at least, had been colorful. McFadden had been attracted to flamboyant women.

The first wife was Sophia Berger, a promiscuous, sexually alluring New York girl who was working as an Assistant Editor at Random House when they met. She was spoiled and bright, wild and egotistical. As a promising author, McFadden must have seemed a good match. He and Sophia became trendsetters in New York for a short time until they took a peyote trip together in Central Park, which turned out to be a life changing experience. Newly enlightened, they fled the New York literary circuit and moved to New Mexico. It was a time when many young people were doing the same, leaving cities for the bucolic countryside, unhappy modern children in search of peace.

But the marriage didn't go well in San Geronimo. McFadden's career was fading and Sophia was bored. Charlie had his writing, but Sophia had no interests except to drift more seriously into drugs. It soon became apparent that Sophia was going mad in the high desert. Her exploits could no longer be explained as simply the antics of a free-spirited individual. The marriage ended when Sophia set their house on fire with McFadden and the 8 year-old Mikaela inside. Sophia was judged incompetent and put into a state institution in Las Cruces . . .

Jack had heard all this before from Howie. Nevertheless, he continued to listen to Nancy's recitation. He believed the answer to the deaths of Zia McFadden and her father was hidden somewhere in these family details.

McFadden's second marriage was to Dorothea Brownwell, an aspiring actress. This marriage lasted two years until Dorothea got a part in a TV soap opera and flew off to Los Angeles, never to return.

The third marriage—to Danielle Hartz, a ski instructor who was an aspiring writer, twenty-two years younger—lasted even less time. Ten months. At which point Danielle decided that if she was going to achieve the great goal of getting published, it wouldn't be with Charlie's help, whose own books were out of print by the time she knew him.

"Okay, Nancy, shut up, please, I need to think," he told her before she could tell him about McFadden's later work and the readings he had done in local coffee houses and bookstores.

It was McFadden's first marriage that interested Jack the most. The second and third marriages were predictable—an actress, an aspiring writer briefly bedazzled by McFadden's fading fame. But Sophia, mother of Mikaela, in turn the mother of Zia . . . Jack felt that there was something here that needed to be looked at more carefully. He couldn't quite put his feeling into words, but Jack had learned to trust his intuitions.

What had happened to Sophia? That was the first thing he needed to discover. Was she still alive?

"Nancy, find a state mental institution in Las Cruces, New Mexico," he ordered after a long silence. "See what you can find about a possible patient named Sophia Berger or Sophia McFadden."

"Got it, Jack. It was called the Sun and Sage Living Institute. The name makes it sound like a resort, but it wasn't. It was a terrible place. It's closed now. She was known there by her married name, Sophia McFadden."

"Where did she go when the place closed down?"

"That's unknown. She was discharged on May 24, 2017, after a panel decided she was no longer a risk to herself or others. There's no information beyond that. The address she gave the medical board on her release turned out to be a fake. No one has seen her since."

"She disappeared?"

"Correct, Jack. The lady vanished."

"How old would she be now?"

"Seventy-three."

"And this Sun and Sage Living Center didn't keep records of where their patients went?"

"There was a fire only a few months after the hospital was closed. Everything burned. All the computers and records went up in smoke."

Jack nodded. *Another fire!*

"Jack, why don't I put on some soothing music? It'll help you relax and go back to sleep."

"I don't want to relax," Jack told her. "Now, let me think!"

In fact, Jack was afraid he wasn't thinking as clearly as he used to. His big fear was that he was becoming slow and stupid. He was surviving his other handicaps: blindness, age, lack of mobility. But he would be damned if he would give in to stupidity!

He needed to focus.

"All right," he said after a while. He had found a place to start. He needed to conduct his own interview with Charles McFadden and do a more in-depth job of it than Howie had done. Howie meant well, but he hadn't known the right questions to ask.

For Jack, this should have been a simple proposition. He had conducted thousands of interviews with suspects and witnesses. He was good at it. But he was stuck at home, which was frustrating in the extreme. McFadden lived only a short distance away but Jack had no means to get to him.

Or did he?

***

Jack met his new caregiver, Shayna, that morning.

Emma had needed to wake him. He had fallen asleep toward dawn and it was nearly 8:30 when Emma came into his bedroom.

"She's here, Jack, and I need to leave for work. If you'll come out for a few minutes, I'll introduce you and you can go back to sleep afterwards."

"Okay," he said grumpily. "I need a little time."

He'd been asleep for less than two hours and had woken in a fog. But by the time he wheeled his way into the kitchen, his hair was combed and his smile benign.

"Jack, this is Shayna," Emma said brightly. "And Shayna, this is my dear husband of many years, Jack. He can be a tad grouchy, but don't pay any mind. If you have any problems with him . . . if he misbehaves," she added cautiously, "be sure to give me a call at the library."

"I will, Mrs. Wilder. But I'm certain Commander Wilder and I are going to get on perfectly."

Shayna had a pleasant voice, clear and polite. It could be taken as the low alto of a woman, but there was an essence, Jack thought, that was male. There was a rural warmth to it.

"Please, you can forget the Commander," he said to Shayna, clear and pleasant himself. "That was long ago. These days even my computer calls me Jack—and Emma, honestly, you can forget about us, we'll be fine."

Emma paused. After her experience with caregivers, she didn't quite trust Jack's makeover.

"Well, you know where to find me," she said as she gathered her things and walked out the door.

Jack remained in the kitchen with Shayna.

"So, Shayna, I hear you were a cop. In Reno, no less!"

"I was only a traffic cop, no big deal. I had hopes to make detective one day, but I never got there."

"Listen, traffic is just as important a job as anybody's," Jack said. "More people get killed on roads than they do in homicides."

"Yeah, that's true. I never thought of it that way."

"Of course it's true! I remember a case I had in San Francisco where a guy was driving and eating french fries from his lap. He had just come from a drive-thru at a Jack-In-the-Box and was headed to the Golden Gate Bridge on Lombard Street. But then, you know what happened?— he dropped a french fry and the idiot looked down to find it. He missed a red light, hit a young woman in the crosswalk, and killed her. All because of a lost french fry."

"That's awful!"

"Yes, and that was only the start of it. The young woman's father happened to be a gangster in Detroit and he hired a hit man to take out the guy who had killed his daughter. This was where I came in. In the end, I was able to get the hit man sent to San Quentin and I took down an entire family operation in Detroit."

"That's pretty exciting stuff, Commander—"

"Jack. Yes, it was a time all right, being a cop in San Francisco. I'm writing a book about it, as a matter of fact."

"Are you? That's fantastic," said Shayna.

Jack waited until he heard Emma's car pull out from the driveway.

"So what kind of wheels do you drive, Shayna?"

"I have a Ford pickup. Why do you ask?"

"Is it reliable?"

"Well, sure, it's only a few years old. An F-150."

Jack smiled.

***

It took a while for Jack to convince Shayna to drive him to Charles McFadden's house. He had to use all his powers of persuasion. Driving hadn't been in Shayna's agreement with Emma and she was worried about Jack's health, that someone in his "stage of life," as she put it, would be better off at home.

"And Mrs. Wilder will kill me when she finds out!" she objected. "Probably I'll get fired, and I need this job!"

"Shayna, I'll answer to Emma. She gave up on me years ago. And believe me, she needs a caregiver much too badly to give you the boot."

In the end, Jack brought Shayna over to his side by interesting her in a stripped-down version of the case, one cop to another.

"It's a tricky case," Jack told her. "Two deaths made to look like suicide. First Zia, then Keir. I'm going to get to the bottom of this with or without you, Shayna. But I'd sure be grateful if you'd help me out. All I'm asking is for you to drive me around a bit. The address is 127 Don Trujillo Road, by the way. You might have to look on your phone to find it."

"I don't know, Jack . . ."

"Look, we'll go to lunch afterwards. I only need to ask McFadden a few questions and then we'll try out the new Thai restaurant. What do you say?"

After much cajoling, Shayna finally said yes. She made sure Jack had his pills and then she wheeled Jack out of the house to his truck.

"Upsy-daisy," she said as she lifted him effortlessly into the cab. Her arms were thick and hard. Jack could feel the bulk of her chest as she plopped him into the passenger seat and buckled him in. Once she had him settled, she lifted his wheelchair with one hand and placed it into the back of her truck.

Jack inhaled deep breaths of New Mexico air as Shayna drove them through town. Except for a doctor's appointment, he'd been housebound for weeks. But the smell of the wind gave him a moment of unbearable sorrow as he remembered how Katya, his guide dog and companion, used to sniff the air through the crack in the window that he always left open for her.

Jack had to close the window to make the memory go away. With an effort, he pulled himself from a sinkhole of sorrow and returned his attention to the story Shayna was telling him, about her childhood in Alabama and why she decided to move west.

Jack found himself liking Shayna. He knew it hadn't been easy to be a black transgender youth in rural Alabama. It had taken a good deal of courage and character to pursue her own particular path. Jack liked original people. He didn't like drones.

Nevertheless, as Jack listened to Shayna's story, his mind was simultaneously deciding on how he wanted to conduct the upcoming interview with Charles McFadden.

What did he want to know? And how was he going to get it? Those were the questions he always asked himself at the start of a case like this.

Most of all, he wanted to know about Wife #1, Sophia—the crazy one who was put away for setting a fire. He definitely wanted to know more about that fire. And he wanted to know where she was now.

Mikaela was next on his list of question marks. He wanted to know more about Zia's mother and her relationship with Keir Aaronson. From there, it was hard to say. Jack's idea of an investigation was to avoid grand strategies, and just go from one thing to another. However, he reminded himself that two people had died, this was a *murder* investigation. They needed to be careful.

"Excuse me, Shayna," he said, interrupting. "We must be getting close to the house?"

"It's just a few minutes away."

"Good. Okay, here's a question, cop to cop. Are you carrying?"

"Are we expecting trouble?"

"Maybe," said Jack. "In my experience, you never know. Routine interrogations can go bad. Are you carrying?"

Shayna was reluctant to answer. "Mmm," she said at last, a vague sound of assent.

"Good. Not that we're going to need it. But sometimes with guns, it's nice to know they're there. What do you have?"

Again, she hesitated. "There's an AR-15 under the back seat."

"Okay, that's good to know," said Jack.

"But I'm not going to use it, not if I can possibly help it," Shayna told him. "After my transition, I said to myself, no more violence. I'm totally with Buddha now. I'm at peace."

"Then why keep the assault rifle in the back?"

Shayna sighed. For the first time since he had dealt with her, she sounded less than cheerful.

"I had to drive through Texas a few months ago," she said. "There are people in places like that who give folks like me a bad time."

Jack got it. It was easy to see that Texas might be a problem for what looked to be a hefty black man dressed as a woman.

When they arrived at Don Trujillo Road, Shayna pulled into the driveway and turned off the ignition.

"Describe what you're seeing," Jack said as they sat in the cab.

"It's a rambling sort of shack. The property's nice, lots of shade trees. But the house is run down. Reminds me of Alabama where I grew up. All it needs are chickens running around loose."

"How about vehicles in the driveway?"

"There's a beat-up old Corolla near the front door with a motorcycle parked behind it. The bike looks new and spiffy. It's a Ducati, expensive, a racing bike. We're blocking their exit. Maybe I should back out and park by the curb?"

"No," Jack said. "Sometimes it's an advantage to have a captive audience . . . what's that I'm smelling?"

"I don't smell anything."

Jack raised his nose and sniffed the air almost like Katya used to. Minus sight, the rest of his senses were sharp.

"It's smoke," he said. "What's burning?"

"I'm not sure," Shayna said uneasily. "How are we going to do this?"

"It's easy. You're going to get my chair from the back, set me in it, and push me to the front door. I'll handle the rest . . . now, there *is* something burning! I can smell it stronger!"

"I'm smelling it now, too . . . Lord, the house is on fire! There's smoke coming out the side window! It must have only just gotten started. This old wooden house is going to explode! I gotta go see if there's anyone inside who needs help."

"Shayna—"

"Jack, I'm going to have to leave you here. I gotta see if there's people inside."

"Okay," said Jack, knowing he couldn't stop her. "Just put down the windows and make sure I'm not locked in."

Shayna stopped long enough to lower the windows before she slammed the truck door. Then, to Jack's astonishment, he heard her running inside the burning cabin.

***

Alone in the cab, Jack couldn't think of anything else to do but phone 911 to report the fire.

The acrid smoke was starting to burn his nostrils. He could hear the crackle of burning wood. The fire was growing quickly and he doubted it was accidental. The truck wasn't far from the house and Jack was starting to worry that the flames might engulf him. He was stuck, unable to escape.

"Shayna! Where the hell are you? Get back here!" he shouted.

It seemed forever, but at last he heard Shayna come out the front door. She seemed to be staggering slightly with the weight of something she carried in her arms. Someone.

The rear door of the cab was pulled open violently and Shayna jackknifed a limp body onto the seat, pushing the legs into the cab.

"It's McFadden," she said quickly. "He's alive but he's going to need help. There's someone else inside. I have to go for him!"

"Shayna, wait—I called the fire department. They're coming. Don't take a chance in there. Let the firemen do the job, they're trained . . ."

"I gotta go, Jack. I gotta do this!"

"Stop and think! If there's somebody still inside, it's the person who set the fire!"

But she was already running back inside the cabin.

Jack felt helpless. He was frankly amazed at Shayna's heroics. She was inside the burning house, possibly with a killer.

Abruptly there was an explosion, a single gunshot from inside the house. It was loud above the crackling flames. Like the crack of a whip.

Jack froze.

To make matters worse, there was a stirring from Charles McFadden in the back seat, a groan.

"Be quiet!" Jack told him. He reached back between the bucket seats until he was able to feel McFadden's leg. "You awake back there?"

There was no answer. At least McFadden wasn't dead. Jack didn't want to be held responsible for a dead author. But the gunshot had changed everything. Who fired, who was in the house? Jack had no way of knowing.

Meanwhile, whoever was left inside would need to get out. If it was the arsonist with a gun, Jack was a sitting duck in the driveway. He could feel the fire getting hotter, the heat on his face. Among his other worries, there was a chance of the gas tank exploding.

He knew he had to hide himself but this wasn't easy. With some difficulty, he unbuckled the seat belt and slumped his body sideways across the two bucket seats. The emergency brake dug into his side, every part of him was uncomfortable. But he was out of sight, he hoped. As long as someone didn't look inside the cab.

Shayna had said there was a gun under the back seat, an AR-15. Jack wondered if there was any way he could get his hands on it. He didn't think he could. He would need to get out from the cab, step onto the driveway, climb in the back door over McFadden's body, and rustle around the rear in a space he didn't know.

Jack knew he was stuck. The only choice he had was to lie quietly on his side and hope that either Shayna was alive and would rescue him, or the arsonist would come out in such a hurry to get away, he wouldn't look closely at the Ford. It was a toss up. If he was lucky, the arsonist might assume that Shayna had come alone.

Jack's mind was racing. It was only seconds after the gun shot that he heard footsteps running from the house. He stayed low, certain it wasn't Shayna. It didn't sound like her. This was a different body.

In the distance, Jack was glad to hear sirens. Fire trucks were on the way. But he still had a few minutes to get through. Unfortunately, bad things could happen in a few minutes.

The motorcycle in the driveway started up with a rumbling growl. Jack listened as the Ducati turned around in the driveway and came his way. It passed within inches of where Jack lay but it didn't stop. He listened as it accelerated down the street, changing gears, and the purr of the engine faded into the distance.

That was good news. But by the time the fire trucks arrived, Jack was unable to move. He had never felt so tired in his life. He was paralyzed. His breath rasped in his chest. He felt a great heaviness.

The last thing he remembered was finding himself on a stretcher that was carried by strong hands—younger hands than his own—hauling him into an ambulance.

"Where's Shayna?" he asked. But his voice was softer than a whisper, and there came no answer.

Chapter Fifteen

Jack's "escapade," as Emma called it, happened on Monday after-noon, but Howie didn't hear of it until 4 AM Tuesday morning. He discovered later that Emma believed Santo had informed Howie of the situation, and Santo was certain Emma had done so. Somehow Howie had been left out of the loop. Confusion, misdirection, and misunder-standings are the heart of the human comedy.

It was Jack who managed to contact Howie from his room at San Geronimo Mercy Hospital where he was being kept for observation.

At 4 o'clock in the morning, Howie was doing what he liked to be doing at that hour. He was sleeping when his phone woke him with the climactic moments of Tchaikovsky's *1812*, Jack's assigned ring. Only Jack, Claire, and Georgie were allowed to get through to him at this hour so he sat up and answered.

"Yes, what is it, Jack? Do you know what time it is?"

But it wasn't Jack.

"Excuse me, Mr. Moon Deer, my name is Melissa. I'm a night nurse at Mercy Hospital." She sounded young. "Mr. Wilder gave me his phone to contact you. He asked me to give you a message."

"He's in the hospital? He's okay?"

"I'm sorry, I can not give that kind of information, I can only tell you his message. I'm not even supposed to do that, but he kept at me. He made me repeat it to him several times. He wants you to know he's banged up in the hospital, and you're to come to the Emergency Room as soon as possible to get him out."

"That's it? He's in the ER?"

"That's it," said the nurse. "He held my wrist until I promised to call you. Normally I would call security when a patient does that. But I'll let it go, as long as he doesn't do it again."

"I'll talk to him," promised Howie. "But what's his condition? Why is he in the hospital? Will it be okay to take him home?"

"I'm sure Dr. Zimmerman will give you an update when you arrive," she said breezily before hanging up.

Howie had a dozen questions that she had left unanswered. He got dressed downstairs trying his best to be quiet so as not to wake up Claire. He left a note for her by the stove saying that Jack was in the hospital and he would give her a call as soon as he knew anything.

He arrived at the hospital when dawn was just lighting the sky. San Geronimo Mercy Hospital was modern, modular style, a maze of interconnecting buildings that were spread out on a single level. Howie parked in the nearly empty lot and went into the side door near the ambulance bay to the Emergency Room waiting area. He was not entirely surprised to see Emma Wilder in one of the gray plastic bucket seats. He went immediately to sit by her.

"How's Jack?"

Emma looked tired. "I'm so angry at him I could scream, Howie! But he's going to be all right, I suppose. The doctor said he didn't see any sign he'd had another stroke. Jack's a tough old bird. But I don't know if I can take this anymore. I swear, I'd move out in a second— but then who would take care of him?"

"Emma, slow down. What happened? I don't understand. The last I knew he was home with his new caregiver."

"Exactly. That was *supposed* to be the plan. His new caregiver, Shayna, was a very nice person. Somehow Jack convinced her to drive him around so he could do some investigating. He wanted to see your client, Charles McFadden. But when they arrived at the house, it was on fire. Shayna left Jack in the cab and she rushed into the house to save the people who were inside. She pulled McFadden out of the fire and then went back into the house again for another person. But this time she wasn't so lucky. Jack heard a gunshot. Then someone, not Shayna, ran out of the house, started up a motorcycle, and drove away."

"And the gun shot?"

It took Emma a moment to speak. "Shayna is dead. The person who set the fire shot her and got away. I feel so bad about it, I can hardly speak."

"Did Jack tell you all this?"

"No, it was Santo. He just left here a while ago. He got Jack to tell him the bare-bones of what happened. Jack won't talk to me. I'm afraid I was so angry I shouted at him and said all the wrong things. But I'm at the end of my rope, I really am. He promised to behave himself! He's retired, Howie—it's ridiculous that he won't accept that he's an invalid and he can't go out on these ridiculous escapades! It's other people who end up paying for Jack's irresponsibilities! Shayna! He got her killed!"

Howie took a moment to take this in. "I'm sure Jack's very upset about Shayna." he said. "Of course, he cares."

"Oh, he feels guilty all right! He knows he's responsible. He's almost catatonic with depression—Dr. Zimmerman is worried about it, actually. But that doesn't get him off the hook."

"He cajoled a night nurse to phone me to ask that I come and get him out."

"You're not getting him out, Howie. No way. He needs to stay here at least another day. You have to tell him that. I'm too angry to deal with him right now, but he'll talk to you. Tell him he's off the case! No more, Howie. Jack's detective days are finished!"

Howie nodded. But he thought he would let someone else deliver the news that Jack's detective days were over. You might as well tell a bird not to fly.

"By the way, Howie," Emma said as he was leaving. "Charles McFadden is in the hospital, too. He was unconscious when they brought him in. But he's alive."

***

Howie found Jack in the same private room where he had recovered from by-pass surgery four years earlier. Visiting Jack in the hospital was becoming the new normal.

His bulky figure was covered by a white sheet on the narrow bed. His Santa Claus stomach protruded like a beach ball. The back of the bed was reclined nearly to a prone position. Howie was relieved to see that the nurses had allowed him to keep his dark glasses. Without his glasses, Jack looked like a mad prophet from a Greek tragedy.

"How are you feeling, Jack?"

There was no answer. Jack was hooked up to a machine that showed his heartbeat, otherwise he might have been dead.

Howie pulled up a chair near the bed.

"Well, Jack, you've done it again. Emma is furious with you. You're old and retired, you're recovering from a stroke. What in the name of heaven possessed you to go off on a crazy escapade to McFadden's house?"

There still was no answer.

"Look, I understand," he said. "You want to involve yourself in the case. You're bored. But you have to accept the reality of your situation. You're as smart as ever—okay, I'll give you that. But your mobility is zero."

"Really?" Jack muttered. It was his first sign of life.

"Jack, you've had a long interesting career. Now's the time to relax and enjoy your golden years."

"Do you have a gun with you, Howie?"

It was a surprising question. "No, I do not."

"That's too bad. If you're going to kill me, I'd rather you do it with bullets than words. Golden years? Did you really say that?"

"Jack, we're trying to look after you. You're not making it easy when you act like a two-year-old."

Jack pressed a button by his right hand and the back of the hospital bed came up slowly until he was sitting up.

"All right, let me tell you how things stand. I'm sorry," he said bitterly. "I'm very, very sorry about Shayna. I liked him."

"Him?"

"Her, whatever. That's not important, don't worry about it. Shayna was amazingly brave at the end, going into that burning house to rescue people. But I wasn't the one who killed her. It was the bastard who set the fire, and I'm going to get him. I'm thinking it's the same asshole who murdered Keir and possibly Zia. So my question for you, Howie, is this. Are you going to help me nail this son of a bitch, or are you going to get in my way?"

Howie was taken aback. "Jack, relax! I'm in. And so is Santo, by the way. We all want to find the person who's doing these awful things. But *you* need to take a back seat. I know this is frustrating, you want to do everything yourself. If you had questions you wanted to ask Charlie, you could have given me a call and told me what you wanted to know. *I* would have gone and done the interrogation."

"Howie, with due respect—my way of questioning people is different from yours. I have more experience, frankly."

"Jack—"

"Listen to me, Howie. Shayna was in my employ when she got shot, and if you think I'm going to forget about this, you're crazy. Nobody kills someone on my team and gets away with it! Nobody! I'm going to nail this jerk and no one is going to stop me. Not you, not Emma, not Santo. I refuse to let this stand!"

Howie sighed. "You know, sometimes I fantasize the life I might have lived if you hadn't hired me to mow your lawn. I would be teaching in some happy university—rural New England, maybe, me and my students sitting on a grassy knoll in the shade of a big maple tree!"

"Howie, shut up. Now, listen closely because here's what we're going to do. You're going to go out and be the eyes and the feet, and I'll be—"

"Right, you'll be the brain. I got it, Jack. Has it ever occurred to you that you have a very large ego?"

"Howie, okay, you're smart, too. I'll say it. Nevertheless, I'm still your boss and I'm calling the shots. Now what are you going to do?"

Howie shook his head. As far as Howie was concerned, Jack was *not* still his boss. But he didn't want to inform Jack of this when he was in a hospital bed hooked up to machines.

He took a deep breath. He told himself it was a waste of time to argue with a crazy old coot.

"What do you mean, what am I going to do?"

"What are you going to do next when you leave this room? How are you going to pursue this investigation?"

"Okay," he said reluctantly. "As it happens, our client, Charles McFadden, is also in this hospital. I checked when I stopped at the desk. He's been moved from ER into the main building, and that's where I'll be heading next. I presume he's recovering. I'm going to ask him if he saw the person who set the fire. I'm hoping I can get a coherent account from him. With luck, we may find who the killer is right there."

"Okay," said Jack. "That's good. Be sure to ask him about his first wife, Sophia. I want to know what happened to her."

"Why are you interested in her?"

"She's a loose end, Howie, and I don't like that. We don't know where she is. And she likes to set fires, too. We can't forget that. All right, what are you going to do after you interview McFadden?"

"I want to confront Mikaela in Albuquerque. My main focus is to find the identity of the Dweeb, the boyfriend who was molesting Zia. I see a motive for murder here, especially if he turns out to be somebody in a respectable position who doesn't want to be exposed. I'm going to put Georgie on an online search to see what she can find out about Mikaela's private life. I'll question Mikaela in person. Zia's diary has given me enough ammunition so that I think I can make her talk."

"You believe the Dweeb is the killer?"

"I think it's a very good place to start. Don't you?"

"Maybe, Howie, maybe. But why would he kill Keir then attempt to burn down McFadden's house?"

"He was afraid Zia had told Keir about being molested. The same with her grandfather. The Dweeb is trying to cover up his crime."

"Maybe," Jack said again. "Okay, go and do it. When you see Mikaela, ask about Sophia. See if you can find out where her mother went after she got out of the loony bin."

"Jack, we don't use expressions like loony bin any more. You should know that better than anyone. We respect people with disabilities."

"Hey, I do respect people with disabilities!" said Jack. "Now let's get on with this investigation! I want you to keep me updated every step of the way."

"Okay, okay," said Howie, throwing up his hands. "I'll try."

Chapter Sixteen

Georgie got a ride into town with Claire, who had a t'ai chi class. Howie had left home before dawn. He phoned while they were having breakfast to say that Jack was in the hospital, but showing signs of life—his old self, in fact, was rising from the ashes. Howie would tell them all about Jack's misadventure when he saw them. He couldn't do justice to the story now because he was in transit to see their client, who was in another part of the hospital.

"Jack and Howie would get along better if Jack treated him more like a colleague and less like the son he never had," Claire said as they were driving.

"Couldn't Emma and Jack have children?" Georgie asked. This was a conversation they wouldn't have had if Howie were present.

"It was Jack who at first didn't want children, back when he was in San Francisco. He said his job was too dangerous, too stressful, and he couldn't bring a child into a situation like that."

"Emma told you this?"

"She did. We're family, really. You are too, of course. I don't think she'd mind me telling you this. When Jack lost his eyesight in that hostage situation, that's when *he* started talking about having a child. But Emma was past forty, she was busy with her own career, and this time it was she who said no. That's how Howie became Jack's pseudo-son, filling a sort of blank. At least, this is how Howie sees it."

"It sounds like a problem," said Georgie.

"It is. Howie had his own father, a wonderful old man—I met him just once. And he's not looking for a father figure with Jack. A boss, yes. That's different. It doesn't have the psychological tangles."

Georgie found family talk interesting, how generations pass down. Ray and Carol had always been her family. Such decent people. They had always been so kind to her. But she had never thought of them as mom and dad, they had always been Ray and Carol—even before Howie found her.

So who am I really? was Georgie's constant question to herself. Half Lakota, half Anglo. This was her heritage and it always led her to wonder about her mother—the mother she had never known. The beautiful Grace Stanton—as Howie always called her, ironically. Her father's first love, the golden girl who had come from a family of New Mexico aristocracy, land barons and politicians. For Georgie, this made for a complicated mix.

"Maybe none of it matters," she said as Claire pulled into the rear of the agency building to drop her off.

"What doesn't matter?" Claire asked with a laugh.

"The drama we make of things. I'm not sure I'll ever understand any of it, anyway. So why take it seriously?"

Inside, Georgie opened the windows to let in the New Mexico morning that was only slightly tainted with the scent of downtown traffic. She made coffee and spent the next hour doing some long-overdue cleaning, vacuuming and scrubbing the bathroom. The adobe walls were lovely but they shed a lot of dust.

It was nearly noon when Howie came in the back door looking irritated and bedraggled. He settled into the big rocking chair behind Jack's old desk with a sigh.

"Everything okay, Da?"

"Basically, yes. It's been a frustrating morning, but that's just the way some mornings are. I'm not going to let it get to me."

"I can see that."

"But our client, *he's* a challenge! He was dead drunk when the fire broke out so he couldn't tell me anything about it. He didn't see who set it."

"What fire?"

Howie had to back up and tell Georgie about the fire and Shayna's death. This took a few minutes. At the end of it, Georgie was very quiet.

"It's incredible how Jack was able to persuade Shayna to drive him there!" Howie said with frustration. "I suppose it's good he wants to stay involved, but honestly, he's no longer able to take care of himself—he needs to stay home! I mean, getting his caregiver killed! Georgie, this is the last straw! It's tragic. I feel for Jack. But his antics have become a danger to everybody near him."

"You're starting to sound a bit like Emma, Da."

"Well, Emma is upset. I talked with her on the phone as I was driving here from the hospital. Most of all, she's furiously unhappy about Shayna. She's asked me to locate Shayna's parents to make sure the agency pays all the funeral expenses and do whatever we can to make amends."

"Is the agency financially liable?"

"I don't think so. But we'll have to see. In any case, Emma is determined to set things as right as she can make them. Meanwhile, she's not sure how she is going to continue working at the library without a caregiver for Jack. Her work is important, not just to Emma but to the community. She's in the midst of an epic legal battle against a group that wants to ban "To Kill a Mockingbird" from public libraries. They believe patriotic taxpayers shouldn't be required to subsidize leftist literature that suggests America has a history of slavery and racism. They don't want writers to write the truth. Under Emma, the library is fighting back. But this is taking a lot of her time. All this week she's supposed to be attending hearings in Santa Fe—but with no caregiver, she's going to be stuck at home. Jack's going to be home from the hospital tomorrow and someone is going to need to be with him."

"Why don't we take it on together?" Georgie suggested. "You and me, Emma and Claire. We could do it in shifts so one of us doesn't have to get stuck with Jack duty forever."

Howie smiled but shook his head. "Look, I don't want you to feel obligated to take care of Jack. I'm not going to saddle you with him. Emma, Claire, and I will somehow cover Jack."

"Da, honestly, I like him. I think there's something wonderful about Jack refusing to retire. He won't ride off into the sunset as he's supposed to. It's heroic in a funny way. I admire him."

"Not heroic. Foolish, Georgie. That's the word I'd use here."

"Okay, but sometimes foolish is what being heroic is all about. So put me on the rotation, please."

Howie resisted the temptation to give his daughter a big hug.

"Okay," he said. "Now let's find the Dweeb. I'll leave you to the online search. I'm going to tackle Mikaela."

***

For the next hour, Howie sat in his office, phone to his ear, working his way upward through the hierarchy at television station KABB, trying to reach Mikaela McFadden, the CEO.

Starting with the switchboard, he was put on hold and passed from one office to another. He was disconnected several times, either accidentally or deliberately, and had to start all over again. By the time he reached Mikaela's secretary, he had his rap down.

"Hello, my name is Howard Moon Deer. I'm a private investigator working for Mikaela's father, the author, Charles McFadden. I need to see Mikaela today about an urgent personal matter."

"Please hold," said the secretary.

After five minutes of insipid music, he was disconnected yet again. Fortunately, private detectives learned persistence or they perished. He began from scratch with the main switchboard.

At last he reached a woman who described herself as Mikaela McFaddens's executive assistant. She had a faint British accent.

"Ms. McFadden has no openings in her schedule (she pronounced it *shezule*) but if you will tell me what this is about, I will make sure she gets your message at the end of the day."

"I'm afraid I can discuss this only with Ms. McFadden," Howie replied. "But you can tell her it's about the death of her daughter, Zia. This is about to become a police matter and she will want to talk to me as soon as possible."

"I see. Please hold," said the executive assistant.

He was just thinking he'd been disconnected once again when the assistant came back on the line.

Howie scribbled on a notepad as he listened. "Okay, okay, one o'clock, the station on Central . . . I'll be there. Yes, I got that. The fourth floor."

He stood from his desk and hurried to where Georgie sat at the desk computer in the front room.

"I've got to go. The only time Mikaela can see me is when she comes into the station at one. She's giving me fifteen minutes of her time, that's it. I've got to leave right now."

"Do you want me to come with you, Da?"

"No, it's best you stay here and keep digging. Have you found anything yet about the Dweeb?"

"Not yet," Georgie admitted.

"Well, keep looking. And give me a call the second you find out who he is. If possible, I'd like to know that before I talk to Mikaela. Will you be okay on your own? You can get a ride home with Claire."

"Da, of course I'm okay on my own. I'm quite independent, if you haven't noticed. And if Claire can't pick me up, I'll sleep in the office. There are restaurants nearby. Bars. It's quite an interesting night life around here. So don't worry."

"Of course not," he told her.

***

Georgie settled in at the big screen Mac in the front room to search for the Dweeb. She was good at online research, it's what had gotten her through university. But she always felt a bit squirmy sitting at a desk in an office. She liked to be outside.

Mikaela was the obvious starting place. As the CEO of a TV station, she would have a professional presence online, and hopefully information about her personal life. Georgie began by googling her name and she followed the leads from there. There was a good deal about Mikaela online. KABB, which went by the slogan Albuquerque Big Boy, was part of the Cypress Media Corporation which included a dozen TV and radio stations in New Mexico, Texas, and Oklahoma.

Georgie made notes on a pad alongside the computer in the front office.

How did M get job?

There was nothing to indicate how a carefree teenage party girl had transformed into somebody responsible for running a television station. Georgie wanted to look into this. But first she scanned trade publications, newspaper morgues, and YouTube videos for anything that might disclose her private life.

Georgie spent the next two hours searching the Internet. She solved one mystery almost immediately, how she got her job. In her late twenties, Mikaela had married a man whose family owned the Cypress Media Corporation, the company that owned the Albuquerque station.

The marriage lasted three years, was childless, and ended when the husband was killed in a motorcycle accident. Men didn't do well after they hooked up with her. Mikaela inherited a sizable minority share of stock in Cypress which paved the way for her to become the CEO of Albuquerque Big Boy. Apparently she enjoyed the power of running a TV station, though the trade publications gave her a mixed review. An article in the online journal, *Broadcasting & Cable*, claimed that her rough management style had made her disliked at the station. Under her leadership, a number of the most competent workers had quit, to be replaced by Mikaela's picks who were often friends who had little idea of how to run a TV station.

Fortunately, KABB had Joe Ochoa, who was possibly the most popular weatherman in the state, and this kept their ratings high. Joe was king of the hour-long 10 o'clock News. He did gardening segments, told homeowners when it was time to bring their plants inside, and was adored by grandmothers everywhere. Small town TV stations lived or died on the popularity of their weathermen, the weather report being generally the most watched segment of the local news.

Mikaela kept her personal life to herself, but by early afternoon, Georgie was fairly certain the Dweeb was none other than Joe Ochoa, the charismatic weatherman. She had found three photographs of Mikaela and Joe together—one at a media conference in Denver, another at a fund raising dinner for a new cancer research center, and the third at a UNM football game where the Lobos lost to the Colorado State Rams.

It was the photo at the football game that convinced Georgie there was some hanky-panky going on between them. Joe was in his early forties, and though he wasn't especially handsome, there was something appealing in his manner. In the photograph, Joe and Mikaela had their heads close together and whatever they were saying had brought a smile to both their faces. There was an intimacy in their manner, sharing a joke, that made Georgie think of Ashton Woolridge the Third.

No, she would not think about Ashton Woolridge the Third!

After more research, she discovered that Joe was married to a woman named Cindy and that they had three children together. They were a Christian family who often spoke of their faith. Joe liked to say that the Bible was his "user manual." The three children were all girls: Mary, Carey, and Sherry.

"Poor kids!" said Georgie.

There was one more interesting piece of information Georgie discovered about Joe. It was gossip, really, but if it was true it gave Joe a possible motive to kill.

The item came from a column in *Broadcasting & Cable*, the trade journal. It said that Joe Ochoa was being courted by CNN to be their main weatherman, which would pluck him from small city obscurity into national TV. For Joe this could be the opportunity of a lifetime. But he wouldn't get the job if it came out that he was a child molester.

Would he kill to keep his secret? By mid-afternoon Georgie felt confident enough to phone Howie, hoping to reach him before his meeting with Mikaela. She got his voicemail.

"Hi, Da, I think I have it. The Dweeb is the KABB weatherman, Joe Ochoa. I've seen three photographs of them together at different events and their body language looks just a pinch intimate. Also, he has a possible motive. Joe's married, he has three kids, he's up for a job on CNN and he would lose everything if Zia decided to talk about what he did to her. I'm going to keep looking, but right now I'm 80 percent certain it's Joe."

70 percent certain would have been more accurate.

Face it, 60 percent. If that.

Three photographs and an unproven motive weren't much to go on. But she had a feeling she was right.

After leaving the message for Howie, Georgie locked up the office and set off in search of lunch. She had been working intensely all morning, her back was sore from sitting so long, and she was starving.

***

Georgie walked four blocks to Mama Lama, a café on the south edge of the historic district, a local hangout that hadn't yet been overrun by tourists. Mama Lama had the best vegetarian food in town as well as a pleasant patio where you could eat in the shade of a grape arbor.

Georgie found a table outside and ordered the Persian Shirazi Salad tossed lightly with a Tibetan Yak Milk dressing.

"What would you like to drink?" asked the tattooed, multiply pierced waitress.

Georgie was tempted by the Third Eye Stout, mindfully brewed in San Geronimo, but decided to go non-alcoholic with a Passion Flower Mint Seltzer.

She was perfectly comfortable eating alone in a restaurant. As soon as she ordered, she took her laptop from her daypack, connected to the café's Wi-Fi, and resumed her research. Now that she had found the Dweeb (hopefully), she turned her efforts to locating more of Zia's classmates. Uma had been helpful but Georgie was hoping that Zia's other classmates—perhaps teachers—would be able to tell her more.

Georgie returned to the San Geronimo Valley School graduation photograph she had found earlier that had given her a last name for Uma Rothenstein. It was a small school and there were only twenty-five graduates, boys and girls. There was a Maya, a Rainbow, a Cosmo, Beckett, Arrow, Zarin, Kade, and several more. One unfortunate kid, probably an outcast, was stuck with the name Steve. Most likely he received a lot of grief from his classmates. Zia was not on the list because she was dead by the time of the May graduation.

Georgie found a pen and notebook in her daypack and was copying the names when she was surprised to see Edward Rothenstein and another man seated at a table beneath the arbor a dozen feet away. Both men were looking her way, obviously discussing her. The second man at the table was much younger than Edward, in his early thirties. Quite good looking.

Georgie looked away and resumed her work, paying no further attention to the two men ogling her. But a few minutes later she felt a shadow hovering by her table.

"God in heaven, it's my Lakota princess!" said Edward, peering down at her.

Georgie was incensed. "I am not a Lakota princess, Mr. Rothenstein," she told him curtly. "And if I were, I would certainly not be *your* princess!"

"Have you thought over my offer to paint you?"

"I haven't given it any thought at all. The answer is still no."

"I can make you famous, you know. You'll be hung in a museum."

"I don't want to be famous. And I certainly don't want to hang in a museum."

"Then how about cash? I don't expect you to model for free. Let's say a hundred dollars an hour? I work slowly, so it should be worth your while."

"I don't want your money either."

"You're a mystery, aren't you?" He studied her with his amused bad-boy blue eyes. "You don't want to be famous, you don't want money—what *do* you want?"

She gave him the hardest hard-boiled look she could manage. "What I want Mr. Rothenstein, is to eat my lunch in peace and be left alone!"

He smiled sadly. "Ah, life has its disappointments. It's what makes us human, I suspect. Grief. But as you wish." He made a small bow, and returned to his table.

Georgie considered having her lunch put into a to go container, but she didn't want to give Rothenstein the satisfaction of driving her away. For the next twenty minutes, she ate her salad, decided she would never again order anything with Tibetan Yak Milk dressing, wrote in her notebook, and made a point of not looking across the patio to where Edward Rothenstein and the other man were seated.

It was only as she was looking about for her waitress that she noticed Rothenstein had left. The younger man was sitting alone at their table with a small leather folder and paying the bill. When he was finished, he put the credit card slip in the folder, stood up from the table, and walked her way.

"Excuse me," he said. "May I have a word? I'm Jean-Claude Maurot. I'm curating an exhibit of Edward's work next year at the Guggenheim. Do you mind if I sit a moment? I'd love to ask you a few questions."

He was French and had a pronounced accent. Parisian, Georgie decided almost immediately. He had that look, everything Georgie thought of as Paris. She had been intrigued by the French men she had known on her trips there. Students mostly, ardent intellectuals.

Jean-Claude was cosmopolitan from head to toe. He had a thought-ful, clean-cut, delicately handsome face. His eyes were an intelligent shade of brown. He was dressed in a classic summer style of city peo-ple: tan slacks, a light blue long-sleeved Oxford shirt, sleeves rolled up on his wrist, revealing a watch that looked more expensive than a Rolex but less blatant. His smile was the essence of well-bred charm.

He was still waiting, politely, to be allowed to sit down. Georgie wanted to tell him no, but the word wouldn't quite form.

He took this as an invitation and sat.

"The Guggenheim?" she asked.

"Yes, but not the New York one. Bilbao. Have you been there?"

"I have," she answered. Travel had always interested her and she found herself babbling more than she intended. "I didn't have as much time as I would have liked. I was on a two-week break from university. I spent the first five days in Madrid at the Prado, then three days in Bilbao, and the rest of the time in Barcelona for Gaudi."

Jean-Claude nodded appreciatively. "For Gaudi! I'm impressed! The English girls I've met usually go to Spain for the beach and sun tans. But you went for art!"

Georgie sensed he had known quite a number of English girls. "I'm not English," she told him. "I'm Scottish."

His smile became a laugh. "My apologies! But you're Native American, I believe. I'm not sure I've ever met a Scottish Indian lass before."

"I'm only half Lakota," she told him, putting a damper on any Scot-tish Indian lass nonsense. She found Jean-Claude definitely attractive. But she wasn't about to be bamboozled by latin snake oil.

"So, you're curating an exhibit for Edward Rothenstein," she said, returning the conversation to safer ground. "Are you in San Geronimo looking for work to include?"

"Yes, and to write the catalogue. Most of Edward's work is in New York at the moment. Much of it is in private collections, which means I have to go about to various wealthy homes to convince people to lend to the Guggenheim."

He shook his head sadly. "It's not my favorite part of the job. In any case, Edward's new work is really very good and I want to include a good sampling of it in the show. The work he's been doing here in New Mexico these last few years. His style has completely flipped around to an unusual neo-realism that I think is brilliant."

Neo-realism? Georgie had to think about this.

She decided to be foolish and ask. "I'm trying to visualize what you mean by neo-realism?"

"That's a good question. A kind of super realism, really. Nature and people in exacting detail—Edward is a master craftsman, believe me. But there's an added element to his realism, a certain glow that's almost . . . surrealism."

Jean-Claude let the word surrealism hover in the air for a long moment. Georgie imagined he could charm a million-dollar painting from a rich person's living room and spirit it away across the Atlantic with a mere batting of his eye lash.

"You would have to see the new work to understand exactly what I mean," he told her. "There's a girl he drew and painted again and again. He was obsessed with her. The work he did with her is profoundly good."

"A girl?"

"There's one painting of her that I think is the best work he's ever done. He called it *America Girl*. It's a nude and it's unforgettable. It sums up something about America that's on the razor end of being profound, on one hand. And total kitsch on the other."

"I see," said Georgie. "More or less."

"I like it so much, I want to make it the center of the exhibition. In a sense, all the rest of his work radiates from this one painting."

Georgie was glad she hadn't taken her honors degree in Art History, as she had once intended. There was only so much of this sort of talk one could take at one time. Fortunately, she had a sense where Jean-Claude was going. Zia McFadden. It would explain the tension she felt at the Rothenstein estate at the mention of her name.

She looked up from the remains of her salad and found Jean-Claude regarding her intently.

"I'd love to see this painting," she told him.

He shook his head very slightly. "Edward told me you're a journalist and you're doing an article for the Guardian about a teenage girl who killed herself. Is that true?"

"Well . . ." Georgie was about to lie, but found she couldn't. "Actually, I did write an article once for the Guardian about student life at Cambridge. But I'm not a real journalist. I'm working for my father here in San Geronimo. He's . . . actually, he's a private detective."

Jean-Claude smiled. "You went to Cambridge?"

"I did."

"And now you're a private eye! This is quite *fantastique!*"

"No, I'm not a private eye. I only work in the office to help out my Da."

"But you're investigating the death of that teenage girl? It's why you went to visit Uma. Edward told me that Uma and the girl were classmates."

"Yes, her name was Zia McFadden and I'd very much like to find out everything I can about her. My father and his partner were actually the ones who found the body."

"Zia McFadden. Is she related to the author?"

"She is. Charles McFadden was her grandfather. I'm surprised you know about him."

"Like a lot of French people, I'm fascinated with the American West. When I was a child I read *Blood Red Mountains* under the covers with a flashlight. I fantasized wild adventures in New Mexico with coyotes howling rather than my boring life in Paris."

"Paris isn't really so boring," Georgie informed him.

"No, but *I* was bored. Look, there is something I want to ask you. This is a delicate matter, actually. I'm trying to discover the precise origins of *America Girl*."

"You suspect the girl in the painting is Zia McFadden, don't you?"

"Well, yes, I do. But I'm not certain, that's the problem. Edward has taken artistic liberties. As I said, there's a kind of neo-realistic glow that becomes almost semi-abstraction."

"Yes," Georgie said with some impatience. "But tell me this. In the painting, the girl . . . you say she's naked?"

"She's nude, yes. But of course artists paint life models all the time. Now here's my predicament. *America Girl* is absolutely the best painting Edward has done in years, perhaps ever. I'd very much like to have it in Bilbao. But if it gets out that the model was a teenage girl who took her own life because of her relationship with Edward, it could become a scandal. I would need to leave the canvas out of the show."

Georgie had to keep her mouth from falling open. This changed everything. She wasn't sure how, but she knew it did.

"That lech! He asked *me* to pose for him, you know!"

"Yes, he told me. He's quite disappointed you said no. He thinks you have a very interesting face."

"Right. My face."

"Ah, I see what you mean. Well, what can I say, Georgie. The human form has fascinated artists for centuries."

"I'm sorry if I sound provincial. But Edward Rothenstein, honestly! The man is too much! And if he seduced Zia, that's awful. She was only seventeen. This certainly could have something to do with her death!"

"Well, as I said, I'm not entirely certain the model really is Zia. If by any chance you would look at the painting and tell me what you think, I'd greatly appreciate it. I can't take the canvas from Edward's studio, that would be impossible. But perhaps I can snap a photo on my phone."

"I'd be glad to tell you what I think," she said, trying not to be too eager.

"I tell you what," he said. "I'm going to be taking photographs of a number of Edward's works later today, and if you'll have dinner with me tonight, I'll show them to you. If the girl is Zia, I am going to have to change the entire show. I may even have to cancel it."

"Dinner tonight?" This wasn't what she had in mind.

His smile was so charmingly French, it made her feel giddy. "It would be a pleasure. I'd be very grateful, really. And I promise to be on my best behavior."

What could she say? "Well, all right. I suppose."

"Wonderful. Let's say the Blue Mesa Café at 8 o'clock? I hear that's a very nice place to go."

It was a nice place to go. It was also a very romantic and expensive place: candles, low ceilings, adobe walls, good food, spirits, intimacy galore, even a musician playing a baby grand piano in the corner. Georgie wasn't certain, but it appeared she had just agreed to go out on a date.

They lingered at the table for another half hour. Along with the Guggenheim, Jean-Claude had done work for the Musée d'Orsay in Paris, the Met in New York, and the Tate in London. He had fascinating stories to tell of famous artists and the art world. As he spoke, she realized that Jean-Claude was himself a person of importance in this glamorous world of talent and money.

Walking back to the office, Georgie chided herself about saying yes for dinner.

Get a hold of yourself, Georgie! This is the last thing you need in your life right now! A charming, handsome, interesting Frenchman!

Yet a rogue voice whispered as she opened the back door to the office—that perhaps this was exactly what she needed.

Chapter Seventeen

Howie ran into road work just north of Albuquerque and made it to KABB with just ten minutes to spare.

The TV studio was on the 4th floor of a rectangular, brutal-looking office building on Central Avenue that took up a large corner of a city block and was eleven stories high. It was a skyscraper by New Mexico standards.

Central Avenue was what remained of Route 66, the famous highway that was once the main route west, but the romance was long gone. The identical windows up and down the skyscraper were receded, set in indented squares that must have looked very modern in the 1960s, but today seemed monotonous and drab. On the roof, there were a bewildering array of electronics and blinking red lights to warn off aircraft.

Since he was in a hurry, Howie parked in the building's underground garage rather than search for a cheaper spot on the street. He took the elevator to the fourth floor and made it just in time to the receptionist, a young woman who sat at a desk in a glass cubicle guarding against those who might try to break into television without a station ID card or an appointment. Howie was early. It was 12:59. He was out of breath.

He said his name and told her he had an appointment with Mikaela McFadden at 1 o'clock. The receptionist smiled, picked up a phone, said that Mr. Moon Deer was here, smiled again, and told him to have a seat, someone would be with him shortly to take him down the hall to Mikaela.

Shortly turned out to be a relative term. Howie settled on a black leather couch by a potted palm and watched the minutes pass on a digital clock on the wall next to a TV screen that showed KABB's current broadcast, a quiz show in which everybody appeared to be having a hilarious time. The reception area was antiseptically modern. After a half hour wait, Howie returned to the glass cubicle.

"Hi, I thought I'd check on that person who was supposed to take me to Mikaela McFadden."

"And your name is?"

"Howard Moon Deer," said Howie.

"Let me find out."

Again the young woman picked up the phone. Again she smiled. It was the most ruthless smile he had ever seen.

"I'm sorry, but Mikaela is tied up right now. She won't be able to see you until eleven."

It took Howie a moment to absorb this. "11 o'clock? Tomorrow morning?"

"No, 11 o'clock tonight." Her smile brightened. "After the 10 o'clock News."

Howie was about to object.

He was about to tell her that he had rushed down from San Geronimo, a three hour drive because Mikaela McFadden said she could only see him at one. He was about to blow up. But the young woman's smile defeated him. She was beyond reach.

"Thank you," Howie managed, with only a hint of sarcasm. "I'll be back."

He went off fuming. He had ten hours to kill! In Albuquerque! It was beyond reason. He couldn't imagine what he was going to do with himself for ten hours!

He took the elevator to the lobby with a growl on his lips.

He walked out onto Central Avenue, stood on the sidewalk, and reached for his phone to call Claire to let her know he would be home late. Very late. The screen told him there was voicemail from Georgie as well as a text message. His phone had been on the passenger seat throughout the three hour drive. He had been half an hour south of Santa Fe at the time she called, so he should have heard the ring.

He brought up Georgie's text.

The Dweeb is Joe Ochoa the KABB weatherman. I'm 80% certain. Check your voicemail. Left you a bit more.

Georgie knew that Howie often forgot to check his voicemail. It was one of his many problems with the modern world. It was difficult to hear Georgie's voice with the traffic of the busy boulevard behind him.

"Hi, Da, I think I have it," she said. "The Dweeb is the KABB weatherman, Joe Ochoa. I've seen three photographs of them together at different events and their body language looks just a pinch too intimate. I think he has a possible motive to kill. Joe's married, he has three kids, he's up for a job on CNN and he would lose everything if Zia decided to talk about what he did. I'm going to keep looking, but right now I'm 80 percent certain it's Joe."

Howie tried to call her back in person, but now she didn't answer. He left a voicemail.

"Hey, I'm stuck in Albuquerque. Mikaela changed our meeting to eleven tonight! Can you believe that woman? Anyway, Joe Ochoa! Good work! I've seen him. He's everybody's favorite weatherman, a real celebrity in this state. This is going to give me some serious ammunition when I see Mikaela tonight. But you say you're only eighty percent certain? Where's the twenty percent doubt? Call me when you can. Love you!"

Love you was more casual than *I love you*. Howie adored his daughter, but he had only known her a few years and he didn't want to scare her off.

145

Now he only had ten hours to kill!

***

It turned out to be easy to kill ten hours in Albuquerque as long as you didn't mind spending money.

Howie drove to Montgomery Boulevard where he knew of an Asian supermarket and bought a number of spices that weren't available in San Geronimo. Claire was going to be happy. From there he drove to Page One Bookstore, killed an hour browsing, and left with a pile of books. He phoned Claire from an all-you-can-eat Chinese buffet where he stopped for a late lunch.

"Did you get my message? I'm going to be home late, Claire. I'm pissed off about it, really. But I have to see Mikaela. There's a lot about this family that isn't clear."

"I know, Howie. And Zia, that poor girl! I'll never forgot the sight of her body in that river at Eagle Falls!"

"Will you be able to pick up Georgie tonight in town?"

"Yes, of course. But she's here right now. She's in the shower. She's going out for dinner at the Blue Mesa with a French man she met who she says may have some important information about Zia."

A French man? Howie was slightly alarmed by the idea of a mysterious French man taking his daughter out to dinner.

"Relax, Howie. He's an art expert in town to curate an exhibit for Edward Rothenstein. That's the artist who's the father of Zia's school friend, Uma. I don't know anything more. I drove Georgie back home after my t'ai chi class. After her shower, I'm going to drive her back into town. She says not to worry, she'll sleep on the futon in the office, the restaurant is only three blocks away."

"So it's a date then?"

"It's sounds like half-date, half-investigation. I'm sure this art expert from Paris is very nice."

"Paris?"

"I advise you to leave this alone, Howie. Georgie's a young woman and men are going to show an interest in her. It's not entirely out of the question that she might show some interest back."

"I see," said Howie, taking this in. "Well, maybe she can give me a call when she gets out of the shower."

"Howie, give her some space. Truly, it's for the best. Why don't you wait and talk with her tomorrow."

"Okay," he agreed unhappily.

In fact, Howie knew she was right. He didn't want to make Georgie feel penned in. Still, it was annoying. He had intended to ask her why she was only eighty percent sure of the Dweeb's identity. But she clearly had other things on her mind. Men.

His late lunch and cell phone conversation with Claire took up nearly an hour and a half. By the time he was finished, he had only a few more hours to kill.

He was back at KABB, Albuquerque Big Boy, by 10 o'clock. He parked once again in the underground garage, paying the exorbitant fee because he didn't want to be late. There would be a TV screen in the reception area and he didn't want to miss the weather forecast.

***

The 10 o'clock News had a cheerful, friendly, small city feel to it. If it weren't for the stories about murders, rapes and robberies—of which Albuquerque had its share—you'd almost feel you were in Mr. Roger's Neighborhood, an alternate universe where everybody overflowed with civic virtue and good will.

After checking in with the 4th floor receptionist, Howie ensconced himself on the black fake-leather couch by the TV monitor on the wall that was showing the news. The receptionist kept an eagle eye on him. It was a different person from the one earlier, the robotic woman with the impenetrable smile. This was a young man who appeared to take his job seriously. Nobody was going to get past him who didn't belong.

Joe Ochoa, the weatherman, kept appearing throughout the hour to promote the weather segment that was coming later in the show. He dropped teasers to raise the suspense, warning viewers that "big changes were in store." New Mexicans might need their umbrellas later in the week. Howie had to admit, Joe was good. He radiated fun. He made it sound like it was a big deal whether it rained or not.

Physically, Joe wasn't much. He had a slight, spidery figure. He was dark complexioned but it was hard to say if he was Hispanic or Lebanese or something else entirely. About forty years old, Howie guessed. He wasn't handsome, but he wasn't plain. He was just nice looking with dark hair, even features, and a tremendous smile.

It was the smile that had made Joe's fortune.

After keeping viewers in suspense for nearly an hour, he came on camera to let viewers know that yes, there was a 60 percent chance of thunderstorms on Saturday. Howie watched closely, trying to find the Dweeb beneath the friendly face, the creep who had come into Zia's bedroom to molest her. But that side of Joe, if it was there, was well-hidden. This amiable weatherman was somebody you'd trust your grandmother with. Or your teenage daughter.

Howie wasn't sure what he thought. On one hand, Georgie had done research and had decided—80 percent decided—that Joe was the Dweeb. Howie trusted Georgie's research. But looking at Joe, it was hard to see it. There was an aw-shucks quality about him that made it impossible to imagine him having an affair with anybody, much less Mikaela—much less using the opportunity to molest Zia on the side.

When the news was over, a young Hispanic woman with a clipboard came through a security door promptly at 11 o'clock to take him to Mikaela's office. She led him through another door and down a wide industrial hallway that was large enough to move scenery and lights around. She came to an open door, knocked and discreetly vanished.

The office was cavernous with only a single light showing, a desk lamp. Mikaela McFadden sat behind an enormous desk studying him. The desk was a slab of modernity, sleek and shiny. Behind her, the nightscape of Albuquerque was spread out panoramically through floor to ceiling windows on two sides. It was a city that looked better at night than it did in the daytime.

"Okay, let's get this over with," she said, setting a combative tone. "Sit down."

Howie sat. "I assume you know about your father?"

"What about my father?"

"He's in the hospital. Somebody tried to burn down his house yesterday while he was inside. If my partner hadn't gotten there in time, he would be dead now," Howie added.

"But he's alive?"

"They might keep him in the hospital for a day or two, but he's okay."

Mikaela snorted a kind of negative laugh. "Funny, my father used to say God takes care of drunks and little children. That was his motto. God takes care of drunks all right, but little children have to fend for themselves!"

Howie studied Mikaela as she sat half-hidden in the shadows. She was overweight, in her late thirties, and she looked as though she had lived a damaging life. Her hair was blonde, cut short, but it didn't look natural. Her skin was a little loose, and it didn't look natural either. She wore a frown that Howie imagined had become a permanent fixture of her face. He had gotten her attention, but she didn't seem unduly disturbed that her father had been nearly burned alive.

"When's the last time you saw your father, Ms. McFadden?"

She shrugged. "I don't know. A few years ago. He was down here for some literary conference and we had lunch together. I don't see him often."

"Would you say you're estranged?"

"Estranged? Not really, just not interested in seeing him. He wasn't always a drunk, that only came in recent years. But he was always an arrogant prick who had no interest in anything but himself and the books he was always writing. I got tired of that. I like to live my own life."

"I understand," Howie said sympathetically. He'd had hours to consider how he was going to conduct this interview and had decided to start softly. "Anybody who grows up with a famous parent ends up needing to find their own life. But you know what's odd here? This isn't the first time somebody tried to burn down your father's house with him inside. In fact, you were inside with him the first time. That time your mother did it."

Mikaela sighed in an exaggerated way and shook her head. "My family!"

"Your mother was sent away to a mental institution in Las Cruces. Do you have any contact with her?"

"Are you kidding? I have no contact with her at all! Would you, after she did something like that?"

"I don't know. As I grew older, I would consider the fact that she was ill."

"Oh, gimme a break! She tried to kill me when I was eight!"

"I gather the hospital closed in 2017 and she was let free. Has she made any attempt to get in touch with you?"

"No."

"Do you have any idea where she is?"

"Not a clue. Now, look, Half Moon or whatever your name is— why are you asking these things?"

"Moon Deer," he told her. "As I told your assistant, I'm a private detective. You father hired me to find out why Zia died. He doesn't accept that her death was suicide. He thinks it could have been murder."

"Murder! That's ridiculous! My father always had a melodramatic streak and too much imagination. But the cops said she jumped. She even left a suicide note. It's a tragedy, but there's no mystery about it."

"The supposed suicide note was scratched into the cliff, but it could have been put there by anybody. The Sheriffs didn't do a thorough in-vestigation. Suicide was more an assumption than anything else. And now with everything else that's happened, people are taking a closer look."

"What do you mean, everything else that's happened?"

"Keir Aaronson is dead also. Zia's father, your old boyfriend from your ski days. That's just too much dying in one family to be a coinci-dence."

"I heard about Keir," she said, and for a moment she went almost soft with the memory of him. "Hanged himself from a tree, didn't he?"

"He was in a tree, but he didn't get there by himself. The medical examiner says he was dead before someone put a rope around his neck and hoisted him up there."

Mikaela shrugged. "Well, I'm sorry. He was a lot of fun a long time ago. Probably it was a drug deal gone wrong. How would I know?"

"Was Keir into drugs when you knew him?"

"Not really. Weed, of course. We all smoked a lot of weed back then."

"But no hard drugs?"

"Not that I know of. Look, I haven't seen Keir in years so I can't say."

Howie nodded. "All right, let's talk about Zia. Why do you believe she committed suicide?"

"I've already told you that. It's what the cops said!"

"I mean, what reasons would Zia have to kill herself?"

"Oh, come on—every teenage girl considers suicide at some time or another. It's not easy being a teenage girl. But it's a phase most of us get through. I'm sorry Zia didn't."

"How did you get along with her?"

"Get along with her? I didn't! She hated me!"

Mikaela laughed so hard she threw her head back into the shadows outside the small circle of the desk lamp.

"Yep, she hated me!" she said again. "The irony was she was finally old enough to be a buddy, somebody who might be fun to have around. Honestly, I couldn't stand her when she was little. I don't like little kids. I've always been waiting for her grow up and be a pal, not a burden."

"I see," said Howie. He decided it was time to take the leap. "But here's something else. She didn't like the man you were involved with—Joe Ochoa, the weatherman. Zia told a friend at school that when he stayed overnight at your house, he came into her bedroom and molested her."

Mikaela went pale. For a moment she appeared too shocked to speak. Howie waited, praying that Georgie's 80 percent guess was right and Joe was the Dweeb.

"Where did you hear this?" she demanded.

"I'm sorry, that's confidential," he said. "My team has been talking with a number of people who Zia confided to during the time she lived in San Geronimo, and we've been collecting information. But she was very clear about Joe. She was even specific about exactly what he did when he came into her bedroom. She said he masturbated on her leg."

Mikaela looked away. Howie had stretched matters considerably. He certainly didn't have a team. He had his twenty-one year old daughter and a blind old man in a wheelchair. Meanwhile, Mikaela sat deep in her thoughts, saying nothing, hardly aware of him.

Howie kept at it. "Your daughter came to you and told you what Joe was doing, but you did nothing to stop it. Nothing. That's why she moved to San Geronimo to live with her father. She had to get away from you and the situation here in Albuquerque."

Mikaela came out of her silence blazing mad. "That's not true! Joe would never try something like that with my daughter! Don't you get it? I'm his fucking boss! I would fire his ass!"

Howie nodded. He had his confirmation. Almost. "But Zia told you, and you didn't believe her?"

"Of course, I didn't believe her! The entire thing was in her imagination. She *wanted* Joe to come into her room—all the girls want that. But Joe didn't do that, because Joe belongs to me."

"I see," said Howie, his go-to phrase.

"Okay, sure, she came to me with these stories," Mikaela admitted. "But they weren't true. My daughter just didn't want me to have a boyfriend and be happy. That's all there is to it. If you knew Joe, you would know he would never do a thing like that! He loves me."

"I'm sure he does," Howie said insincerely. He wished he was recording this. He now had full corroboration that Joe was the Dweeb, but he had pushed too hard. Mikaela knew she had let anger get the better of her and she had said too much. She stood up.

"Okay, now you know. If you tell anyone about Joe and me, I swear you'll regret it. Now get out! Your time is up. Get out of my office before I call security!"

***

It was nearly midnight when Howie signed out at the security desk on the ground floor.

The building had emptied out and Howie's footsteps were loud in the hallways. In the lobby, four TV monitors were showing the current broadcast, a talk show from New York, a national feed. For Albuquerque Big Boy, only a robotic workforce was needed to keep pre-recorded programs on the air for insomniacs. The station had slipped into its late-night hibernation.

What a horrible woman! Howie said to himself as he was leaving. He pitied Zia having had a mother like that. It was hard enough to bear half an hour with her!

Tired and disgruntled, Howie walked down a final flight of concrete steps into a dank basement parking lot, a subterranean half acre underworld. Howie's Subaru was off by itself in the P-section. The garage was nearly empty. In the half-light, he could only see a handful of other vehicles. His footsteps echoed against the concrete walls. There was no one else around.

Howie suddenly knew that he shouldn't be here. He couldn't see anyone, he heard nothing, but he had a sense of danger. An underground garage was a lonely place at night.

He walked a little faster toward his car. His Outback was only a dozen feet away, his key fob in his hand, when he heard footsteps running up behind him. He whipped around to face his attacker. A man wearing a mask was coming at him waving a gun. He looked like a

154

madman. Howie barely had time to react before the man lunged at him and he was pushed backward violently against the side of his car.

"Dickhead!" the attacker screamed in a high voice.

Howie had been caught off-balance. He slipped down the side of his car onto his butt, scraping his back against the door handle.

From above, he saw the heavy shape of a gun coming down toward his head. He flipped onto his stomach and curled into a ball to protect himself. But the blow he expected never came. Instead, he felt the hard barrel of the pistol press against the back of his neck.

"Listen to me because I'm only going to tell you once! You stay away from here! You hear me? You stay away from all of this. Because if I see you again, I'm going to kill you, dickhead. You'll be dead, dead, dead! A goddamn dead dickhead!"

The guy was nuts. "You will die, die, die dickhead!" he kept saying in his high hysterical voice. "You hear me?"

Howie managed a kind of nod from his curled up position.

"Keep your damn head down, dickhead!"

The attacker vanished as quickly as he had come. Howie heard his steps as he ran toward the garage exit that gave out onto Central Avenue. By the time Howie raised his head, he could see only the rear silhouette of a man in jogging clothes disappearing up the ramp toward the street.

He believed he knew who his attacker was. It was the Dweeb. The monster beneath the friendly face.

He was 70 percent sure of it.

Chapter Eighteen

Here's the question that bothered Georgie: Was it a date tonight, or was it not?

Of course, it wasn't a date! This was work, a chance for Georgie to see the painting that Edward Rothenstein had made of Zia McFadden. This could help explain Zia's death. This could be important.

Meanwhile, if this was work, why was she wearing her one good dress?

Get a grip on yourself, Georgie! she told herself firmly.

"So, he's French," Claire said as she was driving back into town. Georgie had told her a little about him when they were driving in the other direction, to the land, and now she was pressing further. "You say he's an international art expert?"

"He's curating an Edward Rothenstein exhibit for the Bilbao Guggenheim. He's a traveling expert, quite a big deal in the art world, from the look of him. Personally, I hate how art has become overcome by money!"

"How old is he?" Claire asked.

"Mid-thirties, I'd say. He's ridiculously handsome, Claire. And charming, too. I know you're sending me warning signals, you're looking out for me. But honestly, you have no need for concern. I'm totally off men. Maybe one day there will be someone, but not now. This is work, really."

"I can see that, Georgie. Personally, I think you should have a fling if you want to. But don't tell Howie I said that. For God's sake, you're single, you're twenty-one! This is your time, girl!"

Georgie loved Claire. She was more of a sister than a faux-step-mother. But she had no intention of spending the night with Jean-

Claude Maurot. It was dinner only. Along with her one dress, she brought a bathroom kit and backpack full of books, electronics, and clothes into town with her, what she would need later at the office.

Claire dropped her off at 3:15—she had agreed to teach a chamber music class at the art center—and because it was early for dinner, Georgie made a point of spending the next hour working on Howie's books.

She didn't think about Jean-Claude once. Until she received a text a few minutes before 4.

I booked us a table at the Blue Mesa at 7. Shall I pick you up?

She had to think about that. Should he pick her up? She pictured Jean-Claude coming to the office, the two of them alone in the building.

I'll meet you at the restaurant, she texted back.

***

The Blue Mesa Café occupied an old adobe building whose interior was a maze of small rooms, each with four or five tables. With the thick mud walls and the hundred year-old timbers overhead, there was an intimate, cave-like feeling to the candlelit spaces.

Georgie arrived at exactly 7:05, not early, but not really late.

She entered through the bar which was crowded with people waiting to get tables. Though the bar was small—only four stools and three little tables—the owner had managed to fit a baby grand piano into a corner, where a young woman in a tuxedo was playing Chopin. Later in the evening, there would be jazz. The crowd, most of whom had drinks in their hands, spilled out onto the sidewalk where there were two benches. If you didn't have a reservation, you weren't going to get in. Not for months. How Jean-Claude had finagled a table was an open question, but Georgie assumed he was the sort of person who knew how to get through lines.

At the far end of the bar, an attractive young woman stood at a lectern checking reservations. Georgie knew her from her yoga class. Her name was Athena.

"Georgie!" she cried when Georgie, with some slithering, managed to make her way through the crowd. "Look at you!"

"Oh, this is just an old thing I brought over from Scotland," she said modestly. "It's my only dress, actually."

This was true. But it was Dolce & Gabbana, quite expensive, not just an old thing. It was beige, simple, nothing ostentatious, but it was cut perfectly. Georgie had bought the dress in order to attend a snooty party at a country house in Surrey with Ashton. It wasn't an occasion she wished to remember. In San Geronimo, no one had seen her in anything other than jeans, shorts, and shaggy old sweaters.

"I'm meeting a man by the name of Jean-Claude Maurot." Georgie chose her words carefully, hoping Athena wouldn't think she was on a date. "He made a reservation for 7 o'clock."

"The French guy?" Athena studied Georgie with new interest. "He's at the table waiting for you. I'll show you the way." She smiled knowingly. "He ordered a bottle of champagne."

"Did he?" Georgie wasn't entirely pleased.

"Taittinger," Athena added.

Georgie had to admit, she liked good champagne, ice cold. The kind with tiny bubbles that made your nose tingle. But she hoped she hadn't given Jean-Claude the impression that she was easy prey. She wasn't.

Athena led the way through two of the small dining rooms to a third room, where Jean-Claude was at a table next to a kiva fireplace that had a pot full of flowers on the hearth.

He stood and smiled as she approached the table. He looked very stylish in a tan summer suit, dark blue shirt, no tie.

"You're stunning," he told her. "I love your dress!"

She was about to repeat the fiction that it was just an old thing she had brought from Scotland, but she decided it was best to accept the compliment and sit down.

"I've ordered us a bit of bubbly," he said almost apologetically, waving his hand over the ice bucket and the bottle. "It takes me back to my childhood. We had an old family house in the Champagne region where we often spent our summers. It was cheaper than Paris and it was a relief to get out of the city in August. My father was a failed artist who drank too much and we didn't have much money. But he had a friend at one of the vineyards and somehow we always had champagne . . ."

Jean-Claude was off, telling her one interesting story after another about his summers in the Champagne district. He was a good conversationalist. His stories were smart and entertaining, especially his tales about his father, who he made sound like a character from Balzac.

Georgie drank a glass of champagne slowly. She ordered modestly—a salad, a vegetarian pasta—and she did her best not to let herself get carried away by Jean-Claude's charm. The table was so intimate that their legs touched from time to time, though she did her best to keep her limbs to herself.

"So, tell me about you," he said. "What was it like growing up in Glasgow?"

"Not very interesting, I'm afraid. My parents were school teachers and we lived a quiet life. I always knew I was adopted. I was an odd kid, really, not very popular. I studied a good deal of the time. I was a grind. School work was very important in our house."

"I can't imagine your life was as dull as that," he said. "And your actual father is Howard Moon Deer, the private detective. That doesn't sound boring at all."

Georgie laughed. At lunch, she had said her father was a private eye, but she hadn't mentioned his name. Which meant Jean-Claude had been asking about her.

"No, Howie isn't boring. Somehow he always manages to get himself into trouble. That's what Jack says, anyway. Jack Wilder is his old boss who's supposed to be retired now. We're all a bit worried about Jack because he's very old and eccentric."

"And you've decided to go work for your father? Is this a permanent career? Georgie the P.I.?"

"I don't know." He was making fun of her, a little, but she answered honestly. "I honestly don't know what my future holds."

"Well, none of us do," said Jean-Claude. "That's what makes life an adventure."

He was easy to be with. He was clever, he was fun. But Georgie kept her focus where she wanted it to be. On work.

"Did you get the photograph of *America Girl?*" she asked before she let him pour her a second glass of champagne.

"I did. It's on my phone. It's a fairly large painting so you won't get a full idea of it on a small screen. Would you care to see it?"

Georgie nodded.

Jean-Claude found his phone in the vest pocket of his jacket and brought up the photo of *America Girl* on the screen.

Georgie thought it was a stunning painting, realistic, a psychological portrait that was very different from the Rothenstein works she had seen in the Tate Modern. Zia was shown against a dark blue background. She was naked, revealed in detail, a lovely young woman who was sexual but sad. The power of the painting was in her expression and the penetrating sorrow of her eyes.

"As you see, Edward is no slouch," Jean-Claude said as she studied the screen. "He's caught something in the girl that's quite subtle. So what do you think? Is that the girl who killed herself?"

"It's Zia, without any doubt. And as for Edward Rothenstein, what a horrible old lech! He was sleeping with her, wasn't he?"

"I don't know, Georgie. I suppose so, yes. But it's not the sort of question I've ever asked him. I'm only the paid help, you see."

"Did you meet Zia?"

"Yes, briefly when I was here in April for a few days to discuss the catalogue."

"What did you think of her?"

"I had only a surface impression of a young girl with a nice smile. I see now that I should have paid more attention, but I was in a rush that trip. One of the great hassles of moving expensive art works around the globe is the insurance. The company I had worked with in the past wanted to charge us an outrageous fee so I spent most of my time on that April trip on the phone to Lloyds of London trying to get a better price."

"When you saw Edward and Zia together, did they appear to be . . . well, a couple?"

Jean-Claude smiled and shook his head. "I can't say there was anything overtly intimate in their behavior, but of course they would take care not to let that show. Catherine was always nearby and she can be jealous."

Georgie was interested in this. "What do you think of Catherine Rothenstein? Or Van Gieson, I should say—she uses her maiden name?"

"Only for her art. At home, she's Rothenstein. That's a difficult question. Catherine can be funny and smart at times, but she can also be very nasty. To be honest, I've never been sure exactly what Edward sees in her. She seems to have some strange hold on him."

"Really?" Georgie was interested. "Why would you think that?"

"No reason, really. It's just a feeling. I don't think Edward likes her very much, yet he stays. He's a mystery to me. He's very talented, and very talented people defy normal conventions. They live by their own rules."

They talked about genius, and how so many of the great geniuses of the world were unpleasant human beings. The French, in her experience, loved to argue philosophical abstractions, and with half a bottle of champagne bubbling in her brain, Georgie enjoyed the conversation. She said no, however, to his suggestion of a second bottle. And though they decided to split a single desert, a slice of Black Forest cake, Georgie only had two bites and left Jean-Claude to finish the rest.

As before at lunch, he told wonderful stories of the artists he had met through his work, including a week he spent with David Hockney in Los Angeles. All the artists were eccentric and made for funny anecdotes. After the Black Forest cake, he stretched out the evening by suggesting a cognac and Georgie couldn't find it in her nature to say no. Feeling very relaxed and talkative, she told him more of her childhood in Glasgow and how she had never been entirely at home there.

"The problem for me in Glasgow was I always looked different. I was a Native American, I wasn't Scottish. And some of the kids gave me a hard time about it. A lot of them thought I was a Paki, but the Pakis knew I wasn't one of them either. So I was always an outsider. Then when I was fifteen, I met Howie, my real father, and I understood the missing piece. It's like Hans Christian Anderson. I thought I was a duck, and found out I was a goose."

"Not a goose," Jean-Claude told her. "A swan."

Georgie hadn't voiced these private thoughts to anyone, not even Claire, with whom she was close. So she wasn't sure why she was being so candid now with Jean-Claude.

"But it made you strong," he said. "I've been to Glasgow. It's a fascinating city, a tough working-class town. You learned to defend yourself there, didn't you? You see, it's good to be the Ugly Duckling. Either it defeats you, or it sets you on a journey to find yourself. Which is a very good thing."

He seemed to understand her. Not everything, of course. But for some reason, they seemed to live on the same planet. It was easy to talk to him.

He insisted on walking her back to the office after dinner, though it was only a few blocks away. Georgie led him to the front entrance on Calle Dos Flores and they stood in the doorway while she found her key.

She expected to be kissed and she wasn't sure what she thought about that.

He looked at her with his warm, gentle eyes and took her right hand. He seemed to read her mind.

"You are the most fascinating woman I've spent time with in a long time. But I'm not going to kiss you."

Georgie was intrigued, and somewhat disappointed.

"Why not?" she asked.

"Because I can tell you're uneasy about it, and I don't want to do anything to cause you distress. I want to see you again. And when we do kiss, I want it to be momentous!"

Georgie laughed. "You're very sure of yourself, aren't you?"

"No, alas. Not really. The only thing I'm sure of is that I would like to have dinner with you again. Will you do me the honor? What do you say to Friday night? Perhaps we can try the new Moroccan restaurant on the Plaza? Do you like falafels?"

"Yes," she managed. Falafels were fabulous.

"Then let's meet there at eight. I'll make a reservation."

With delicacy, and the finest French manners, he lifted her hand to his lips. Then he smiled and let her go.

Georgie unlocked the door to the office with a hand that wasn't entirely steady.

Chapter Nineteen

Jack didn't like being in a hospital, lying in bed doing nothing. He had been in hospitals too many times over the past few years. Hospital world. A place where terrible things happened—you could die here. Yet at the same time it was insanely boring.

His brain was working a good deal more efficiently than his body. He still had questions for Charles McFadden, and it was frustrating to know McFadden was somewhere in this very hospital, nearby. But he had no way to get to him.

"Damnation!" Jack said aloud contemplatively.

"I'm sorry?" said a male voice.

"Don't mind me. I'm just complaining about the state of the world."

"Yes, the world is damned, certainly. Even here in this lovely country of yours, this land of milk and bananas."

"Milk and honey," Jack corrected.

"Whatever," said the man. He was a janitor and had an accent Jack couldn't identify. He had come into Jack's room to empty the garbage and clean.

"Where are you from?" Jack asked.

"Syria," said the cleaner. He said it proudly, like throwing out a challenge.

Jack sighed. He knew that there were people on the planet whose lives were worse than his own, though that was hard to imagine at the moment.

"What's your name?"

"Arif. In Arabic, this means knowledgeable. In Aleppo I was a physicist. Here I clean rooms in a hospital. But I am alive. That's enough."

"How would you like to earn a hundred dollars, Arif?"

"A hundred dollars? These days, that's barely enough to buy a hamburger!"

"I'll make it two hundred dollars. You'll be able to get a side of fries."

"I don't think so, mister. I think you wish me to do something that isn't good."

"All right, three hundred dollars. You'll be able to add a soft drink to your order."

Arif was silent as he considered the proposal. "Okay," he said after a moment. "Tell me what you want."

**

Arif pushed Jack's wheelchair down a long hospital corridor toward the wing where Charles McFadden was a patient. Mercy Hospital was small but it was spread out.

Every now and then, Arif made a comment as he pushed the chair.

"You should have seen the hospital in Aleppo! Blood on the floor, dying people everywhere. The noise, the screams!"

Jack found these descriptions unbearable. He didn't feel well. The terrible assault of guilt, sorrow, and anger over Shayna's death made him feel like a balloon about to explode. It was beyond his endurance, on top of this, to listen to stories of blood and screams in Syrian hospitals. It made him want to scream himself.

"Arif, please. If you don't mind, I'm preparing myself for a conversation. Perhaps we can go easy on the war stories."

"Okay, you need to think. I get it. But I have to tell you, thinking is dangerous. In Aleppo one of my friends was a doctor who thought so much he ended up in prison . . ."

Jack tuned out stories of horror and death as he rode through a hallway that seemed to go on forever. Patients were often transported from one department to another and Jack hoped they wouldn't be stopped. So far Arif was handling the situation very well. He even managed to bluff their way down an elevator to the main floor.

"Okay, Mr. Wilder, here's the reception area," said Arif. "Would you like to talk to the nurse in the kiosk?"

"I would."

"One moment . . ."

When it was Jack's turn, he asked the nurse which room Charles McFadden was in.

"Are you a relative?" she asked.

"I work for Mr. McFadden." This was true, in the broader sense, since McFadden was a client. But from here, Jack got creative. "I need to speak to him about his insurance. It's lapsed, I'm afraid, and he's going to need it if he's going to pay his hospital bill."

This got her attention. "Let's see," she said as she scanned her computer screen. "Oh, he checked out two hours ago! He's gone."

This was a disappointment. Arif pulled him back from the kiosk into the waiting area.

"Let me sit here for a moment," Jack told Arif. "I need to think."

As he was thinking, a voice spoke from close by.

" 'Scuse me, but I couldn't help overhear you asking for Charlie. He's gone, brother. Gone, gone."

"And who are you?"

"Can't you see me? No, I guess not. I'm in the wheelchair right next to you, getting some air. Charlie was my roommate."

Jack was interested. "Was he feeling well enough to go home?"

167

"Oh, sure, he was. He'd inhaled some smoke, that's all. I think he was faking it, really. Hiding out from the world. The guy was sort of over-dramatic, if you know what I mean."

"I do," said Jack. "He's a writer. Writers are often over-dramatic. Did he say anything about his experience?"

"How he got out of that burning house?"

"No, I'm more interested in what happened before. Did he see who set the fire."

The roommate lowered his voice and moved closer. "He said people were asking him that. The State Police, some detective who came by—everyone wanted to know if he saw anybody."

"Yes, and?" Jack encouraged when there was a pause.

"He said sure, he saw who it was. But he wasn't going to give it away, not for free. He told me this was his ticket back to New York."

"No kidding? He wanted to travel?"

"No, he meant it figuratively. He was going to write the true story of his granddaughter's death and it was going to bring him back into big time New York publishing. No more small presses. Until then, he was going to keep what he knew to himself."

"He didn't tell the cops what he saw?"

"Nope. He didn't tell anybody. Not even me. That was another thing he said about writing. A writer, he said, should never discuss his story in advance. If you *tell* it, you won't be able to *write* it."

"So, let me get this straight. He knows who this guy is, very likely a killer, and he's not going to say because he's keeping it for his book?"

"That's the gist of it," said the man in the wheelchair next to him. "Says it's going to make him a million dollar advance!"

Jack's first response was to be outraged. But then, to his own surprise, he leaned back and gave a mighty laugh.

***

Emma picked up Jack at the hospital an hour later, after receiving a call saying that he had been wandering the halls. The hospital official spoke in a curt, patronizing tone, as though it was Emma's fault for having a husband like that.

She drove Jack home in silence, one that she broke from time to time with sharp bursts of irritation.

"I don't know what to do with you, Jack, I truly don't! Thank God Georgie can come over and stay with you for a few hours this afternoon or I would have to cancel an appointment with the Superintendent of Schools. This means a lot to me, Jack—I'm not sure you understand that."

"I do, Emma. Honestly, I do."

"You don't act like it."

"You say Georgie's coming over?"

Emma sighed as she turned at the intersection to their street.

"Georgie had a big night last night apparently. She's glad to get out of the office for a while and just sit and read a book. She says she's nursing a hangover, Jack—so let her read in peace. I think she went out on a date."

"A date!" He chortled. "I bet Howie's spitting blood!"

"Jack!"

"He's the classic possessive father!" Jack said merrily. "He doesn't want some outsider stealing his darling!"

"Jack, it's not like that," Emma said. "Personally, I think he's making a very good father. Especially when you consider that fatherhood came to him rather unexpectedly. So I want you to behave yourself today. Claire is going to spend a few hours with you tomorrow, we're taking shifts so you won't be alone. But you need to do your part!"

Jack sat in the kitchen feeling like a bad boy who was out of favor with the world. He cheered up slightly when Georgie arrived, full of fresh air and energy from riding her bike. Her youth was contagious to an old man.

"If I get too comfortable, I might fall asleep," Georgie warned. "So be sure to give a shout if you need anything."

Jack smiled. Young people could sleep anywhere, any time, in an instant. He envied that more than any other part of lost youth.

"You didn't get much sleep last night?" he asked.

"No, I just couldn't. Not a wink. I was tossing and turning—going through my life."

"Well, Georgie, insomnia may not be good for your body—but every now and then it's good for your soul."

"Ha!" Georgie was happy to laugh it off, but she had felt like a fool lying awake on the office futon thinking about her dinner with Jean-Claude. She wasn't entirely pleased with herself. She re-lived the sense of his lips on her hand again and again, until that one kiss on the back of her hand swelled into an erotic wave of almost embarrassing horniness. She hadn't meant for that to happen.

Before she left, Emma told Georgie to feel free to use her library, take any book she liked—no need to return it, she was paring down.

The library was in a front room of the house facing the street, originally a parlor, an old-fashioned room with bay windows that looked out onto Emma's front rose garden. The room had cheerful Victorian wallpaper, a pattern of small wildflowers, and thousands of books arranged neatly on shelves that were high enough to need a stepladder. Emma had the books in categories—philosophy, world history, earth sciences, social sciences, literature, everything from Lao Tzu to Artificial Intelligence.

Georgie settled with a volume of Chekhov stories in the upholstered platform rocker in the center of the room, Emma's reading chair. It was an ugly old chair but fabulously comfortable. Georgie was just getting settled into 19th century Russia, her eyelids heavy, when a dark van of indeterminate make pulled into the driveway. There were three men inside.

Coming more fully awake, she watched through the window as the two men in front got out of the car and stood on guard flanking the opposite sides of the vehicle. To Georgie, they looked like military types. Beefy bodies, short hair. From the back of the van, a lone man, their passenger, stepped out onto the driveway.

He was fairly young, tall and thin and gangly. He wasn't in any way impressive so it was hard to imagine why he deserved such an escort. He wore jeans and a red T-shirt that had Bob Marley's face on it.

Was he a rock star? He looked somehow familiar, but it wasn't until he was approaching the house that her heart took a leap.

"Buzzy!" she cried, putting down her book and rushing from the library to the hall. She flung open the front door. "I can't believe it! Look at you!"

She gave him a big hug as they stood in the doorway.

Long ago, Buzzy Hurston had been Howie's Little Brother in the San Geronimo Big Brother program. Georgie had known him for years from her previous trips to New Mexico. There had been a time when Buzzy had almost been a boyfriend, but probably it was better that had never happened.

The Big Brother program for Buzzy had been mandatory, court ordered after he had been caught selling pot to his 5th grade classmates. He had always been a problem. Howie gave Buzzy his first used Mac laptop when he was ten, and by the time Buzzy took that laptop apart and had it together again, he was set on a path that took him from a half-starved hippie commune in the desert to a highly secretive cyber department within the CIA. Georgie didn't actually know what Buzzy did there. Nor did she dare ask.

"Come in, Buzzy! How long are you in town?"

"Only a few days," he answered in a subdued voice. "My mother died. I'm here for her funeral."

"Buzzy, I'm so sorry!"

He took both her hands in a gesture of despair.

"I don't have much time, Georgie. I need to see Jack."

***

"I'm sorry about your mother," Jack said as they sat in his office. Jack was in his wheelchair behind his desk, Buzzy in an old-fashioned wooden rocker that wasn't far away. Rockers abounded in the Wilder house.

Buzzy's mother, in Jack's opinion, had been a casualty of 60s idealism and psychedelic drugs. The back-to-the-earth movement brought many communes to the Southwest, but few of them lasted long. There were still ruins of abandoned school buses and geodesic domes and strange pyramids in the desert miles from any highway.

"I'm sorry about my mother, too," said Buzzy. "I wish I could have done more for her. She'd been sick for a while, but it was a stroke that got her. She was only fifty-seven. It was the booze, that's what got her in the end. She should have stayed with peyote."

A stroke! Jack didn't like to hear about people dying from strokes. It sent a chill up his spine. It was a good thing he had cut down to two glasses of red wine per night.

"So, Buzzy, how long are you going to be in town?"

"Three days. There's going to be a small ceremony tomorrow out on the land. A kind of Celtic/Viking death ritual, or whatever they've dreamt up. I need to stay for it and then I'm planning one more day to clean up all the Tibetan bells and junk in her bus. I might even take a day longer. Honestly, Jack, it feels good to be back in New Mexico. Sometimes I'm not sure just how much more I can take of Langley."

Jack nodded. "I can understand that, Buzzy. Knowing you're an anarchist, it must bother your principals to work for the CIA—"

"Jack, don't even joke about stuff like that," Buzzy said lowering his voice. "I mean it. It's easy to get into trouble with these people."

"Who are these people?"

"Leave it alone, Jack. Now look, I have a favor to ask you. I'd like to use Nancy for a few minutes."

"Nancy?" Jack repeated with some apprehension. Buzzy had built Nancy, she was his invention. This request shouldn't have made him uneasy, but it did.

"I'll take a look at your software at the same time. There's newer stuff out these days. I'll make sure you have it. You wouldn't want to be obsolete, Jack."

"It's a little late for that. But let's talk about this," said Jack. "I'm assuming you want Nancy for some secret purpose that your two body-guards outside won't know about—"

"Jack—"

"No, don't Jack me. I don't like this but I'm willing to make a deal. I could use some help finding someone."

Buzzy gave Jack a hard look. He sighed with resignation. "Okay, who?"

"Her name is Sophia McFadden. She's the first wife of the author, Charles McFadden. She tried to set fire to their house while McFadden and their daughter Mikaela were inside sleeping. This is 1992 we're talking about, a while ago. Sophia was put in a mental institution in Las Cruces until the hospital closed down in 2017. Sophia was released and she disappeared. I can't find out what happened to her, whether she died or moved somewhere else. I need to find out."

"And you think I can do this for you?"

"I'm hoping your computer skills allow you to search far and wide," said Jack with a strong touch of irony. He knew that Buzzy didn't always walk a legal line.

"All right, okay," said Buzzy. "Give me a few minutes with Nancy and then I'll look for your Sophia."

"Thank you. However, I need to ask you—are you planning to do something illegal with Nancy?"

"Absolutely not," said Buzzy. There was a new tone in Buzzy's voice that had come with money and position. It had changed him. He was more sure of himself. "I'm simply going to enjoy my right of free speech under the Constitution!"

"Oh, for chrissake!" Jack shook his head wearily. "All right, Buzzy. Go for it."

***

Jack waited tensely as Buzzy typed at a furious speed on Nancy's keyboard—a keyboard Jack never used. He didn't like anybody messing with Nancy besides himself, not even Buzzy, who had built her.

"How is it going?" he asked when it seemed to be taking forever.

"Mmm . . . fine," he answered distractedly.

In fact, it took Buzzy less than five minutes to find Sophia McFadden.

"Okay, Jack, I got her. But you really didn't need my help with this. She was easy."

"Buzzy, where is she?"

"She lives here in San Geronimo. She's been here since 2018. She runs The Elf and Toad."

Jack wasn't surprised often, but this was unexpected. "She's here? That's the children's shop, isn't it?"

"Yeah, sure. They sell kiddie books and cute hand-made toys. She goes by the name Sophia Sunshine. Probably why you didn't spot her."

Jack knew The Elf and Toad. It was a small store, crowded with gifts and knick-knacks. Emma sometimes bought toys there for the children of her friends.

How Jack and Howie had missed this was incredible. Sophia McFadden was only a few blocks away.

Buzzy spent a few more minutes with Nancy, doing whatever it was he wanted done.

"Okay, thanks, I'm done," he said after a short time. "I'm afraid I have to split, Jack, or they'll start wondering about me."

"Your keepers?"

"That's right, Jack. My keepers. Go ahead and laugh."

Jack didn't laugh. He had never found the Central Intelligence Agency even slightly funny.

When Buzzy was gone, Jack felt he needed to have a word with Nancy.

"All right, Nancy—tell me what Buzzy did just now."

"He did what you asked him. He found out where Sophia McFadden was."

"I mean after that. What did he do after that?"

"I'm not allowed to tell you that, Jack."

"Sure, you are. I'm your boss, aren't I?"

"Yes, you are. But I've been engineered with certain restraints."

"Screw the restraints, Nancy. I want to know."

"Jack, I don't know if I can. This is uncharted territory for me, dealing with contrary commands. I might bust a circuit."

"Give it a try, Nancy. I'm not kidding."

"Okay . . ." Nancy stuttered for a moment. "He . . . Buzzy . . . all right, here it is. He sent an email to *The New York Times*. It had a long attachment."

Jack sat back in his wheelchair with a groan.

"Oh, fuck!"

Chapter Twenty

In the morning, Howie felt awful. His left shoulder was bruised from being thrown against the side of his car. He had more bruises on his hands and arms. He felt like a herd of cattle had stampeded over him.

The pain had settled and deepened since last night when the attack happened. He had been able to pick himself up from the concrete floor of the underground parking garage, slump into his car, and make the three-hour drive north to San Geronimo. It took him forty minutes longer than usual.

He arrived home at four in the morning, and when he awoke he was so sore he could barely move. Claire took one look at him and refused to let him leave the house. She threatened to take away the ladder to the sleeping loft so that he wouldn't be able to climb down if he didn't promise to take a day off from work and stay home.

"Howie, you're a mess. You need time off," she told him. "And besides, would it be so terrible for the two of us to spend the day together?"

He had to admit, a day off was welcome. It was good to stay home, rest his aching body, and have time to be with Claire and think.

In the afternoon, after a nap with Claire, Howie spent several hours in his computer nook on his laptop and on his phone. He spoke with Georgie several times, and with Jack. Georgie was more or less living in the downtown office for the time being, and Howie told her that was fine, though he would miss their evenings together on the land.

"I'll be back with you soon, Da," she promised. "I just need time to . . . I don't know, to think, I guess."

"Thinking is good," he assured her.

"Here's something odd," she said, directing the conversation away from herself. "Zia was modeling for Edward Rothenstein. Without her clothes on. I think it's possible they were having an affair—a 60 year-old man and a 17 year-old girl! I mean, honestly! What a lech! There's a painting he did of her, *America Girl* he calls it. It's actually very good. The lech has talent. But it's definitely Zia."

"Could Rothenstein have painted it from his imagination? Maybe she didn't actually model for him."

"Aye, I suppose that's possible. But then she ends up dead. I've been thinking, what if she got in over her head, having an affair with someone like Rothenstein—a famous, older man. What if it *was* suicide? What if the affair got too emotional for her?"

"Sure, that's a possibility. Can you send a photo of this painting? I'd be curious to see it."

"I can't, Da. I don't have it. It's on Jean-Claude's phone. He probably shouldn't have it either, but he showed it to me."

"This is the art expert . . ."

"Jean-Claude, Da. Yes, he's putting on a Rothenstein exhibit at the Bilbao Guggenheim."

She didn't encourage further questions about Jean-Claude, and Howie was wise enough to leave the subject alone.

Georgie sent him links to the Internet articles and YouTube videos that she had found for Joe Ochoa, the 10 o'clock weatherman. Howie spent much of the afternoon examining them. There were dozens of online articles about Joe, many of them concerning his annual Christmas drive, Kristmas For Kids, in which he solicited toys and warm clothing for disadvantaged children.

In the late summer, he ran a contest that had become an Albuquerque tradition: a prize for the best front yard rose garden in the city, a weekend stay at the Kiva Casino Hotel, with a $200 coupon for gambling. The ten runners-up in the contest got a year's supply of Big Glo potting soil. The contest was promoted nightly, with TV coverage and interviews.

Everything about Joe was perfectly full of cheer and neighborliness. He and his wife were active members of the High Desert Temple of Christ. There were three children who were polite and well-spoken and were involved with their parents in raising money for Christian missionaries.

Howie wasn't fooled. There was no sign of the secret Joe beneath the friendly weatherman, and it was hard to believe this outstanding citizen could be the Dweeb. But Howie had heard Mikaela admit that Joe was in fact her lover.

Late in the afternoon Buzzy phoned to let him know about the funeral tomorrow for his mother. He was hoping Howie would come. He told Buzzy, yes, of course.

He had known Buzzy's mother, though not well. Her name was Sharon, though she had changed it to Cheyenne by the time she migrated to New Mexico from Santa Barbara, where she had been a student at the University of California before joining the bleakest, poorest, most idealistic commune in the Southwest. Buzzy had grown up almost feral in the desert.

"I paid a visit to Jack," Buzzy told him. "I thought you should know he wanted my help with an investigation. Isn't Jack supposed to be recovering from a stroke?"

"He is!" Howie said with irritation. "So what did he want you to do?"

"I'll tell you tomorrow when I see you," Buzzy said. "Look, Howie, I need to go. *Mañana*, bro."

Howie held the phone thoughtfully after the call was finished.

He could use Buzzy's help himself. There were times when it was good to know someone who knew the wormholes of the Internet.

Jack himself phoned soon after Buzzy.

"I thought you'd like to know a thing or two about *your* client," Jack said in a voice that could have cut through a steel pipe.

"He's not *my* client, Jack. He's the agency's client. Charles McFadden. What about him?"

"Let's start with his first wife, Sophia. The mad one who set the house on fire and was sent away to Las Cruces. She's been living here in San Geronimo since 2018. Did you know that? She runs The Elf and Toad Bookstore."

"Seriously?"

"Yes, seriously, and she needs to be checked out. But here's the kicker. I spoke with McFadden's roommate at Mercy Hospital. And do you know what he told me?"

"Okay, Jack, what?"

"He said McFadden told him he saw the person who set the fire but he's keeping it to himself. He doesn't want to give it away because he's saving it for the book he's going to write."

Howie's mouth fell open. Literally. "A book? You're kidding? He's writing a book about all this?"

"I'm sure you'll be his star character," Jack said cattily.

"I doubt it," Howie replied. "The only star character in Charlie's writing is himself!"

"I guess he figures it's a good story, money in the bank. A true life crime drama. But he's lied to the cops and you might want to pay him a visit and set him straight."

"I will!" said Howie angrily. "First thing tomorrow. I can't believe that idiot! I swear, if he saw the killer, I'll choke it out of him!"

***

Howie began Thursday with a 9 a.m. visit to his client, Charles McFadden. He was aware the genius might be asleep at this hour, but he didn't care.

McFadden's rambling shack looked mostly untouched by the fire. In Jack's telling, it had been a roaring inferno of heat and flame, raging everywhere. But the truth—as far as Howie could tell—was more modest. A far side of the building was blackened and partially destroyed. There was also some blackening on the trunk of a giant Siberian elm that hovered over the roof. But the main structure where the author lived was intact.

Howie knocked and when there was no answer he tried the door. It was unlocked. He found McFadden asleep on a mattress on the living room floor, covered by an Afghan rug that looked like it had been expensive long ago. He was surrounded by a clutter of papers and books and objects that included a disembodied car engine.

"Good morning!" Howie said loudly.

McFadden groaned. "Christ, what time is it?"

"Almost 9 o'clock. We need to talk, Charlie."

McFadden sat up bare-chested in bed. His chest was sunken and gray, an old man's chest. If he was naked, Howie hoped he stayed under the rug. He really didn't want to see Charlie in the natural.

"Look, I didn't pay you to wake me up at some ungodly hour!" Charlie complained. "Now, go away and come back this afternoon."

Howie got down on his haunches so that they would be on the same level. "Actually, Charlie, you haven't paid me a thing. You were supposed to send a check. Remember?"

"What? You're worried about a check? Of course, I'm going to send you a check, Moon Deer! But give a guy a few days, for chrissake!" He pointed about helplessly at the messy state of his living situation. "First, I gotta *find* the checkbook, okay? That's a big project. You're not going to start acting like some Nazi, are you?"

"All right, all right," Howie said to calm him. "We'll talk about money later. I want to know if it's true that you're writing a book about Zia's death and this investigation?"

"Well, I'm thinking about it, why not? It's a good idea—narrative non-fiction, something that reads like a good novel. Truman Capote, *In Cold Blood*, life, death, drama! I've been looking for a story like this for decades! Something I can use to really explore what it's like to be . . . me!"

Howie couldn't speak for a minute. He decided to move on.

"Okay, here's where you need to start thinking clearly because otherwise you're off to jail. Did you tell your roommate at the hospital that you saw the person who set the fire but you were holding it back because you wanted to put this in your book?"

"Hey, Moon Deer—when you got something juicy like this, you don't want to go public too soon. It's called building suspense."

"Charlie, it called obstruction of justice. Now, tell me what you saw."

"Okay, okay. The problem is, I didn't actually see anything. Only a kind of shadow. . . a dark deep shadow . . . no, a dark forbidding shadow . . ."

"Charlie, for chrissake, did you see the person who set the fire, or did you not?"

"No, I guess I was bragging a little to that guy in the hospital. Kind of building up the project."

"Was it a man or a woman?"

"I don't know. I'd tell you if I did, Moon Deer. I'm trying to be straight with you."

"Sure," said Howie.

"To be honest, I passed out drunk as a skunk earlier in the evening and I didn't see a thing until I woke up in the hospital."

"This is true?"

"I swear! Of course, in the book I'll need, you know, to exaggerate a little."

"Lie, in other words. But you must have some idea of who set that fire. Somebody who bears you a grudge. Maybe someone who doesn't want you to tell something you know," Howie added.

"I know many things," McFadden said with an authorly smile.

"What about your first wife, Sophia? Would she do a thing like that?"

"Sophia? Oh no. No, no, honestly. Not Sophia. We made peace in the end."

"Do you know she's been living here in San Geronimo for several years? She runs The Elf and Toad Bookstore."

Charlie nodded. "Sure, I know. I've seen her several times. Like I said, there's no animosity between us. Look, let me tell you what that fire was all about. It's about the books I write. Words are dangerous, great art is revolutionary. Someone's trying to stop me because my books are a threat to the system!"

Howie was tempted to remind McFadden that nobody read his books anymore, so it didn't really matter if he was a threat to the system. But he kept these thoughts to himself. If Charlie still thought of himself as someone who shaped world opinion, Howie didn't want to be the one to break his bubble.

***

The ceremony for Buzzy's mother began at three. It was a sad affair. The wind picked up and whistled among the canyon rocks in a minor key. Howie stood next to Buzzy on a hilltop overlooking the once-bustling Lodestar Commune as the ashes of his mother, Cheyenne, were scattered to the New Mexico sky.

The commune had been in decline for decades and now there were only half a dozen residents, most of them old and ailing. They had arrived full of youth and idealism, but utopia was easier to imagine than achieve. First, you had to be willing to wash dishes when it was your turn, and forgo lusting for other people's partners.

Howie felt a tug of depression as he watched a squat, red-haired women in a patchwork dress recite a Mary Oliver poem about wild geese. Another woman recited a poem she had written herself about the radiance of love. A man who didn't seem entirely sober rambled incoherently about the evils of Capitalism and the need to tear everything down so that life could begin anew.

After the remains of Buzzy's mother were released into the sky, the group walked down the hillside in a small procession to the commune below where the festivities were set to begin—dance, drink, song, and whatever pagan madness a gathering of aging hippies could manage. For Howie, he felt like he had wandered into a post-apocalyptic time warp.

Halfway down the hill, Buzzy left the trail and walked toward a rock shelf where he sat down with a dispirited grunt. Howie sat beside him. There was a wide view from here across the desert to the mountains twenty miles away. They were etched clearly against the blue desert sky with patches of snow on the highest peaks.

"This is where I used to come to get away," Buzzy told him. "I lost my virginity here when I was eleven."

"*Eleven?* Honestly?"

"We were advanced thinkers at Lodestar. You know, Howie—you saved me from this place. When you became my Big Brother, you showed me a way out."

"You would have got out without me, Buzzy."

"I'm not sure. When you gave me that old laptop, you opened a gate."

"You opened your own gate. You should be proud of yourself, Buzzy. You've made a success of yourself."

"Have I?"

Howie wasn't sure what to say. Buzzy had persuaded his two CIA minders to remain in their vehicle while he attended his mother's funeral, but they were there waiting to reclaim him.

"You know, I could start World War Three if I wanted," Buzzy said unexpectedly. "I shouldn't tell you this, but I'm the head of a secret Russia department. We have their entire energy grid in our sights. I could shut it down with a few strokes of the keyboard and Russia would come to a halt. The problem is they would know we had done it and they would retaliate. That's what the next war will be. Someone like me in a darkened room on one side of the ocean, and another person like me in a darkened room on the other side."

"There will still be blood and gore on the battlefield," Howie told him. "Real people will lose their lives. Look, Buzzy, "I sense you're under a lot of pressure. Maybe you should take some time off."

Buzzy laughed at Howie's naiveté. "Time off? They don't let me out of their sight!"

"Then quit. With your credentials, you could get a great job in the private sector."

"I don't know, Howie. It's a dark world out there. I've seen some really bad stuff in the last four years. Sometimes I think maybe it would be best just to put this planet out of its misery. Other times I think it's

time to fight back. I could make those assholes at Langley sorry they
ever met me . . ."

Howie was becoming alarmed. He had never seen Buzzy like this.

"Look, Buzzy, you got yourself kicked out of Stanford because you
were a bad boy. You went too far, you got yourself into trouble, and
you don't want to run that route again. That's a bad direction. I hope
you understand that."

"I do, Howie. Honestly."

"If you need a vacation, I'm sure you can get it. Just don't do anything crazy. Please."

Buzzy pulled out a joint and pointedly changed the subject.

"Do you mind if I smoke this while we talk? It's been a stressful
day."

Howie laughed. "I never managed to stop you in the past, did I?"

Buzzy lit up and the pungent scent of marijuana drifted into the late
afternoon.

"Not me, thanks," Howie said when the joint was offered his way.

"You want something else though, don't you?" Buzzy took a long
puff. "Just like Jack did."

"Look, Buzzy, when you put it that way, it doesn't sound good. So
forget about it. You have enough on your hands."

"No, go ahead and ask. I'm glad to help my friends while I can."

Howie felt something was off with Buzzy, but wasn't certain how
to ask. "What does that mean? While you can?"

"It doesn't matter. How can I help you, Howie?"

"I'm interested in a guy by the name of Joe Ochoa. He's the chief
weatherman for KABB. He's very popular in New Mexico, everybody
loves him."

"I know who Joe Ochoa is, Howie."

"Yes, but what you don't know is that secretly he's a sleaze. He's married, but on the sly he's been having it off with Mikaela McFadden. There's evidence that he molested her teenage daughter, Zia, when she was fifteen. That's the case I'm working right now. Zia either jumped or was pushed off a cliff at Eagle Falls and I'm trying to find out how it happened. Unfortunately, there have been a string of incidents. A total bystander was killed, Jack's caretaker. Zia's father was killed as well, Keir Aaronson, and somebody tried to set fire to her grandfather's house while he was inside sleeping. The grandfather is Charles McFadden, the author. He's my client."

"Jack was telling me a little about this. Sounds like a family with more problems even than my family."

"The premise I'm working on is that Joe is trying to cover up what he did with Zia. It would be the end of his career if it got out that he likes to jerk-off over teenage girls while they're sleeping. It wouldn't do much for his image. The grandmothers of Albuquerque wouldn't adore him anymore."

"So, Joe Ochoa?" Buzzy looked skeptical. "I've seen the guy on TV. You really think he's a killer?"

Howie took his phone from his back pocket. He brought up the photograph that Georgie had taken during the office break-in.

"This is a picture Georgie took of someone who tried to break into the office last week. He's wearing a mask, but the way it clings to his face, you can almost make him out. I'm hoping your people have some software that can imagine what this face would look like without a mask. I believe this is Joe."

"Sure, we can do that," said Buzzy. "Send me the picture."

"I call him the Scream," said Howie, as he sent the photo to Buzzy's phone.

"Is that a neo-punk band?"

"It's a painting by Edvard Munch," Howie said patiently. Computer nerds like Buzzy rarely knew much about art.

"You really want to nail this guy?"

"I do. Among other things he attacked me in an underground garage in Albuquerque on Tuesday night. I'm still banged up. I'm hoping to examine Joe's life as closely as possible and see if I can come up with some evidence of what he does when he thinks no one is looking."

"Would you like to follow him wherever he goes?"

"You bet I would!"

"Well, okay. Do you have pen and paper?"

The notebook and pen were in the pocket in the front of his jeans. He wiggled them out and handed them to Buzzy.

"Okay," he said as he wrote. "Type this address into your browser . . . here's the password."

Both the URL and the password were long numbers mixed with letters that looked more like a physics problem than an Internet address.

"Do that and a screen will come up, a blank page with a blank square. Type two words 'Casanova Cloud' into the square. A new page will come up, also with a blank square. Write 'Hot Sauce.' Capital letters at the start of each word."

"Casanova Cloud," Howie repeated dubiously. "Hot Sauce?"

"Hey, you gotta be creative wherever you can. If you've put in the correct passwords, you now should be in. The next box you see you simply put in the name of the person you want under surveillance. Put in the name Joe Ochoa. There will be a place where you can add a photo of Joe. Next you will be asked questions about the subject—where he lives, his profession, his employer, the more you can fill in the better the search will be. If you can't answer one of the questions, just leave it blank. Press OK and you're off."

"Off where?" Howie asked. "What's going to happen?"

"What's going to happen, Howie, is that you are going to be able to watch Joe Ochoa's life in real time as it happens. If he's at home sleeping, you'll know. If he's sneaking off to see his girlfriend, you'll know that too. Once the software has him spotted every security camera in America will follow him. You'll be able to watch him live on your screen. There's an additional link if he goes international."

"There are enough cameras out there to make this possible?"

"Howie, there are cameras everywhere. Maybe not here in the desert, but in San Geronimo, for sure. There are cameras attached to traffic lights. Security cameras on buildings. In stores, in elevators, in lobbies, in supermarkets. Most people aren't aware of it, but unless you live miles from anything, you're most likely on somebody's screen."

"So what happens when Joe is sleeping? You don't have cameras in his bedroom, do you?"

Buzzy shrugged. "Probably not. But you never know. Sure, there will be breaks in the feed where he's lost from view. My advice is don't watch live unless something important is happening. You'll be able to record the feed and jump forward through the parts where nothing happens. Meanwhile, let me work with Georgie's photograph. I'll let you know what I find."

"Thanks, Buzzy. This is tremendous! I'll owe you."

Buzzy stubbed out the joint against a rock and stood up. "Look, I need to speak to some people here. They were friends of my mom, they saw me grow up, they expect me to say hello."

"I understand," said Howie, rising to his feet as well. "Now, please, get some rest, bug them in Virginia until they give you a vacation—and whatever you do, don't start World War Three!"

Chapter Twenty-One

On Friday, Jack had a new caregiver, a pleasant elderly woman by the name of Joanne Ferris who was a volunteer at the San Geronimo Public Library.

Joanne and her husband, Dwight, were retirees, recent arrivals to New Mexico from Cincinnati where Dwight had been an insurance executive and Joanne a high school science teacher. Arriving in San Geronimo, they were fresh prey for the many non-profits looking for volunteers. Elderly newcomers arriving with civic idealism and a bit of money were always good for free labor for a year or two.

Jack liked Joanne, though she wasn't—by his standards—particularly interesting. She was a very decent woman, however, eager to help Emma in any way she could.

Emma had become a minor celebrity, a librarian who was fighting against the banning of books. It was a hot topic and Emma had received a lot of press. Many people in San Geronimo supported Emma, though she had also received several death threats (a fact she kept from Jack). Joanne was happy to join the struggle by being Jack's caretaker—not forever, she hoped—if this gave Emma more freedom to go off to battle the culture war.

"Joanne has gone out of her way to be helpful, so I want you to be nice to her," Emma warned Jack. "If you misbehave, I swear you'll be heading straight to the sleaziest, rat-infested nursing home I can find! I'll let *them* take care of you!"

"I'll be good," Jack promised. He meant it, too. Like Emma, he wanted to safeguard school children's right to read American classics like *Huckleberry Finn* and *To Kill a Mockingbird*. Of course, there was racism in America! He had seen it himself again and again as a cop, on the streets, and in high mucky-muck offices. He was glad his wife was speaking up—and in a sneaky way, he believed this let him off the hook, family speaking, from getting more civically involved himself.

Meanwhile, he had a problem. While he very much wanted to keep his promise to Emma, he also very much wanted to question Sophia McFadden. Unfortunately, he had no way to get to The Elf and Toad Bookshop, the business she owned. The sort of interview he had in mind couldn't be done over the phone.

The answer was obvious once it popped into his mind a few minutes later. The senior center in San Geronimo had a wheelchair friendly van to drive housebound elders to doctors appointments and grocery stores. Jack retired to his office and was able to make an appointment for the van to pick him up at 12:15. At shortly before noon, he wheeled his way into the living room where Joanne had set up camp and told her he was going to take a nap. Since he hadn't slept much last night, she shouldn't worry if his nap was a long one.

Jack returned to his room where there was a seldom used door from his bedroom outside to the side of the house where the garbage bins were kept. From here he could escape to the front yard without being seen from the living room. With luck, Joanne would never know he was gone.

At 12:15, Jack was in his chair on the sidewalk in front of his house waiting to be picked up. The driver was an elderly Spanish man who at first balked at driving Jack to a bookstore rather than a doctor's appointment or the supermarket, but when Jack explained that he needed to buy a gift for his favorite grandson in California, he soon gave in.

The driver's name was Manny and it turned out that he also had grandchildren in California. Jack and Manny told stories about their grandchildren—Manny's real granddaughter, Jack's make-believe grandson—all the way to The Elf and Toad.

***

By the time the van arrived at the bookshop, Jack and Manny were great friends, grandfathers-in-arm.

Jack knew all about Manny's twenty-two year old granddaughter in Van Nuys, Consuela—and Jack had told a tale or two about his grandson, Thomas. Jack rode in the back of the van where he and his wheelchair were secured in place. He enjoyed making up stories about Thomas, but it was also a little sad since Tom didn't exist. When they reached the store, Manny came around from the front seat to open up the rear. He lowered Jack in his wheelchair on a hydraulic lift to the pavement.

"I'm hoping to find a present for Tom's new baby—this is number two for him with his partner."

"So you're actually a *great*-grandfather!" said Manny. "Now, that's something!"

"Makes me feel old," said Jack comfortably. "Hey, why don't you come in with me, maybe you'll find something for Consuela."

"Well, she's twenty-two, Jack. A girl that age, it's hard to know what she wants."

"Yeah, but why don't you come with me anyway," said Jack. "I'd really appreciate help picking something out. And you can tell me about this place, describe it to me. I can't see, you know."

Jack liked Manny. Authentically. But this didn't stop him from using the driver for his own ends.

Manny was good at describing. The Elf and Toad was on a side street, not in the main downtown district, occupying an old house that was made completely of smooth river stone. Two flags flew from the front porch, a yellow flag that had an elf on it, and an orange flag with a toad.

192

Manny pushed Jack through the front door into a darkened room with narrow windows and many shelves full of books and handmade toys that were often ingenious.

In another section, set on tables, there were packs of Tarot cards, Ouija boards, crystal balls, and astrological charts of the heavens. The old woman behind the counter had long white hair that fell nearly to her waist. She wore a voluminous dark red dress. Manny whispered that he thought she looked a little witchy. "It's kind of spooky in here," he whispered nervously.

There was a single customer, a young woman in shorts and a T-shirt who bought a silver chain necklace with a small crystal dangling on the end. The witchy woman behind the counter said it would be certain to protect her from just about anything. When the customer was gone, Manny wheeled Jack to the counter.

"Well, look who's here," said the old woman. "It's Jack Wilder! I was wondering when you would show up."

"You've been expecting me?" asked Jack, surprised.

"I see the future, I see the past, few things get by me, Jack. I tell you what, let me put the closed sign on the door and we'll go into the back and have ourselves a chat . . . not you," she said to Manny when he attempted to follow. "You wait out here."

***

"You know, you were a hard person to find, Sophia Sunshine. I have to admit it," said Jack. "And here you were the whole time, in San Geronimo. Just the person I was looking for!"

"Seekers often lose their way," said Sophia.

"How did you know who I am?" Jack asked.

193

"Oh, I know lots. I know that you're looking into the death of my granddaughter, Zia."

"Do you know how she died?"

"I know only what the wind tells me."

"Really? And what does the wind tell you?"

"It says . . . *whooosh, whooosh, whooosh!*" said the old woman dramatically, summoning up a storm.

Sophia McFadden, *née* Berger, came from an upper-middle class East Coast family and her voice still had traces of what Jack regarded as privilege. The back room in which they sat—he wasn't sure if it was a store room or an office—felt close and velvety.

"Do you consider yourself a seeker, Sophia?"

"Oh, yes! Hide and seek! What fun! Not all those who wander are lost, Jack. Pilgrims occasionally find their way."

Jack smiled warily. He knew the Tolkien quote. But he wasn't sure Sophia Sunshine was as mad as she pretended.

"You were in a mental institution in Las Cruces until 2017?" he asked. "Is that right?"

"Yep. Good old Las Cruces Hospital for the Insane. That was the original name for the place until 1962 when they renamed it the Sun and Sage Institute. This was supposed to represent a new sensitivity toward people with disabilities. I played a lot of card games there."

"You were hospitalized because you set fire to your house with your daughter and husband inside."

"Yes, that's what they said."

"What do you mean, what they said? Are you saying it's not true?"

"True?" she echoed. "True blue? A true screw? What does truth have to do with anything?"

Jack smiled to show he was a good sort. "I realize truth has become a scarce commodity today, something people argue about on TV. But I look for it anyway."

"You see, you *are* a seeker!"

"Sophia, when the hospital closed they let you go. That must have been nice for you. But there doesn't seem to be any word of you after that."

"You looked me up? How flattering!"

"You returned to San Geronimo? Why's that?"

"I'm a homing pigeon, I suppose."

"You returned because Charlie was here?"

"Charlie? Well, it's always an event to see him. I used to hear music playing every time I looked at him, now it's something of a dirge. But I had a life in San Geronimo, too, besides being the author's wife." She lowered her voice. "Do you know what it's like being the author's wife? It sucks, I tell you. But I had fun anyway. I made out with a lot of guys! This was back when I was young and lusty, before I went nutsy-cuckoo and they had to put me in the loony bin."

"You think this is funny?"

"Actually, I do. I think the only answer to life is to laugh your head off."

Jack made a thoughtful hmmphing sound. Sophia Sunshine seemed very sane to him. He wanted to keep her talking.

"How long have you had this store?"

"Since I got here. I needed a way to support myself. I've never been a freeloader."

"I imagine you're doing well now. A cute little store in a town full of tourists is a good fit. But it must have taken money to get this business off the ground. How did you come up with that?"

"Charlie helped me. Didn't you know?"

"You're friends with your ex-husband?"

"I wouldn't say friends. He wanted me out of his hair. Guilt money, more accurately. It wasn't a lot. Charlie had just gotten paid to rewrite a screenplay behind three other screenwriters. It wasn't a great assignment, and the script was never made into a movie. It was bad luck for him, but he had enough to give me ten grand to fix this place up, pay the first month's rent, and get enough stock to open up. The rent is cheap, luckily. The place is owned by an old Spanish family of *penitentes* who like having me here."

"And you see Charlie from time to time?"

"Not often. Usually in passing somewhere. He would rather pretend I don't exist. But here I am."

Jack nodded wisely.

"Well, Sophia, history repeats itself. On Monday somebody tried to set fire to Charlie's house while he was in a drunken stupor. Except for the fact that Mikaela wasn't there, it was *déjà vu* all over again. Almost like the fire you set that got you sent away. Unfortunately, a very decent human being died getting Charlie to safety. My caregiver. Someone who was working for me, who trusted me. This makes me angry. In fact, I'd go farther and admit that this makes me fucking furious. So I'm going to find who set that fire and I'm going to nail him. Or her."

"You think I set the new fire?"

"I think it's a distinct possibility."

"Well, I'm sorry to disappoint you, but no, I didn't set the fire at Charlie's house. I don't do things like that."

"But this is a pattern with you. You did it before, Sophia. You confessed to it."

"Ah, yes, I did it before! I confessed. But you see, sometimes I didn't tell the truth back then. To be honest, I was a liar when I was young. I made things up. It's something I've grown out of. Life beat the shit out of me and I got old. Today I only—believe me, *only*—speak of what is true. Life is too short to pull your punches."

Jack didn't speak for a moment. "Are you saying you didn't set the fire when Mikaela was eight?"

"You catch on, Jack. I like smart men. If we were twenty years younger, God only knows what we'd end up doing in this room!"

"But why did you confess if you didn't do it?"

"You're the detective. Figure it out."

Jack frowned furiously. "You're not lying to me, are you?"

"I told you, I do not lie," she said firmly.

Oddly, he believed her. The truth hit him with a jolt.

"Mikaela set the fire! My God! It was your daughter! And you covered for her!"

"You got it, darling! Funny how no one suspected that, not even Charlie. Mikaela was always a bad child. Charlie hated her, he called her a monster. She destroyed one of his manuscripts once, he lost an entire novel, a year's work. You should have seen him chase her around the house! To be honest, I've never liked her very much either, but I felt sorry for her. Mikaela was just a small child. She hated me and Charlie. I always understood why she did it. I saw her get out of bed that night. She went outside with a box of kitchen matches, set the fire, then got back in bed and pretended later she had been fast asleep and barely escaped alive. She wasn't a happy girl, I'm afraid. Her karma is complicated."

"I don't care about her karma. Am I supposed to believe you spent all those years in a mental institution to cover for something Mikaela did?"

"I was going through a period of egolessness, Jack, fighting my natural narcissism. I think maybe I *was* crazy. I said to myself, why not? What else do I have to do with my crazy life except give my daughter a second chance? You know what I decided?"

Jack was stunned. This changed everything. If it was true.

"What did you decide?"

"I decided my life was unimportant. I was nothing, less than the tiniest dust of stardust. My life would only have meaning if I gave it to my little girl. It's the final lesson, Jack. You can only keep your life by giving it away!"

Jack sighed. "I don't know, Sophia. It seems to me you need a bit of ego to keep things together on this planet. Bluster has its place. Now, Mikaela knows that you covered for her. I hope she's grateful. What's your relationship with her like now?"

Sophia changed the subject. "Would you like me to do a Tarot reading for you, Jack? I could give you a look into the future!"

Jack gave her a wintry smile. "Sophia, at my age, in my condition, I have a very good idea what the future holds. A Tarot reading would be wasted on me. Now, let's stick with the subject at hand. Has Mikaela come to San Geronimo to see you recently?"

"I'm not going to lie to you, Jack. I've promised you that. But I'm not going to answer all your questions either. Now, you'll need to excuse me for moment."

Jack listened as Sophia walked across the room and closed a door behind her. He sat for several minutes absorbing what she had told him, trying to understand how the case stood now. To Jack, it felt as though a thousand piece puzzle he had nearly completed had been picked up and thrown to the ground.

He was so deep in thought that at first he didn't notice how long Sophia had been gone. He waited another five minutes for her to return before he realized she wasn't coming back.

"Manny!" he called. "Are you there?"

Manny came through the door ready for action. He was surprised to see Jack sitting alone in a musty, crowded store room.

"Where did she go?"

"Wherever she went, she's not coming back. We're finished here," said Jack. "You can drive me home."

On the way home, there was no more talk about grandchildren. Manny drove in silence.

In his wheelchair in the back of the van, Jack found his phone and called Howie. He was transferred to voicemail.

"Howie, call me!" he commanded. "I need to know everything you can tell me about your meeting with Mikaela. From now on, she's our focus. Mikaela McFadden."

Chapter Twenty-Two

On Friday morning, Georgie returned to the office from the Dos Flores Bakery with their morning tea, as she called it—she drank tea, Howie drank coffee. She found Howie in the back office on the phone with Buzzy Hurston.

She set Howie's cappuccino and bear claw on the desk and then pulled the client chair closer so that she could sit and listen. They were talking about the photo she had taken of the man who had broken into the office.

"You couldn't get a definite match?" Howie was asking. "Here I thought you guys could find anybody! I see . . . look, hold on a second, Georgie just arrived with goodies. I'll put you on speaker . . ."

Howie took a quick bite of the bear claw.

"Buzzy couldn't ID the photo you took!" he said to Georgie with his mouth full. "I mean honestly! The CIA!"

"Let me finish," Buzzy replied patiently, his voice coming from the small speaker on the phone. "The software couldn't make a definitive match, but there are sixteen runner-ups. The list descends in order of likelihood. Your weatherman is number twelve, Joseph L. Ochoa. So you got something. A probability of 67 percent. He's not a sure match, but the fact he's on the list I think gives you what you need."

"It gives me everything I need except proof. You'll send me the list?"

"Not in writing. We're not going to leave a paper trail. You can memorize, can't you?"

"Well, yeah . . . sixteen names? I mean, that's a bit of work for an aging brain, but go ahead."

"I'll help you, Da," Georgie told him. "Memory is what got me through school. We'll do it together. Go ahead, Buzzy. We'll get it."

***

Georgie had the sixteen names memorized before Howie, but she kept quiet. She wanted to see how long it took him to nail it. In fact, Howie got it quickly enough. Though later, when he tried to repeat the sixteen names, she had to correct him three times.

"It's number twelve we're interested in," he emphasized, somewhat defensively. "The others aren't as important. We'll check them out, of course. But I'm starting to have a good sense of who the Dweeb is, and what he's up to."

"You've been following Joe on that camera app Buzzy gave you?"

Howie paused his attack on the bear claw long enough to sigh. "It's a site on the dark web. Buzzy gave me a bunch of passwords. I hate to go there. The dark web is a sewer, the absolute underbelly of human existence!"

"The id," she said.

"Sure, let's call it the id."

"I like underbelly better," she allowed graciously. "Hell with Freud!"

Howie thought of himself as well-educated, but he often found himself struggling to keep up with his daughter. He didn't mind that, in fact. The thought of it made him glow.

They were finishing morning tea when a call came from the State Police. It was Sergeant Rodillo, one of Santo's detectives. He said Santo wanted to see Howie in his office. As soon as possible. Pronto.

"Okay, give me an hour—"

"Now!" said Rodillo.

"Be right there," said Howie. "I'll try not to drive too fast."

"Get here!"

Howie sensed he was in trouble. Nevertheless, he paused long enough to get Georgie set up on Buzzy's secret site. He sat her down at his desk and leaned over her shoulder as he showed her how to get on and off the dark web and gave her the site passwords. Getting off the dark web was especially important when she wasn't following the feed. These were shark-infested waters where you didn't want to linger.

"It's mostly very boring," he warned. "I spent an hour this morning watching Joe's house, waiting for him to do something. Nothing happened at all. But I'd like you to keep an eye on the feed as much as you can. If Joe goes anywhere, be sure to text me, even if I'm with Santo."

"I'll keep an eye on everything, Da."

"And look, Georgie, if for some reason I'm arrested . . . I mean, I'm *not* going to be arrested, but just suppose—call Jack and he'll set our attorney in motion. He's in Santa Fe, but he'll come up here if we need him. His name is Matt Heldman and he's good."

"You think you're going to be arrested?"

"Well, tampering with evidence is a dicey matter."

"Then I'll get arrested, too! I was there, Da—I was part of it."

"Yes, well, let's keep this to ourselves for the moment and see how it plays out," he told her. "Maybe we'll be lucky."

Howie gave Georgie a quick hug then drove off, leaving her alone in the office.

She settled at Jack's old desk—a desk as outsized as Jack—and kept an eye on the surveillance feed. The screen showed a static scene of Joe's garage and front yard. It was a home she regarded as the epitome of suburban America, a house she had seen hundreds of times growing up in Scotland on the telly, the American cop shows Glaswegians devoured. It was semi-modern, two stories, on a quarter-acre lot.

There was a wrought-iron fence around the property that had sharply pointed spikes on top. A sign by the driveway showed the outline of a gun and the name of a security company, as well as a warning of an armed response.

Georgie wondered where the security camera was positioned that was taking this feed. Across the street, she presumed. But how would that be possible in a residential neighborhood?

Georgie set up her own laptop alongside Howie's that was showing the front of the house. She was bringing up Google Maps, hoping to investigate Joe's Albuquerque neighborhood, when her phone rang. To her surprise, it was Uma Rothenstein.

"Hey!" Uma said. "Look, I'm in town and I need to see you. I'm at the Nuestra Señora church. In the park. Can you meet me there now?"

Georgie knew the old Nuestra Señora de las Montañas church. It was an historical adobe church from the early 1800s a few miles from the center of town.

"I'm alone in the office," Georgie told her. "Can't you come here?"

"I can't! And honestly, I have to see you. I remembered something about Zia that I need to tell you."

"Are you all right Uma?" Georgie asked. She didn't sound all right. She sounded like she was in overdrive.

"Please, I need to see you. You gotta come, please!"

Georgie found herself holding a dead phone. It didn't take her long to decide that she would go to the church to see what Uma wanted. Howie would understand the need for it. The ride was mostly downhill so she could get there quickly.

She texted Howie:

Uma Rothenstein called in a tizzy and asked me to meet her in the park by the Nuestra Senora church. Says she has something to tell me about Zia. I'm going to hop on my bike and see what's up. Later!

***

Georgie walked her bike into the hot summer afternoon. She set the alarm and left the agency building with a feeling of relief. It felt wonderful to jump on her bike and pedal away.

She slowed down when she reached Calle de los Nubes, a high tourist district of galleries and gift shops. But she wasn't going slowly enough. She had to slam on her brakes to avoid a sunburnt couple who appeared out of nowhere, crossing in the middle of the street. Her first instinct was fury at such a clueless pair. They hadn't even noticed that they had almost been run down. But she quickly decided that they were best forgotten, cancelled from her brain.

As soon as she was free of downtown traffic, Georgie slipped the mountain bike into a high gear and got her body into an easy rhythm. She rode gloriously fast. She loved living at 7000 feet, 2133 meters, in a high mountain valley where the air was like champagne.

But the thought of champagne brought up an image of Jean-Claude. She remembered sitting so near to him that their knees occasionally touched at the small table in the Blue Mesa Café.

This disturbed her in a way that she wasn't ready to examine. With an effort, she turned her thoughts to Howie, knowing he would be happy to see she was wearing a helmet. For Georgie, this was a concession. She would rather feel her hair free in the wind.

She road on side roads through a mix of residential and commercial neighborhoods until coming to a large piece of land that had the old church on it, Nuestra Señora de Las Montañas. It had originally been a morada, built by the Penitentes. Over the centuries it had morphed into more mainstream Catholicism although it had long ago ceased to have regular services. Today the church was kept up by its aging parishioners and only opened on Christmas Eve and Easter. There were occasional funerals and weddings, but only for the families of longtime parishioners. There was a small local park behind the church that had become a hangout for San Geronimo teenagers.

Georgie found Uma in a group of half a dozen teens who were standing in a loose circle smoking weed in the shade of a Siberian elm. She was laughing at some boy's joke and didn't look like there was an emergency.

"Hi, Uma," she said as she approached the teens.

"Oh, it's you," Uma said, deadpan turning to Georgie. You wouldn't have thought that she had phoned half an hour ago begging Georgie to meet her.

Georgie's smile was hard. "Is there somewhere we can talk?"

"Well, I guess."

"Come on, then." She turned and walked away with her bike at her side.

"Be back soon," Uma said to her friends as she followed after Georgie. "Wait up, there's a bench on the other side of the church where we can sit. This way."

The park was a maze of overgrown paths. Georgie and Uma followed the barely paved path around to the back of the church.

"So what's going on, Uma? What did you remember about Zia?" Georgie asked while they were walking.

"It's just something I remembered," said Uma. "But maybe I shouldn't tell you. I mean, she's dead, maybe it's best just to let it ride."

"What did you remember?" Georgie didn't hide her impatience.

"Okay, you asked me about guys. What guys were interested in her at school. I mean, it's just a small thing. But I thought I ought to tell you."

"Yes?" Georgie urged. There was something bovine about Uma that irritated her immensely.

"So I said all the boys at school had the hots for her, but she wasn't interested in anyone."

"Right. I remember you telling me that."

"Well, it's true. I mean, true about the boys at school. But older guys had the hots for her, too. And that's what I remembered. But now I'm not sure I should tell you."

Georgie stopped on the path, her patience gone. "Uma, I hurried over here because you said you had something to tell me. Are you trying to tell me that your father and Zia were having an affair?"

"No, not my father!" Uma protested. "Zia modeled for him, sure. But that doesn't mean anything. When you're an artist, women model for you all the time. It's art. It means nothing. All Daddy wanted was to draw her."

"So what are you trying to tell me?"

"It's that French guy. Jean-Claude whatever. He was the one who was all hard for Zia. I caught them together one time."

Georgie felt as though she had been stabbed with an icicle. "What do you mean you caught her together with Jean-Claude?"

"I walked in on them. They were together in Daddy's office and they didn't know I was there. You should have seen the look he was giving her!"

"What look?"

"It was a look that said I want to fuck you forever! I mean, his tongue was hanging out."

"Were they . . . fully clothed?"

"Well, yeah. They were in Daddy's office, what do you expect? But they looked like they were tearing off each other clothes in their minds."

"In their minds? So this was just a look?"

"I thought I should tell you, that's all. I thought you would want to know."

Georgie was baffled. She didn't know whether to take Uma seriously.

"When did this happen?" she asked. "How long before Zia died?"

Georgie didn't get an answer.

"Over here!" called a woman who was sitting on a bench at the side of the old church. Georgie was surprised to see it was Uma's mother, Catherine. She turned to Uma for an explanation.

"She wants to speak with you," Uma said sullenly. "I can't help it. She made me call you."

"Come here!" Catherine ordered from the bench. "Sit beside me!"

Uma was already hurrying away. Georgie sighed. She leaned her bike against a tree, preparing herself for a bad time.

Georgie was unhappy at being ambushed, but she joined Uma's mother on the bench.

***

Georgie could tell immediately that Catherine wasn't going to be her new best friend.

She smiled as Georgie sat down on the bench beside her, but it wasn't a happy smile. It was the smile a shark might flash, all teeth, before it bit off your arm.

"So, my dear, I thought it might be nice to have a chat," she said.

"Well, all right," said Georgie hesitantly. "What would you like to talk about?"

"You're from Scotland, I hear. Isn't that lovely! I always picture uptight Calvinists living cold dreary lives in the rain. But you're not at all like that, are you? You're young and full of sparkle."

Georgie was starting to feel a little sharkish herself. "Cultural stereotypes are a mistake," she answered. "In the UK, we often regard Americans as overweight idiots with guns who speak English with a rather silly accent. But you aren't like that either, are you?"

There were more smiles all around.

Georgie had no idea what this meeting was about. She had only seen Catherine briefly once before, and this was the first time she was able to study her more closely. She was a blonde woman in her fifties and you could tell that she had been very pretty at one time, an It Girl of the Blondes-Have-More-Fun era. But that was long ago. Her face had been hollowed out by time and struggle. Her eyes were deadly.

"So, do you like it here in New Mexico?" Catherine asked.

"I do," said Georgie. "The land is so big and open, and there's so much sky. I like the people here also. Most of the time."

"Uma tells me you've been poking around asking questions about Zia, that girl who used to come around."

"Yes, that's true. I wouldn't call it poking around, however. It's more focused than that. My father is a private detective and we're investigating the circumstances of her death."

"The newspaper described it as a suicide."

"They did, and that may turn out to be correct. Uma said you didn't want Zia coming around anymore. Didn't you like her?"

"My dear, it wasn't a question of like or dislike. It's my husband, I'm afraid. He has a weakness for fluffy little girls like Zia. He always wants to put his pecker in their pretty little pussies. I try to discourage that, being his wife. A famous artist with plenty of money—there's a certain sort of girlie who finds that irresistible. Over the years, I've found it's best to stop these flirtations early before they get out of hand."

"You think Zia was trying to get her hands on your husband?"

"My dear, I think *you* are trying to get your hands on my husband! Don't deny it. I saw how you shook your pretty little ass at him!"

Georgie was dumbfounded. "Catherine, I find lecherous old men repulsive! Especially the kind who try to bully you with their wealth and position in life. I have no designs on your husband, believe me. I prefer guys more my own age."

"Oh, really? Then explain this!"

Catherine pulled out a crumpled sheet of paper from her handbag, and uncrumpled it as best she could. It was a drawing of Georgie's face, astonishing in its accuracy considering the brief time she had spent with Edward Rothenstein.

Georgie could only shake her head. "I'm sorry but I didn't pose for this. He said he wanted to draw me but I said no. He must have done this from memory."

"Oh, you think you made a big impression on him, do you? Well, let me tell you something. You're nothing special. He likes all young girls. It means nothing!"

"I'm sure that's a problem for your marriage," said Georgie. "But it's not my problem. If I were you, I'd give him the boot."

"Give me your phone," Catherine demanded.

"I'm sorry?"

"Your phone. I want your phone."

Georgie shook her head. "No, absolutely not!"

"You will give me your phone or I will make you sorry!"

"You're kidding?"

"I am not. I want that photograph. I know Jean-Claude gave it to you and I want it."

"Jean-Claude did not give me any photograph," Georgie said firmly. Which was true. She knew now what Uma's mother was after. But she was mistaken. Georgie didn't have the photograph of the painting. Jean-Claude had told her he couldn't give it to her. *America Girl* was a work with the potential to be worth a great deal of money. There were serious proprietorial lines he couldn't cross.

"Let me be clear," Catherine said so softly it was like a hiss. "If you try to peddle that picture, I'll take you to court and screw you over so bad you'll wish you were dead!"

"Catherine, I do not have any photo on my phone that would interest you, period. And that's the end of the matter."

"But you know about *America Girl*, don't you?"

"I know of its existence, that's all," she admitted. "Was Edward having an affair with Zia McFadden, Catherine?"

"Give me your damn phone! Let's see if you're telling the truth!"

Catherine lunged at Georgie and tried to tear her daypack from her lap.

"Is that where you keep it?" she cried, trying to get to her phone. Georgie jumped up from the bench and managed to get free. It wasn't easy. The woman was all over her. It was like trying to fend off an octopus.

"Get off me! You're crazy!" Georgie cried as she stepped backward to the tree where she had leaned her bike. She worried that Catherine might come after her, but she only stared at Georgie with scorching anger.

Georgie climbed on her bike and pedaled away as fast as she could. As she rode past the church she had a glimpse of Uma who was in the field again with her friends. Uma frowned as she watched Georgie ride away.

What a family!

She liked Jean-Claude, but he definitely had some questions to answer. If Uma had told the truth, he had known Zia much better than he had indicated. And how did Catherine know that he had shown Georgie the painting of Zia? This was turning into the sort of sex melodrama that Georgie didn't want.

Men!

Jean-Claude certainly had some explaining to do tonight. But just as she was coming into town, she heard the ding on her phone signaling an incoming text. She pulled over to the side of the road to answer, holding the screen in the shadow of her body so she could see the message on the screen.

It was Jean-Claude and he was canceling!

Sorry I can't make our dinner tonight. A crisis, I'm afraid, and I have to deal with it. Will you forgive me? Will you have dinner with me tomorrow? I will explain everything. There will be roses and champagne and apologies.

Georgie shook her head. What a smooth talking charmer! He was ridiculous, obvious in the extreme, but she couldn't help liking him.

Okay for tomorrow, she texted back. But forget the roses, I have some questions for you.

She waited straddling her bike on the side of the road expecting an immediate answer, a word or two, probably a funny quip. But there was nothing.

Chapter Twenty-Three

Lieutenant Santo Ruben's office was a cramped space full of bulletin boards and filing cabinets. There were framed photographs on every surface of friends in uniform who looked like they were either dead or long retired. The room had a single narrow window with a dismal view of an alley and the chain-link fence with razor wire on top that made a fortress of the station.

Several of the photos on the crowded shelves were of Santo's daughter, Sharon, who had died at the age of 27 of a drug overdose. Santo carried a burden of guilt for this loss that had aged him. He drank too much in periodic binges. His eyes sharpened to stilettos as he studied Howie.

"Don't think about holding out on me, Moon Deer. That would be a test of our friendship that you wouldn't like!"

Howie smiled his most open, honest smile. "Santo, ask me anything. I'll do my best to answer!"

The office was so small that there was barely room for Jack in his wheelchair and Howie alongside him on a folding metal chair. It was Santo's idea to bring in Jack and Howie together. He had sent a town EMT unit to pick up Jack, who seemed happy to be out of his house. Howie hadn't seen Jack so perky in some time.

A uniformed trooper brought in Chinese take-out and spread out the cartons on Santo's desk along with a scatter of plastic utensils and packets of sauces that were impossible to open.

"Thought we might as well have a little lunch while we talked," Santo said as he began making up a plate for Jack. "How about some orange chicken, Jack? You like that, don't you? Maybe some of the Szechuan shrimp?"

"Just a small portion," said Jack.

Santo and Jack had a cop-brotherhood thing between them, one that left Howie on the outside. Jack and Santo spoke the same language. Howie didn't.

Howie had a moment to check his phone and find two messages from Georgie. The first, sent at 11:24 AM:

Uma Rothenstein just called in a tizzy and asked me to meet her in the park by the church. Says she has something to tell me about Zia so I'm going to hop on my bike and see what's up. Later!

Howie always worried about Georgie riding her bike in traffic. He hoped she had taken her helmet. The second text came five minutes ago, at 1:34:

I forgot it's t'ai chi day! Missed last week so can't miss today. I have lots to tell you. See you later!

Lots to tell him? Howie was impressed with her work, and he was curious what she had learned. Zia's school friend, Uma, probably could tell them more about Zia than anyone. Teenage girls confided in each other. Hopefully.

He looked up to find Santo smiling at him in a knowing manner. "You got a text from Georgie! You have that look on your face."

"What look?"

"Fatherly concern. Howie, you gotta stop being such a helicopter parent. Georgie's an adult. She can take care of herself."

"Helicopter parent?" Howie repeated, pausing to see himself in this possible light. "Well, yes. But she's new here in America. I know Glasgow is a tough town to grow up in, but in New Mexico she still looks the wrong direction when she crosses the street."

"Howie, the girl's *agile*," Santo said sarcastically. "She can cross the damn street!"

"I guess," said Howie. "Right now she's off meeting with one of Zia's school friends, Uma Rothenstein. Uma's father is Edward Rothenstein, the artist. Zia posed for him without her clothes on. Whether this means anything or not, I don't know. I've been trying to convince Georgie to take driving lessons and let me buy her a car but all she's said so far is she'll think about it."

"Sometimes I think that girl is more Indian than you are, Moon Deer. You should buy her a horse."

"These days Indians prefer pickup trucks, Santo," Howie answered with a small dose of sarcasm.

The question of the car, Howie knew, had nothing to do with being a Native American. For Georgie, it was a question of whether she was going to stay in San Geronimo, and for how long. A car would be an obligation and an anchor. She was at a time of life when she wanted to be free. Howie hoped she would stay but he didn't want to pressure her. Tomorrow she might decide to fly off to Thailand.

"Okay, let's settle down and put our heads together," Santo told them. "I brought you in here because I want to know exactly what the two of you are doing. It's time to share information, gentleman. I'm not going to tolerate evasions. And I have to start by telling you, I'm still not entirely convinced Zia didn't commit suicide. She left a note, after all."

"Anyone could have scratched those words in the side of the cliff," Howie objected. "So what's happening with the State Police investigation? Information is best when it works both ways."

"You want to know what's happening? We're doing the boring stuff while you geniuses are off with your big theories. Going door to door looking for witnesses, getting background info, doing forensics, collecting evidence. You wouldn't be interested, Howie. It's painstaking work and it doesn't pay well."

"Santo, I do *very* painstaking work when I take on a client—"

"Forget it, it doesn't matter. The truth is there's really nothing so far. I have ideas, but I sure don't have enough to bring anyone in. What do you think, Jack?"

Jack was working methodically on his orange chicken. He had a look on his face that said: *I grew up in San Francisco. I know what Chinese food is supposed to be. This New Mexico version is a parody!*

"Jack, maybe I should get you a fork," Santo suggested. "Those chopsticks seem to be giving you trouble."

"Listen, my friend—I've been using chopsticks since I was 5 years-old!" Jack said, getting a little huffy. What he couldn't see was that the majority of his lunch was ending up either in his lap or on the floor.

"So Jack, I know you've been following this investigation," said Santo. "So let me ask again, what are you thinking?"

"What am I thinking? I'm trying not to think. This is the time to keep an open mind. This is the time for information gathering, thinking's for later."

"I understand, Jack," Santo said patiently.

"However, I've learned a few things that are interesting. Let me tell you about my interview with Sophia McFadden. She claims she didn't set the fire that got her committed down in Las Cruces. She says she took the blame for her daughter. It was Mikaela who set the fire. Mikaela did it."

Both Howie and Santo paused to take this in. Howie shook his head. "I don't know, Jack. Mikaela was 8 years old at the time."

"Matches are easy to use. Eight isn't too young to start a fire. In fact, I'd say eight is a perfect age to be an arsonist. All id, no superego, no restraints on your rage."

"You're kidding, Jack—id? superego?"

"You're not the only one who can throw around bullshit terms. Let's face it, Mikaela was always a monster. Everybody says so. A screwed up 8 year old without any self-control."

"I'm not sure I buy this," Santo said. "I mean, come on—all these years later the mother steps up and says she took the blame for little Mikaela. I mean, to spend all those years in a nut house! That's one hell of a sacrifice."

"Well, she's a bit crazy," said Jack. "Probably more than a bit. But I believe her somehow. There's something innocent about Sophia, truthful. I can see her sacrificing herself for the sake her daughter. I'm not sure if this changes everything, but it sure gives this drama a spin. Old crimes tend to fester and resurface years later as something bad. If she set that first fire, she may have developed a taste for it and set the recent fire too. And we're talking about a fire in which my caregiver lost her life. I'm not going to let that pass!"

"But what's Mikaela's motive?" Howie objected. "Why would she kill Keir?"

"Howie, you've answered that already," said Jack. "Mikaela and Joe did it together. They believed that Zia told her father about the abuse."

"All right, let's pause on the abuse for a moment," said Santo. "Howie, you've left this somewhat vague. I need to know exactly how *you* know that Zia was being sexually abused."

Howie felt bad about his need to lie about Zia's diary. When you tell a lie, it comes back to smack you.

"It was just a theory I had, Santo, based on rumors, nothing more. Georgie went to Zia's school here in San Geronimo and spoke to some of the girls in her class. There was talk that Zia had left Albuquerque because her mother's boyfriend was bothering her. That's all, unconfirmed talk. It wasn't much, but it was a start. With Georgie's help on the Internet, we found that Mikaela has been seeing Joe Ochoa on the sly. None of this was certain until I interviewed Mikaela in Albuquerque. It was a weird meeting late at night in her office, but I bluffed and fooled her into admitting the truth. She told me that yes, Zia had accused Joe of abusing her, but Mikaela didn't believe it. She said Zia was making it up, but that's nonsense. Zia was telling the truth."

"You don't know that for certain, Howie. Did you record your conversation with Mikaela?"

"No, I did not."

"Were there any witnesses to it?"

"No."

"Then you got nothing, Howie," said Santo. "Nothing!"

"I got what I know," said Howie. "I know what happened."

"And a lot of good it will do you!"

"Okay, okay!" said Jack. "Let's not argue. This is really very simple. When I know someone is guilty but I don't have evidence, I've found it's useful to stir things up. Make the suspects squirm. Force them to make a mistake."

"Great. But how do we do it?" Howie asked.

"Easy. You have a man and a woman who are lovers. Joe has a lot to lose if he's found out. He's married, he's a big church-goer, and if he can remain free of scandal, he's hoping to get hired to do the weather on national TV. Now, here's what you have to do, Howie. Pretend you're a Greek god watching these mortals from up in the clouds, figure out what makes them tick then throw some thunderbolts down to shake up their world."

"Jack, I'm not going to pretend I'm a Greek god."

"Sure, you are. Make them quarrel. Turn them against each other. Destroy their status quo and see what crawls out. What could be easier?"

"I can think of many things that are easier. What God-like trick do you have in mind, if I may ask?"

"For chrissakes, Howie, I'm retired! I can't do everything myself! You're running the show now, I'm only a useless old man. Put your thinking cap on, lad. I'm sure if you put your mind to it, you'll come up with an idea."

***

Howie was the one who came up with the idea, but it was Georgie who thought up how to make it work.

The plan was to use social media to show that Joe was having it off with a pretty young woman whose photograph they found online. Her name was Melinda—in fact, she did not exist, she had died some years earlier. With some creative photoshopping, Georgie worked to produce an image of Joe and Melinda snuggled up together in a casino restaurant. This required finesse and it took a few tries. Once they had a convincing photograph, the plan was to post it on Instagram, Facebook, Tik-Tok, every platform Georgie knew under the banner, JOE THE WANKER WEATHERMAN.

Georgie was the one who came up with the word wanker. She didn't imagine that Mikaela would take kindly to the Dweeb cheating on her.

It was fun to dream up ways to cause Mikaela and Joe to have a falling out. It was satisfying to throw darts at them from a distance, anonymously, on the Internet.

But after an hour of planning their online campaign, they found themselves slowly coming to a halt.

Georgie gave her father a good look. "We're not going to do it, are we?"

"It's so tempting, isn't it? You can do a lot of harm on the Internet. You can win by foul means. It's so damn sneaky!"

"Aye, but that kind of victory doesn't bring much joy," said Georgie. "If you sell your soul to the devil, there's a price to pay. I'm glad we're not doing this, Da."

"Me, too. Well, maybe it wouldn't have worked anyway," Howie consoled. "Let's keep thinking about this overnight. I bet we'll come up with something."

At 5 o'clock, Georgie said she didn't have anything planned for the night. Her dinner date had been put off until tomorrow but she was hoping to stay in town anyway. She would grab take-out from the falafel cart in the Plaza and see Howie in the morning.

Howie felt a pang of disappointment that Georgie didn't want to spend the night with him and Claire on the land. But he was wise enough to encourage her independence. At half past five, he drove home by himself, leaving Georgie in the office.

As always, it was good to be home. As the summer twilight lingered in the forest, he and Claire had a bookish, low key evening. They sat outside. Claire in the rocking chair by the vegetable garden reading *Madame Bovary* in French—she was working on her French, which she spoke with an Iowa accent.

Howie settled on a lawn chair by the fire pit with the photocopy of Zia's diary on his lap. He knew he had to get rid of it—he should have burned it already—but he wanted to read it one last time. He had the fire all ready to light, the kindling set into a small tepee with balled newspaper inside.

Howie read once again of Zia's hatred of her mother's boyfriend, the man she called the Dweeb. Her account was graphic, how she had awoken to find him masturbating over her bed. Santo had suggested this might have been a young girl's sexual imagination, but Howie believed her.

Howie stopped reading for dinner, which was a large salad from the garden with a baguette, Irish butter, and different sorts of cheese. He lit the fire and burned what he had read so far, more than half the diary.

They polished off a bottle of cold white wine. They often had nights full of laughter and conversation gathered around the fire, even a song or two. One night they huddled in the tepee by the creek as a lightning storm thundered around them. But tonight was quiet. It was good to be with someone so easy to be quiet with.

Howie put out the fire and they went upstairs to the loft where they made love slowly, gently. That was even better than good. Afterward, they lay comfortably in bed side by side reading. Claire was still making her way through *Madame Bovary* as Howie continued reading the last half of Zia's diary. As committed late-night readers, they each had small, precise lamps that threw sharp but narrow beams on their pages. Howie's over-indulged cat, Orange, lay sprawled on her back between them, waiting for someone to rub her stomach.

Claire put down her book with a sigh. "I wish my French was better! I'm just not a natural when it comes to a foreign language."

"I'd say you're doing well if you can read *Madame Bovary* in French."

"But that's the problem. I'm trying not to look up every other word in the dictionary, so I'm missing a lot. My vocabulary sucks. And in February, I'm playing with a French conductor in Bordeaux. The entire orchestra will be French and they really hate it when some American woman comes in assuming everybody speaks English! Maybe Georgie will introduce me to Jean-Claude and I'll have a chance to practice. I have to say, I'm curious to meet him."

"So is everything going okay with Georgie and this French person?" Howie asked. "She seemed a little down."

"It's not a big thing. She had a date tonight with Jean-Claude, but he canceled. You know what that's like."

"So Jean-Claude," Howie asked cautiously, "is this something serious with her?"

"I doubt it. But he sounds nice. Apparently he knows all about art and artists and Georgie finds this interesting. Whatever happens, it's good for her to get out, even if it doesn't go anywhere."

Howie hoped it was good. But in the end, Georgie would make her own decisions.

"She's twenty-one," Claire reminded, not for the first time. Twenty-one was starting to sound like a disease.

Outside, the forest blew in the wind. A coyote howled.

He felt Claire's big toe touch his toe under the covers. His toe wiggled back encouragingly, but she moved away again. The thought of making love a second time passed between them. In the old days, a second time would have been taken for granted. A third. But for sex she would need to climb down the loft ladder to the bathroom afterwards. They were both comfortable and neither one wanted to move. That, Howie speculated, was the start of middle-age.

Zia's diary was as he remembered it until he came to the final pages, her new life in San Geronimo with Keir.

There was a passage about Zia's friendship with Uma that he had skimmed over the last time he had read the diary, but he took more notice of it now.

Uma reminds me of a cow with her big lazy eyes, Zia wrote. It's her family that intrigues me. The freedom of the artist to do what you like and get paid for it! I'd love to be

221

an artist. But there's some weird vibe between E, C and JC. Sexual? I don't know. Power struggle? Who's the alpha male, E or JC? Their conversation is big city talk, full of references to places and people I don't know. JC is very attractive. I think he's been coming on to me.

Howie moved his right foot so that it touched Claire's left foot.

"Would you say the initials JC are Jean-Claude?" he asked.

"Well, sure. But not necessarily."

"Claire, do you remember when you played in the Granada music festival last summer, you said you met the Spanish Minister of Tourism."

"Yes, Franco Medina. He was in Granada to promote the festival and he was very nice."

"He invited you to visit him on Ibiza," Howie remembered. "At his villa?"

Claire smiled. "Howie, he's in his late sixties. He wasn't propositioning me. He was just being friendly."

"Right. I know all about friendly old men. He gave you his email?"

"Yes."

"Then I'd like you to do something for me. I'd like you to email Franco and ask him about the upcoming exhibition of Edward Rothenstein's work at the Bilbao Guggenheim. Ask him what he knows about Jean-Claude."

"You're checking up on Georgie's date? Howie, I'm not sure you should do that!"

"I think we need to. He's probably a great guy, totally on the up and up. But I'd like to make sure."

***

Howie finished burning the photocopy of Zia's diary in the outside fire pit first thing Saturday morning. He sat next to the fire with a mug of coffee watching the pages burn. He would have liked to keep the diary for further reference, but he knew he couldn't be caught with it in his possession.

Howie tried to keep weekends free to spend with Claire and Georgie, but the case was moving quickly and today both Claire and Georgie had their own plans. Claire was giving a sold-out concert tonight, a benefit for the San Geronimo Art Center, and she was unexpectedly nervous. It was one thing to perform at Albert Hall in front of strangers, another to play in a town where she had lived for years and many people she knew would be in the audience.

Claire was going to have a final rehearsal this morning with a local pianist who was going to accompany her on cello sonatas by Beethoven, Brahms, and Ravel. The pianist was very accomplished, but he was an amateur and she was slightly worried about him. Howie planned to attend the concert and take her out to dinner afterwards. As for Georgie, she had her own dinner plans with the fascinating French man, Jean-Claude Maurot. JC.

They left home at the same time, Claire in her rented SUV and Howie in his dusty Outback. When they arrived at the office, he found Georgie on her phone in the front room answering a query from a prospective client. She explained politely that they did not take divorce cases and the agency was completely booked for the month of August.

Howie settled at his own computer in the back office and logged into the security cameras that were following Joe Ochoa. The software had the ability to back up and show what had happened earlier. From here you could make time fly. You could fast-forward or fast-back.

Howie backed up to yesterday evening and watched as Joe left his house, drove to the TV station, parked in the underground garage, and did the 10 o'clock news. The weather was going to be fine all weekend, but Tuesday morning clouds would be moving into the state.

The view of Joe was passed from one camera to another with astonishing ease. Occasionally there were gaps where the last image would freeze until the subject came once again within range of a new camera. But these gaps weren't long. Howie wasn't sure he liked a world with cameras watching your every move. George Orwell would be snickering from his grave. But as an investigator, it certainly was helpful, just what any snooper wanted.

Howie yawned. He hadn't slept much last night. He felt a vague anxiety, like a coyote sensing there was an earthquake coming.

When she was off the phone, Georgie told him about her encounter yesterday with Catherine.

"It's really a strange family, Da. I don't know what to make of them. It makes me think of that line, the rich are different from you and me. Where does that come from?"

"F. Scott Fitzgerald," said Howie.

"Well, they certainly are self-entitled! Did you come up with some way to make Mikaela and Joe have a falling out?"

"No, I decided not to go that route. I'm sure Jack could pull it off, but I don't think it's necessary. I'm going to focus on the surveillance app. I'm going to keep watching Joe until he makes a mistake. Somewhere along the way he's going to slip and then I'll have him. On camera."

***

Howie was at his desk watching the footage from last night—Joe Ochoa driving home from the studio—when a message flashed on the corner of the screen, LIVE FEED, and the view changed abruptly to the present.

The view was of a hotel lobby looking down from the ceiling. It was a generic lobby, chain architecture, but higher up the scale than a Motel 6. A man had just come into the lobby from the outside, passing through an automatic glass door that slid open for him. Howie didn't recognize him. It wasn't Joe Ochoa. This was an older, larger man with a cowboy hat, boots, and tan slacks. He wore a dress shirt with a bolo tie and he looked as though he had just ridden his pony in from Texas. He carried a leather suitcase. The cowboy wore a white hat, which meant he was a Good Guy.

Howie was mystified. Though this wasn't Joe, a second camera followed him into the lobby and down a hallway toward an indoor pool. The hotel had numerous cameras and the view kept switching as he was passed from one to the next.

On the bottom of the screen, the program was still telling him that this was Joe, though it wasn't. The Texan went into a men's room halfway down the hall just before the pool area. The door closed behind him and now the camera surveillance froze. Most likely a hotel chain wouldn't want to invite a lawsuit because of cameras in the bathrooms.

Howie waited impatiently, wondering what Albuquerque hotel this could be. At the top of the screen, there was a time and date stamp as well as a series of numbers that appeared to be map coordinates. He didn't want to leave the live feed to bring up a new window, but he could use the map app on his phone to check out the coordinates. The joys of technology. He didn't want to miss the man coming out of the bathroom.

He was fiddling with his phone, trying to copy the numbers from the screen, when a different person, a young man wearing sandals and shorts came out of the bathroom. To Howie's surprise, the cameras began tracking him back down the hallway toward the lobby.

Howie had hoped to stay with the Texan. But then he realized, this *was* the Texan—in fact, this was Joe Ochoa who had just changed identities again. However he managed it, it was a clever trick. The hip thirtysomething guy in shorts looked nothing like Joe, and yet—beneath the disguise, Howie was (almost) certain it was him.

Whatever Joe was up to, he was clearly on the move. The leather suitcase was gone, but the young man in shorts carried a fairly hefty daypack. Howie watched as he walked from the hotel into the parking lot and got into a white Honda CR-V.

But where was this taking place? As the Honda backed out of its parking slot, Howie entered the final digits of the GPS coordinates into his phone.

The answer came up immediately and Howie let out a cry of surprise. Joe wasn't in Albuquerque. He was here in San Geronimo. The hotel had seemed generic to Howie, but it was more than that—it was familiar. It was the Sunset Lodge, a Best Western Motel just down the street.

Howie jumped up from his desk and went to Jack's secret stash of weapons in the safe that was behind a bookcase. Jack had been serious about guns and safes. Howie had to push a button to make the bookshelf slide open, then press a digital code on the safe. He chose a 9mm Glock, a standard police gun—not the fanciest gun in the world, but one he knew how to use.

He stuffed the gun in a daypack, swung it over his shoulder and hurried to the front room where Georgie was typing a letter into the computer.

"Georgie, I don't want to worry you, but Joe Ochoa is here in San Geronimo and he's up to something. I don't have time to explain because I don't want to lose him. He just left the Sunset Lodge traveling north. I'm going to try to follow him."

"You should call Santo, Da."

"You do that for me, Georgie. See if you can explain the situation without mentioning the surveillance app. Just tell him I'm tailing Ochoa, you don't know more than that. Everything's going to be okay, but lock the door behind me and turn on the alarm."

Chapter Twenty-Four

Howie raced up Calle Friar Romero at twice the posted speed limit, hoping the traffic gods were with him. If the Dweeb was heading north, Howie could intercept him if he hurried. This would take luck since he didn't have Buzzy's surveillance software with him on his phone, but it seemed worth a try.

He came out onto Camino Real Norte just north of town and there it was— the white Honda three cars ahead of him on the road. The traffic through the center of town had slowed Ochoa down.

Howie stayed back three cars, hoping he wouldn't be spotted. He made an unsuccessful effort to relax his shoulders. The road turned into the highway north to Colorado where the traffic thinned out. After a few miles, there was only one car between Howie and the Honda. He slowed to allow Joe to get further ahead.

There was a final stoplight and intersection where Joe could either make a right turn toward the mountains or a left to the high desert that lay to the west. Howie expected Joe to go right toward a residential neighborhood at the foot of the mountains where there were people, stores, and restaurants, but instead he turned west into the desert. There was very little in this direction but wilderness and small Spanish villages at the end of long dirt roads, villages where it felt like time had stopped a century ago. Some of the larger communities were starting to have gift shops and art galleries. New Mexico had artists and crafts people everywhere.

The Honda gained speed on the open two-lane highway, threatening to leave Howie behind. He was going nearly 70 so Joe had to be doing over 80. Wherever he was headed, he wanted to get there fast.

Howie could see the Honda only intermittently as it ducked in and out of hills and arroyos. He was at least a quarter mile behind. But the land was so open he didn't think he would lose Ochoa completely. Not until they came to the mountains that lay across the wide San Geronimo Valley to the west. Once they left the desert, it was going to be harder to keep Joe in view.

Howie concentrated on driving, making the best speed he could around the many curves. He tried to remember the last time he had taken a really good look at his tires. It was too late to think about that now, but he did anyway.

This far out there were only occasional trailers and strange make-shift buildings signifying solitary characters who didn't have much money. There was little or no water in this part of the desert, which made life hard. But it was cheap. For hermits on a budget, it was ideal.

Staying well back, Howie followed the Honda from the desert into a high hilly grassland that ran north alongside the mountains. After a few miles, Joe turned onto a side road, a narrow two-lane road that followed a creek into a V-shaped canyon.

From here, he didn't try to keep up with the Honda because he knew where it was going.

Howie recalled maybe his favorite line of poetry, T.S. Eliot: *The end of all our exploring will be to arrive where we started and know the place for the first time.*

They were on the road to Eagle Falls, where this had all begun.

***

It helped that Howie had been here before. He pulled off the highway onto a dirt vista point a few hundred yards before the parking area at the trailhead to Eagle Falls.

229

He had taken photographs from here years ago. There was a spectacular view of the high mountains that rose behind the falls.

Howie's binoculars were in the clutter of the back seat, among library books, shopping bags, and a stack of old newspapers he had been meaning to get to recycling for the past month. He took the binoculars from their case and walked toward a large boulder shaped like a giant dinosaur egg at the edge of the turn-out.

From here, Howie could look out on the parking area as well as the first few miles of the trail. The land was strewn with boulders from some prehistoric cataclysm. The trail followed the shallow river into the shadows of the narrowing canyon where it disappeared. The cliffs were straight up and down. This was nature in the rough, a dangerous land.

A wind had come up, dry as bone. Clouds were gathering in the west, darkening the summer afternoon. Howie concealed himself against the egg-shaped boulder and focused the binoculars on the parking area.

The Honda was just pulling in off the road. There were two vehicles parked on the otherwise empty gravel. Howie was startled to see that they were TV vans. One of them had a satellite dish on top. Both vans were white and they had the logo for KABB TV on the side, Albuquerque Big Boy.

The parking area wasn't large, but the Honda made an effort to park as far from the two TV vans as possible, near the split rail fence and cattle guard where the trail began.

Howie watched as the thirtysomething hiker—Joe Ochoa—got out of the car, gathered up his daypack from the backseat, and locked his car. He was in a hurry. He was about to start up the trail when a man got out of the van with the satellite dish and ran across the gravel to stop him. He tried to grab Joe by the arm but missed.

Howie couldn't hear the words but he could tell that the man from the van was shouting at Joe's back as he ran. Joe turned when he reached the head of the trail and shouted back. He was accustomed to being the boss around KABB news crews and the man from the van appeared cowed. He bowed his head with a sad expression as he watched Joe turn and jog away on the path. Probably he had instructions to stay with the two expensive TV vans.

Howie lowered his binoculars and tried to phone Santo, but there was no service. This wasn't a surprise. When Claire had hiked out to phone 911 after finding Zia's body, she'd had to drive for nearly fifteen minutes before getting service. But you never knew in New Mexico when a magic signal might drift your way.

"Damn!" said Howie.

He was starting to get it. KABB was about to do some heartbreak journalism, the kind local viewers love, a segment on Zia's death, the suicide of a photogenic teenager, perhaps connecting her death to newsworthy trends and statistics.

Maybe even Mikaela was here, the distraught mother. And whatever she was about to disclose, Joe was here to stop her.

Howie wasn't sure about any of this but he rushed back to his car and drove the final half mile to the parking area. He took the time to change from sandals into hiking boots because he knew he wouldn't stand a chance otherwise. He dug around the back seat, checked his daypack to make sure it had a bottle of water, sweater, rain shell, and the Glock.

He ran quickly at first, but settled into a more sustainable jog as he crossed the cattle guard and set out on the Eagle Falls trail trying to catch up.

***

Howie ran.

The first two miles of the trail were flat and straight as they followed the river. It was a shallow river, less than twenty feet across.

He had never been much of a jogger. Running jarred his sedentary nature. However, he wasn't in terrible shape, thanks mostly to skiing and strenuous building projects he had been doing over the last several years.

It took him a few minutes to get into a rhythm, but gradually he found his stride. He could see Joe up ahead on the trail but he was a good distance away and gaining. As Howie watched, Joe disappeared into the twists of the box canyon that led to the falls. The canyon appeared to gobble him up.

Howie had to pay attention to the trail because it was uneven. The last mile was steep as it climbed into the canyon. The sound of tumbling water grew louder as he came around the final stretch of the trail. He remembered this place well, the river on his left, the cliff on the right. It was where Claire had first seen Zia's body on the shore.

Howie stopped abruptly when he saw the TV crew on the rocky beach beneath him. They were a few hundred feet upriver closer to the falls, almost exactly where he had pulled Zia from the water. There were three men with cameras and sound equipment, but the central figure was Mikaela McFadden. She was holding a microphone, dressed in a tan hiking outfit that looked like it had come from a store window. They weren't filming at the moment. She and the crew were gathered in a discussion.

Howie hugged the side of the trail gulping air, working to get his breath back. The altitude here was well above 8000 feet and he had been jogging a long way. He didn't want to think about his left ankle, which was starting to throb. An old ski injury.

Mikaela and her crew hadn't noticed Howie. They were below him and they weren't looking up. He couldn't see any sign of Joe Ochoa.

Howie stood very still, hoping he blended in with the rock, wishing he wasn't breathing so hard. With luck the constant roar of the falls had covered any sound of him. But that was hard to say. Sound played weird tricks in a box canyon. The V-shaped end of the canyon created an amphitheater effect and as Howie's breathing grew quieter, patches of what Mikaela was saying drifted his way.

"No, no, I don't want to overdub in the studio, I want live sound, I want this to be real . . . do you understand—*raw!* The grief of a mother betrayed by a man she thought was her friend—"

"Mikaela, the waterfall is just too loud," said one of the men. "I can't dub it out. If you want live sound you'll have to shout."

"Okay, I'll fucking shout. Any more questions?" she demanded. Howie was glad she wasn't *his* boss.

"We need more light," said another man. "I can use a reflector."

"Okay, but I don't want it to look staged."

"I can do real, Mikaela. Trust me. It'll be cinèma vèritè."

"All right! Now everybody shut the fuck up. I need to prepare my inner self."

Mikaela was going for an Academy Award. Neither of the three crew members dared to say a word as their boss prepared her inner self.

Howie was right. It appeared that Mikaela was about to do a tearful human interest segment at the place of her daughter's death, milking it for all it was worth. It was crass exploitation. He wondered how far she was going to go with telling the truth.

Unfortunately, he lost the rest of the conversation. Either the wind had changed or they had begun to speak in softer voices. He never heard about the man who had betrayed her.

Howie still could see no sign of Joe. He hadn't seen Joe for at least ten minutes, not since Joe had disappeared into the canyon. Howie scanned the scree and fallen boulders by the edge of the cliff. There were plenty of places to hide in this tortured landscape. He figured Joe had to be somewhere in the scree which angled upward and was only forty or fifty feet wide. At the far edge of the scree, the cliff shot straight up to places only an eagle could reach.

Howie heard a sound. It was a footstep, only a few feet away. He froze and hoped he couldn't be seen. He was in the shade, fortunately. This time of afternoon, the cliffs cut off the sun and cast the canyon into a deep shadow.

There was a louder crunch of footsteps and Joe came stepping down from where he had been hiding above him in the scree. He was a spidery, goat-like figure who clearly was at home in this landscape. But he hadn't seen Howie. He stood upriver on the trail only a dozen feet away with his back to Howie. In his right hand he held a semi-automatic pistol behind his back, barrel pointed to the ground, hidden from the TV crew below. He was staring at the group on the beach like a bird of prey about to swoop down and make a kill.

"Mikaela, you crazy bitch!" he shouted in a high voice. "You goddamn crazy bitch, I'm not going to let you ruin my life!"

Mikaela and the three men looked up with startled faces to the trail where Joe stood screaming, out of control.

Howie was already in motion. He saw what was about to happen. He moved as silently as he could. One foot after another, he made his way along the trail toward Joe, whose attention was focused on the beach below.

Joe twitched, the tiniest movement. The semi-automatic he held in his right hand was in motion. He was about to shoot.

Howie threw himself forward in a flying tackle, grabbing Joe from behind just as he began firing. The shots were loud, echoing in the canyon, but Howie's tackle had made the gun wobble and the bullets flew wildly into the air.

Howie had a grip on Joe but he was slippery and struggled violently to get free. Kicking and punching, they rolled together off the trail and down the slope toward the river. They bounced for nearly ten feet until they rolled to a stop against a prickly bush.

Every inch of Howie hurt. But somehow he had landed on top. It was sheer luck, heads or tails. They had rolled down the steep slope together, but Joe had ended up beneath him and Howie had the advantage.

It took him a moment to understand that Joe was no longer in a condition to fight. He disentangled himself and managed to get to his feet. Joe was on his back a few feet from the river. He was alive, breathing in raspy bursts, but badly hurt. Howie was bleeding in several places and his ribs hurt, but Joe had taken the brunt of the fall.

Howie picked up the semi-automatic from the ground, a heavy black gun. He was standing with it when Mikaela appeared charging along the beach. She was followed close behind by her three-men crew.

"I don't believe it! It's Howard Moon Deer!" she cried wrathfully. "What are you doing here? My God, what have you done to Joe?"

"He was about to shoot you, Mikaela. This is his gun."

Mikaela put her hand on her heart and couldn't speak for a second. Howie saw the knowledge in her eyes that she had come close to dying. But her expression hardened and she smiled slightly.

"Moon Deer, for God's sake! You've beat up my weatherman!" she spat out.

"I've kept you alive," he answered.

"It doesn't look that way to me. It looks like you nearly killed him! Now, put that gun down. I should warn you, you're on TV, bub! Everything you do from here on out is being recorded."

Howie hadn't expected gratitude from Mikaela, but this was unexpected aggravation. He put the pistol on the ground. He could see one of the men behind her with a portable camera on his shoulder, the lens pointing his way.

"For what it's worth, I've stopped a shooting," he told the camera. "Now, I'm going to hike to my car and find cell service and call for help. Joe needs an ambulance."

"You're not going anywhere," Mikaela said dramatically, posing a little, knowing she was on camera. "I'm sending one of my people to get the cops. You're going to pay for this, Moon Deer! You're done!"

Chapter Twenty-Five

On Saturday night, Georgie arrived at the El Morocco Restaurant at ten minutes past eight, deliberately late. She was wearing jeans and a fleece jacket in case they ate outside.

She had debated over her outfit, wondering if Jean-Claude would find her un-chic. She looked like something that had wandered in from the woods. *Hell with it!* she decided. *I've got only one dress and I'm not wearing it twice. If he doesn't like me in jeans and fleece, he can screw himself!*

Georgie entered the El Morocco in a combative mood. The restaurant was run by a Palestinian family who had come to New Mexico after Israeli bulldozers destroyed their home in the West Bank.

Dr. Aale Said, a gastroenterologist, the head of the family, fled to Marrakech for several years where he reinvented himself as a chef. He promoted what he called pan-Arabic cuisine. Here in New Mexico, he had turned an old Spanish adobe into an Arab restaurant with very little trouble. Both architectures had the same roots, the adobe buildings and rounded arches of North Africa. Dr. Said only needed to convince his American customers to take off their shoes and sit on couches and pillows rather than chairs.

Said's wife led Georgie through the main dining room to the terrace outside. She found Jean-Claude on a nest of cushions at a low table in a kind of three-sided Bedouin tent that was lit only by candle lanterns. Outdoor heaters helped the illusion that they were in North Africa rather than the Southern Rockies.

Jean-Claude struggled to rise from the cushions but fell back with a laugh. Georgie joined him, lowering herself onto her hands and knees to crawl into the nest. She wasn't entirely relaxed to find herself sitting next to Jean-Claude on what was essentially a bed.

"They've rather overdone the atmosphere here," he told her. "But the food is excellent. Edward brought me here the other night."

"Did he? So you and Edward go carousing at night?"

"I wouldn't call it carousing. But Edward likes to get out of the house. Catherine has begun to be a problem."

"I've met her. I can vouch for the fact that she's a problem."

"Really? I'd like to hear about that. But first, why don't we order drinks and pu-pu's?"

"Pu-pu's?"

"It's Hawaiian for appetizer. I lived on Maui for a time. You would like it there."

"I'm not sure I would," she told him. "I'm a northern girl. I grew up in Scotland. I like a cold and stormy sea."

Georgie was glad to chat about Hawaii. She wanted to get the feel of Jean-Claude before she hit him with questions. Charming as he was, she wanted to know how Catherine had learned that Jean-Claude had showed her a photo of *America Girl*. As for Zia, Georgie assumed he was innocent of seducing a teenage girl. But she needed to be sure.

They ordered mango daiquiris and an assortment of North African appetizers. Jean-Claude was freshly shaved and dressed casually— tastefully—in khaki pants, leather sandals, and a peasanty white shirt with the cuffs rolled up. As always, he was immaculately Continental. He looked as though he could discuss Existentialism as easily as punk rock, and do it in three languages. He was everything she both loved and hated about European culture.

Georgie reminded herself not to get too comfortable on the cushions.

"So how is private eye-ing?" he asked with a sympathetic smile.

"You're laughing at me. But it's a serious thing, you know."

"I only think it's a little funny that you earned a degree at Cambridge and here you are in the mountains working as a gumshoe. Girls like you are more easily found as interns in Hollywood or non-profits in Madagascar."

"I would hate being an intern in an office!" she told him. "I belong in the mountains and I love it here. As it happens, working in a private detective agency has been fascinating. It's a rare opportunity to see life at its best and worst, usually in some extreme."

"Oh, I believe it. Like every good Frenchman, I grew up on Maigret and Tin Tin. I understand the attraction of crime. A good detective is an observer of human nature. To be a great detective like Tin Tin, you must be a philosopher."

Georgie laughed. All the French she knew, both men and women—students mostly—were gonzo about philosophy.

"Actually, Jean-Claude, from what I've seen, it's mostly a matter of problem solving. Have you ever played Wordle?" she asked solemnly.

"Wordle? This is the New York Times game?"

"It is. You have six tries to guess a five-letter word, and it's obsessive. Addictive, I'd say. If you're a problem-solving sort of person, a curious person, you can't stop until you figure it out. That's what it's like as a detective. I've seen this with both my father and Jack. Once they're hooked on a case, they're gone."

"So this is all mental, this detecting?"

"And ego, of course. It's competitive, you against an opponent. People who play competitive games like to win."

"And you have this obsession, too?"

"Not at all. I'm only the office girl. My Da doesn't want me to get too involved in the actual case work."

"Naturally, he wishes to protect you. But you have been doing some private eye-ing anyway, haven't you? You went to visit that poor girl, Uma Rothenstein, the other day. I can't believe that was a social call. You've been snooping around the Rothenstein family."

"Why do you call Uma a poor girl?"

"Because she's pathetically lonely and sad. And not very bright. That's the real problem. A smart person can be lonely and sad but still worth knowing. A dull melancholy person is someone to avoid."

"You're a snob, Jean-Claude!"

He laughed. "No, I don't think I am. I certainly don't care about money or social position. I do like to spend my time with people who have good taste in music and art and conversation, those I find interesting. That's why I'm very happy to be having dinner with you tonight."

Georgie took the last sip of her mango daiquiri and shook her head.

"I have no taste at all," she told him. "If you're looking for someone with culture, I'm the wrong date. I've had it with art and music and fancy people. Most days I just want to get into my oldest clothes and walk out into the mountains and live with the animals."

"Really? This is true?"

"Well, not entirely," she admitted. She shook her head, thinking of all her contradictions. "I guess I like my creature comforts too."

He leaned closer. "So, why were you snooping around Uma Rothenstein? You must have had a reason to go see her?"

"Ah, you want information!" She sat up to put further distance between them. "Okay, but you tell me first. Why has Catherine become a problem for the great Edward Rothenstein?"

"Why? Surely you know the reason. He likes young women. Catherine was that sort of young woman herself at one time, but that was twenty years ago. She's the classic scorned woman."

"She grew older, that's all!" Georgie was outraged at the idea of older men ditching their longtime mates for younger women. She'd had older married men come on to her so she knew what these men were like. They were pathetically needy, when push came to shove (so to speak). It was yucky.

"Edward is quite taken with you, Georgie. You know that, don't you?" Jean-Claude said.

"Edward Rothenstein is a dinosaur, a misogynist relic!" she declared. "They should stuff him and put him in a museum! I'm sorry, but I'm not looking for some creepy old Don Juan, thank you very much! When you and Edward go out drinking, I wonder what you fellows talk about? Tits and ass? Your sexual conquests?"

"Georgie, I am not like that!" he said sternly. "You're taking me for a stereotype, something I'm not. I would be bored with a woman who was not my equal in every way. As for Edward, it's my job right now to deal with him. That's my only involvement."

"For the Guggenheim?"

"Yes, exactly that. I'm hoping to curate a seriously good exhibit of Edward's work. For the Guggenheim."

"That's good. I like the Guggenheim. But I have some questions for you," she said firmly.

"Yes, please! Ask what you like."

"What is it about this painting, *America Girl*, that's starting to feel wrong? I got waylaid by Catherine yesterday. She tried to take my phone—we wrestled over it, actually. I just barely got away! She thought I had a copy of the photo you showed me. Jean-Claude, you need to tell me why Catherine is in such a tizzy about *America Girl*. And how she knew you showed it to me."

He didn't answer right away. He shook his head. "I'm sorry to involve you in this, Georgie. I shouldn't have shown you the painting. I needed to know if the painting really was of Zia McFadden. If so, the exhibit was in trouble. I told you that. I wanted your thoughts. But it was wrong to involve you."

"I don't mind being involved," said Georgie. "But I do mind not knowing the truth. *You* should have recognized Zia in that painting, you didn't need me. You knew Zia, you had met her. From what I hear, you flirted with her!"

Jean-Claude shook his head. "I'm sorry if she mistook my polite manner as flirting. It wasn't."

"But how did Catherine know you had taken a picture of *America Girl*?"

"She found it on my phone. She stole my phone when I was taking a shower."

"Oh, really?"

"No, it's nothing like that. It's complicated, Georgie."

"I don't care if it's complicated," she said. "Tell me!"

Jean-Claude didn't look happy. There was a strained expression on his face. But he nodded.

"All right, I will tell you everything," he promised. "From now on, there will only be truth between us."

Georgie smiled but she was suspicious. Jean-Claude was too good to be true. She didn't believe a word he said.

***

Howie didn't get home until three in the morning. He felt worse than a zombie, brain dead, body bruised, exhausted. Fortunately, he had managed to phone Claire at ten last night to say the Department of Homeland Security had detained him—temporarily, he hoped—and he would be late. He would explain when he got home.

242

He found her awake, downstairs in the living area. She greeted him with a worried look on her face.

"Howie, you look awful! How were you able to drive?"

"I'm not sure," he admitted, sinking down upon the small couch.

Claire came up behind him and massaged his neck and shoulders. She was good at body work.

"Ahhhh," he moaned.

"Don't try to talk."

"I won't. This case keeps getting crazier and I don't know what to think anymore."

"Then don't think. Relax, Howie. Let your thoughts drift into the clouds and slowly . . . slowly blow away."

"They're blowing," he told her. Nevertheless, barely a minute passed before he spoke again.

"Mikaela showed up at Eagle Falls with a TV crew to do a segment about her daughter. I presumed it was going to be a weepy piece about teen suicide, but she had something more in mind. She was about to turn on her boyfriend. And do it in a way that would make KABB the most watched station in the state. Mikaela's a woman who keeps her eye on the bottom line. My guess is she understood that Joe's secret sex life was about to come out anyway so her only option was to get ahead of it and pretend outrage. Mothers united against horny boyfriends, and how shocked she was—absolutely shocked!—when she found out he was messing with her daughter. Somehow Joe discovered what she was planning and he tried to stop her."

"Did he?" Claire asked. "Did he stop her?"

"No. That was me. I stopped him."

"Oh, Howie! I wish you didn't always get into these situations!"

"But that was only the start. After I got Joe tied up, Mikaela sent one of her crew to call the cops. I had a lot of explaining to do. First I had to deal with BLM rangers, then the Sheriffs, and then—believe it or not—Homeland Security. They were the worst of the lot. And you'll never guess what they wanted. Information about Buzzy."

"Buzzy? Why would they care about Buzzy?"

Howie snorted a kind of laugh. "Don't get me started! You don't want to know, Claire, you really don't. Buzzy, as usual, has gone off the rails. DHS wanted to know every detail of my relationship with him and everything he did and said when he came for his mother's funeral."

"I hope you mentioned that you were Buzzy's Big Brother when he was in the Fifth Grade."

"I did, Claire. I was hoping to show what a decent all-American Indian I was. But it didn't go over very well. There were two DHS agents, a man and a woman, and they acted like I was some kind of co-conspirator—though a co-conspirator to what, they refused to say. From what I could gather, Buzzy's on the run and he took something with him, something important. He's gone rogue . . ."

Howie would have continued but he realized that Claire had stopped listening. She had faded into her thoughts.

"Claire, what is it?"

She stopped rubbing his neck and came around to sit opposite him.

"Howie, I have something to tell you, but I don't want you to worry. You have to promise me in advance."

"I'll try, Claire. What should I not worry about?"

"You see, I got a reply from the Minister of Culture in Spain. Franco Medina. It was sweet of him to answer so quickly. He says he knows Jean-Claude Maurot by reputation and to his knowledge he's retired and living in Argentina. He's 82 years-old, Howie. And Franco is certain there isn't any future Rothenstein exhibit planned for the Bilbao Guggenheim. As a government minister, he would have known about that."

Howie took a deep breath. "How old did Georgie say Jean-Claude is?"

"She didn't say exactly. But I got the impression he was in his mid-thirties. Howie, what's going on? Is Georgie safe?"

For Howie, after a very long day, this took a moment to fully sink in. His mind was racing. "Let me do some checking."

He went into his computer nook and googled the name Jean-Claude Maurot. There were dozens of articles about him, but Howie quickly saw that they were all five or ten years old, nothing current.

Jean-Claude, in fact, was a well-known art expert. He was known for his knowledge of Greek and Roman art in Syria and southern Turkey. Howie found a photo of Maurot that had been taken at an academic conference in Istanbul. He was a large man with unruly grey hair and a huge walrus mustache. He looked boozy, a guy who could hold forth garrulously about art after a few glasses of malt.

Claire was looking over his shoulder at the screen.

"No, that can't be the person Georgie described," she said. "Maybe there are two Jean-Claude Maurots."

"Both of them art experts?"

Howie didn't believe there could be a Jean-Claude doppelganger, one 82, the other in his mid-thirties. But if the man Georgie was having dinner with wasn't Jean-Claude, who was he?

At 3:27, Howie looked at his watch and decided to give Georgie a call despite the hour.

She didn't answer. His call got routed to voicemail.

"Hi, Georgie—you're probably sleeping. Sorry to call this late. Whenever you get this message, call me back. It's important."

He pressed the red circle, ending the message.

He sat full of worry, despite his promise to Claire. He decided to phone Jack. It didn't matter what time it was, Jack never slept anyway.

Chapter Twenty-Six

The moon rose over the San Geronimo Plaza, a fat crescent in the summer night. Georgie thought it was magnificent.

From the rooftop terrace of the El Morocco, she could hear music and distant laughter. The moonlight silhouetted the high mountain peaks only a few miles east of town. The night was so full of mystery and beauty, she wanted to sink back into the cushions and give in to the languid mood of romance.

But she didn't.

"You have to understand, Georgie," Jean-Claude was telling her, "there are daily dramas between Edward and Catherine. It's awful to be trapped with a couple who are fighting. But I'm their house guest so I have to put up with it. If it weren't for my work, I would be out of there in an instant."

"Your work is that important to you?"

"Well, it is, Georgie," he said. "I don't even think of it as work. Art is my passion."

Georgie was inclined to like men who had a passion. Especially if it was about art. During her visits to London, she had spent hours in the National Gallery and the Tate, soaking it in. She had worn out poor Ashton, who had finally given up and waited in a pub down the street while she spent the better part of an afternoon at the Victoria and Albert. She had hundreds of questions she'd like to ask about what it's like to work for a great museum.

"How did the exhibit for the Guggenheim come about?" she asked.

"Slowly," he answered. "Last autumn I began talking with people I know in Bilbao about a possible Rothenstein exhibit and they were interested. So I contacted Edward and I came to see him here in New

Mexico in December. Unfortunately, I discovered it was Catherine I needed to deal with. She's his manager, you know. She takes care of the business side of his career. Edward isn't interested in any of that. All he wants to do is paint."

Paint and fuck, Georgie might have added. But she left it unsaid.

"Is Catherine good at business?"

"Not particularly. She's too greedy. At first she wasn't interested in a museum exhibit because she didn't see any immediate money from it. She likes her money fast. But I convinced her that the prestige of a Bilbao exhibit would raise the price of Edward's work and the money would come soon enough. As soon as she understood the cash potential, she was on board. But now she hounds me wanting to know every detail of what I'm doing. She wants to be in charge."

"She bosses you around?"

"It's not that exactly. She's devious and suspicious that somehow I'm going to steal from her. She protects Edward's paintings like they were the Crown Jewels."

"Well, they are, aren't they? How much are his paintings worth?"

"The reality? He's at the high end of medium. But not at the top. His canvases sell in the six figures, not seven—and low six figures, at that. Catherine has her heart set on improving this situation."

"So you sold her on the idea that an exhibit in Bilbao would make her rich?"

"Richer. They're not exactly impoverished now. But yes, I played on her greed in order to get her cooperation." He smiled boyishly, a smile that erased several years from his face. "Does it shock you that I use diplomacy to get an exhibit like this together? Believe me, dealing with artists' wives is the easy part of my job. After New Mexico, I need to go to New York to sweet-talk a very good Rothenstein canvas from the living room of a billionaire. *That's* going to be a challenge. I'll need to appeal to his ego—make him feel that he won't only be remembered as a brutal hedge fund manager, but as a grand patron of the arts."

Georgie laughed. "I'm sure you'll have that canvas from him in the wink of an eye! But let's get back to why Catherine thought I had *America Girl* on my phone."

"Yes, off course. I'm glad to explain this to you. When I first got to San Geronimo, Catherine made me sign a contract to play by her rules. I couldn't continue without her consent. There were all sorts of confidential agreements I needed to accept. That's not unusual in my line of work, but she went overboard. She demanded the right to do a spot check on my phone and laptop any time she liked. I wasn't to take photographs of any painting or drawing without her specific consent in writing. She was obsessed with her proprietorial rights. It's all about money, of course. As I said, she's greedy. Greed is one of the Seven Deadly Sins, you know. I think it's second on the list. Catherine Rothenstein personifies it."

"It's sin number three, actually," she told him. "Greed comes after Gluttony but before Sloth."

"You're kidding? You know that? And where is Lust on the list?"

"Lust is number one, Jean-Claude," she told him. "I think you know that. Lust leads the pack."

Jean-Claude smiled. "What a pity! Here, nature gives us this delicious gift—that for a few moments you can have absolute bliss—and then we have to go and call it a sin."

"I was brought up with religion. My adoptive parents were Catholic. I studied the medieval church my second year at university. Do you know all seven of the sins? They're Lust, Gluttony, Greed, Sloth, Wrath, Envy, Pride. It's a list worth thinking about. For myself, I think the first six sum up the downside of humanity. But number seven, Pride—for me that's a virtue."

8

Jean-Claude regarded her intently.

"So, go on," she told him, sitting straighter.

"Well, Catherine did a spot check on me as promised, and it came at a bad time. I was just coming out of the shower with a towel around my waist and I found her sitting on my bed with my laptop. Thinking I had privacy, I'd left the laptop open on the bed with what I had been reading last on the screen, the *Financial Times*. My phone was nearby, and I had left that on as well. It didn't take Catherine long to find the painting on both devices and she was furious. I tried to reason with her. I told her the truth, that I needed to know if Zia had committed suicide in any way that was related to Edward. If so, I might have to cancel the exhibit. She kept at me until I deleted the photo from both devices. She examined the laptop and the phone for a long time afterwards to make sure they were really gone."

"You don't have a back-up?"

"Theoretically, no."

"Hmm," said Georgie. "Theoretically?"

"I'm not going to answer that. In any case, I'm starting to think it may be best to let this exhibit go. Except for meeting you, I'm starting to think it's cursed. But I want to assure you, Georgie, I did not tell Catherine that I had showed you the painting. She guessed that on her own."

"But how could she guess it?"

"She's devious, Georgie. I'm not sure she's smart, but she's very clever. She knows you and your father are investigating this case, and this has made her nervous. Then Uma saw us together the night we had dinner at the Blue Moon. Catherine made her suppositions from there. She not the sort of person to take chances."

"*Uma* saw us?" Georgie frowned. She found this somehow disturbing, though she couldn't say why.

"I believe Uma hangs out at night with friends down the street in the Plaza," he said.

"Okay, Jean-Claude, my last question," Georgie said. "Tell me about your relationship with Zia."

"It wasn't a relationship, Georgie. I met her on my June visit. Zia was introduced as Uma's school friend and it was obvious that Edward was smitten."

"With a forty year age difference between them? She could have been his granddaughter!"

"Famous artists attract young women, Georgie."

"Uma seems to think *you* were the person Zia was after."

"That isn't true. Listen to me, please. Uma isn't someone you should rely on to tell the truth. She's a complicated girl and I don't think she means you well."

Georgie believed him. After the episode at the church, she didn't trust Uma either.

"Now, please listen to me. Zia was very pretty, and of course I noticed her more than I let on the other night," Jean-Claude admitted. "Men notice pretty women. It's how evolutionary biology has made us."

"Oh, you're blaming this on evolutionary biology?"

"It's true, I'm guilty of occasional bursts of lust. But I don't lust for young girls like Zia. I liked her, in fact. From what I saw of Zia—not much—she was appealing and sweet. But unformed. Maybe she would have become someone interesting a decade from now, after a bit of heartbreak and challenge. Life makes people interesting if they let it. Zia was still a child and I prefer adults."

"You know, of course, I'm only four years older than Zia was when she died?" Georgie asked.

"And a hundred times smarter!" Jean-Claude gave her one of his deeper looks. "Georgie, you are not a child. You are a woman. And I'm thirty-seven, only sixteen years older. Is that such a gulf?"

"I'm not sure," said Georgie speculatively. "If we got married, you would be 80 years old when I'm 64. I would have to become your nurse."

"80 years old!" He laughed. "Well, that's a long way off, I hope. The world may end before then."

"Do you think so?"

"The world could end tonight," he told her.

"So eat, drink, and be merry?"

"Be merry, I'd say. At the very least. And if there's eating and drinking . . . who's to say no?"

As the night went on, their conversation drifted away from the Rothensteins and Zia McFadden. There were more interesting things to discuss—books, movies, travel, politics, ideas, the world. Beneath the conversation—beneath the words—Georgie felt a tingle of electricity passing back and forth between them. This was something that she had not experienced for such a long time that she didn't recognize it at first. There was a magnetic disturbance between them, sparkly electrons doing a chorus of high kicks.

They stretched their dinner out so that the wait staff were beginning to clean up around them.

Feeling very relaxed, she told him stories of her childhood in Scotland and her life here in San Geronimo, how she loved to sleep outdoors in her Da's forest, listening to the trees rustle and the calls and scratchings of the wild animals.

"You're a bit wild," he told her. "Like the land."

"Yes, that's me," she answered.

Leaning closer, he kissed her softly on the lips. It was more the promise of a kiss than a real kiss.

"Come stay with me tonight," he whispered. "I'm more than a little in love with you, and I never want this night to end."

No, no, no! said the remaining shred of Georgie's brain.

While her body and soul shouted *yes, yes, yes!*

***

On Saturday night, after dinner—after Jack and Emma had said goodnight to one another—Jack retired to his office and researched a matter that had caught his curiosity.

It was the Dweeb. Jack had been the one to come up with the idea of making trouble between Joe and Mikaela. But Howie and Georgie had decided not to go through with it. Jack had spoken with Howie earlier that morning and he had admitted that he and Georgie had qualms and didn't want to go that route. Yet Joe and Mikaela had a falling out anyway. Joe had showed up at Eagle Falls desperate to stop her. There was something else going on here that he didn't know about.

He had the answer after less than an hour of research. He had to go onto the dark web to do this, but that wasn't a problem, thanks to Buzzy. He found a site that called itself Larky Quarky that specialized in media gossip. The news from Larky Quarky was that Joe Ochoa had received an offer from CNN to move to Atlanta and go national, but Mikaela refused to release Joe from his contract at KABB. Joe was the reason she had the Number One Ten O'Clock News and she didn't want to let him go. This was complicated by the fact that Mikaela's feelings were hurt. Joe and Mikaela were lovers and he was leaving her. According to the article, this had been simmering for more than a month and it was said that Mikaela was furious.

Jack wasn't sure how much to trust Larky Quarky, but he found this particular gossip credible. It explained Howie's adventure yesterday at Eagle Falls. Joe's anger had been simmering for weeks. Mikaela had become his worst enemy and if he allowed her to tape her segment at Eagle Falls, it would destroy him. There would be no spot on family friendly television anywhere for a sex offender.

Jack was glad to understand this situation better, but he still felt he was missing something. He lay down to sleep around midnight, but his thoughts were restless and inclusive and kept him awake. Ironically, he had finally fallen asleep at 3:31 in the morning when Howie phoned.

He had been having a shallow dream that was half-fiction, half real life. In the dream, he was about to solve the Zia Case, but just as the mystery was about to reveal itself—who killed Zia—the phone woke him up.

It was Howie's ring. Jack's phone was programmed so that only Emma, Santo, and Howie could reach him no matter what time it was.

"God damnit, Howie! I almost had it figured out!" he shouted at the ceiling. "And you've ruined it! You destroyed my chain of thought and now it's gone for good!"

Howie didn't understand what Jack was talking about, and didn't care. "Jack, listen, I'm worried about Georgie. I want you to phone Santo and get him to look for her."

"*Now?* At what . . . 3:30 in the morning?"

"I know it's a lot to ask. But he'll do it if you ask."

Jack was still half in his dream. He forced himself to pay attention. "What's going on with Georgie?"

"Jack, she went out on a date with some French man who's not who he claims he is. He's a fraud and I can't reach her on her phone. With all the craziness going on, I'm not going to be able to relax until I find her."

"Okay, Howie, I like Georgie, too. But she's on a date, for chris-sake—not on a safari in Africa! She's a very capable young woman old enough to go on dates without her father going ballistic."

"I'm not ballistic. Let me explain and you'll understand," Howie said, barely patient.

Jack listened as Howie explained how Jean-Claude Maurot—a slithery individual who oozed Gallic charm (Howie's version)—had pretended to Georgie that he was here in San Geronimo arranging an exhibit of Edward Rothenstein's art at the Bilbao Guggenheim in Spain, but it was all a lie. Claire had contacted the Spanish Minister of Culture who said that Jean-Claude, the well-known art expert, was 82 years old and the man Georgie had dinner with certainly wasn't him. Nor was there any future Rothenstein exhibit scheduled for the Guggenheim.

Jack interrupted from time to time. "Slow down, Howie . . . tell me again. Jean-Claude Maurot . . . you say she had dinner with him . . . . Howie, listen to me, we'll find Georgie. The whole thing is probably a mix-up of some kind. And if anyone can deal with a snake-charmer sleaze, it's Georgie . . ."

But suddenly the dream answer that he had been trying to find, the epiphany, came to him. Jack saw with startling clarity how upside down he had been.

His assumption was that Zia McFadden was the central figure, around which all other events revolved. She had seen something, or knew something, that had made her a target. Jack had understood this much from the start. But he saw now that both he and Howie had been looking at this from the wrong angle.

This wasn't about Zia's relationship with her mother, nor the horny weatherman in Albuquerque. It had nothing to do with Sophia, Charles McFadden's first wife. This was about Zia's life in San Geronimo.

In San Geronimo, Zia had become friends with Uma Rothenstein and involved with her father. Jack didn't know everything yet, but he was close. If he was right, this was about more than an inappropriate relation between Edward Rothenstein and the girl. When paintings were worth hundreds of thousands of dollars, crime happens. In his experience, that kind of exaggerated money caused problems.

Jack decided Howie was absolutely right to worry. There was a killer nearby who wouldn't hesitate to kill again. Georgie was in danger.

"Okay, okay, Howie, calm down, I got it," Jack said. "I think you're right. It would be good to make sure Georgie's safe. Let's at least find out where she is. Beyond that, it's not our business. I'll wake Santo. I'll explain it to him."

"Thanks, Jack."

"Don't bother. Just come into town and pick me up—"

"Jack, I can't do that. You know I can't."

"Yes, you can. And make sure you bring a gun."

Chapter Twenty-Seven

Georgie woke up in a strange bed, in a dark room, with the moon touching the curtains with a white triangle of light.

The moonlight was reassuring, but she felt disoriented. It was 4:27 according to her phone on the bedside table. The left side of the bed was empty. She wasn't sure what had woken her.

Georgie yawned and stretched luxuriously. If someone had asked her a month ago, she would have told them that sex wasn't worth the trouble. Men always turned out to be so disappointing.

Well, maybe not all of them. There were one or two . . .

But tonight . . . tonight her world had changed. Every muscle of her body tingled. Making love with Jean-Claude had been a revelation. He was entirely masculine, confident, sure—not like the sensitive Cambridge boys with their hesitant fingers. But he was also gentle in just the right measure. The second time they made love was even better than the first.

Lying in his arms, every pore as unguarded as an oyster on a half shell, she had babbled like a fool. She ended up telling him everything she knew about the case, the death of Zia McFadden. There was such intimacy between them—two beings who had joined—that she was completely candid. She recounted her father's theory that it was the weatherman, Joe Ochoa, who was desperate to hide his sexual assault of Zia. She told him her own part as well, how she had gone to Uma in order to understand Zia better, and to discover what had possessed her to model naked for Edward Rothenstein.

Jean-Claude had listened intently, smoking a cigarette as he lay languidly on his back beneath the covers, his head on the pillow, his shoulders and chest bare. He laughed, he made her feel like the wittiest, smartest woman on the planet. Georgie smoked a cigarette too, though she had given up cigarettes two years ago. It was incredible to find a man who understood her so well, especially after two bottles of champagne. Georgie's memory of last night glowed in a kind of bubbly fizz.

But now, alone in bed, the digital clock at 4:38, Georgie wondered if she had said too much. She knew Jean-Claude was on her side. They had been joined in fire and intimacy. Nevertheless, she knew she should have kept her mouth shut.

And where was he?

***

The guest house on the Rothenstein property was both simple and luxurious. It consisted of a single room with adobe walls—real adobe, flecked with straw—that was spacious and modern in a style that Howie liked to describe as Southwest for Gringos. Every object in the room was perfect, the lamps, the tables, the sheets, the blankets, everything. The windows that covered the entire front face of the room were closed off with ceiling-to-floor straw-colored curtains that looked like an entire tribe in the Peruvian Andes had spent a year weaving them.

There was a kitchen nook, a stylish sofa facing a smallish TV screen, a place to charge your computer, all the comforts of a first class hotel. But the room lacked personality. To Georgie, it was expensively anonymous. Lying in bed, naked, alone, Georgie had the unpleasant suspicion that she was not the first woman who had been brought here for sex.

There were two Rothenstein paintings on the walls facing the bed. They were from Edward's early period, bands of colors that had a subtle radiance to them. They weren't quite abstract. If you studied the canvases, you could see the painting on the right was the ocean at dawn, the one on the left, the ocean at sunset. It was the radiance of the color that had made Edward well-known.

Georgie got out of bed and padded barefoot to the front window. She poked her head out the side of the curtain but she could see nothing. The first light of dawn was still more than half an hour away.

It seemed odd that Jean-Claude should be gone at this hour. Georgie saw a tan suede jacket on a hook by the door that looked like something a stylish man-about-town might wear in Paris or New York, but not New Mexico. It smelled very slightly of Jean-Claude, a scent that would be hard to describe but which she had already come to know. She slipped it on, zipped up the front, and stepped outside onto a flag-stone patio.

The air was cool and fresh and clear. An infinity of stars sparkled in the three-dimensional darkness overhead. She was naked beneath Jean-Claude's jacket which gave her a shivery sense of the immensity of the universe. The faint sound of a human voice floated her way, too distant to make out the words. As her eyes became accustomed to the dark, she saw that there were two men on the meadow across from the guest house a few hundred feet away. Georgie could see them only in silhouette, indistinct shapes. They appeared to be having an animated conversation. She was almost certain the figures were Jean-Claude and Edward Rothenstein. But why would they be meeting outdoors at this dark hour?

It occurred to her that Edward had most likely summoned Jean-Claude. Artists were famously eccentric, after all, and he might not care about the hour if there was something he wanted to say. Georgie tried to find an innocent reason for the two men to be having a conversation at this time of night, but she couldn't find one.

She was curious, naturally. But she decided it wasn't really her business. After watching the two silhouettes for several minutes, she turned to go back inside the guest house and put her clothes on. Whatever was happening, she didn't want to be naked, and she didn't want Jean-Claude to think she was spying on him.

As she was taking off the suede jacket, she felt something flat and rectangular inside a discreetly zippered pocket in the inner lining. She knew lovers should trust one another and under normal circumstances, she would have left the rectangular object alone. But this wasn't a normal circumstance. Jean-Claude had abandoned her in the guest house for some mysterious purpose that didn't seem right.

Georgie gave in to temptation. She unzipped the inner pocket and pulled out two French passports with familiar dark red covers. The first passport had an unsmiling photo of Jean-Claude beneath the banner of the République Français. He was 43 years-old, older than she had thought—he had lied to her—and he had been born in Cahors, not Paris as he had said.

She looked at the stamps on the back pages and saw that he had travelled several times between France and the United States. But there were fewer stamps than she had imagined there might be for an international art expert, and nothing to indicate that he had ever been in Spain. Of course, EU citizens didn't need to get their passports stamped when going from one EU country to another, but still she was surprised. He had mentioned last night a visit he had made recently to Singapore—they were talking about great restaurants—but there was no Singapore stamp.

Georgie opened the second passport and her breath caught in her throat.

There was the same unsmiling photo of Jean-Claude on the signature page, but on this passport his name was Daniel Louis Fourier. The visa pages had numerous immigration stamps from Singapore, Hong Kong, Argentina, several trips to Russia, and more.

She could only conclude that this was the real passport and Daniel Louis Fourier was the man with whom she had just had fabulous sex. Georgie had to sit down on the edge of the bed to take it in.

It was at this moment that Jean-Claude—whoever he might be—came in the door. He looked at Georgie sitting naked and vulnerable on the bed, and then at his suede jacket on the floor and the two French passports in her hand.

He shook his head. "Get dressed," he told her harshly. "We must leave. Hurry!"

His voice was different. He didn't sound like the same man at all. This person was a stranger.

Georgie did what he said and hurried into her clothes. He looked away while she got dressed, but she had never felt so naked and she didn't like it.

"So Daniel," she said angrily. "Maybe you'd like to tell me who Daniel Louis Fourier is? God, I'm tired of men who lie!"

"Georgie, it's a long story and we don't have time for it now."

"I'd say we don't have time for anything further between us. So please leave. I'll walk back to town."

"You can't walk back to town."

"You bet I can! It will only take an hour or so and it will give me a chance to work off the dirty feeling I have from last night. Now, leave!"

"Georgie—"

Before he could finish a voice called from outside. It was Edward and he sounded even angrier than Georgie.

"Jean-Claude, get out here, you son of a bitch! I'm not finished with you! And bring that girl with you. You have a hell of a nerve fucking that Scottish lass in my guest house!"

Georgie blushed with mortification. She avoided looking at Daniel/Jean-Claude while she finished dressing. When she was safely in her jeans and fleece, she turned to him in order to leave him with a final withering look. But her expression turned to dismay when she saw he had a gun in his hand, a black pistol.

"Georgie, you need to trust me," he told her. "Stay inside while I sort this out. We'll talk later."

Before she could answer, he stepped outside and closed the door after himself.

Georgie sat down on the edge of the bed to think. More than anything, she wanted to get away from here. She remembered seeing that the guest house had a back door in the kitchen area to take out the trash. She might be able to escape that way.

She was deciding whether to leave, or whether there was a slim chance that Jean-Claude could be trusted, when there was a loud explosion from outside, a shotgun shot.

This was followed by two shots from a smaller gun, a pistol. And then after a pause, there was a second loud shotgun shot.

Then there was silence. Even the crickets had stopped their throbbing chorus. Georgie sat rigidly on the edge of the bed, listening intently. The silence gave no clue as to what had just happened.

She was surprised to hear someone call her name from close by.

"Georgie, we've got to get away! Come quick!"

It was Uma. She had come in through the back door so quietly that Georgie hadn't heard her.

"Uma! What are you doing here?"

"Please, there's no time for questions. We have to leave! *Right now!*"

Uma was upset. She was dressed in pajamas and slippers and looked as though she had just gotten out of bed. Georgie hesitated. The last time she had listened to Uma, she had been lured into a nasty encounter with her mother.

"Georgie, for God's sake, come with me! We've got to go. He'll kill us!"

"You need to tell me what's going on, Uma."

"It's my father! He's drunk and crazy! Now come on!"

Jean-Claude had also told her they needed to get away and Georgie was starting to think this might be good advice. Uma could show the way.

"Okay," she said. "Let's go."

They went out the back door and ran together across a field and up a hill into a grove of aspen trees.

"Don't look back!" Uma urged.

It was one of Georgie's faults that when someone told her not to do something, she often did it. She stopped and looked behind her. Edward Rothenstein was standing outside the guest house in silhouette against the grey dawn. He carried a shotgun in his arms and he was walking their way, coming after them with strange deliberate steps.

There was no sign of Jean-Claude.

Despite herself, Georgie's eyes blurred with tears as she turned to Uma and ran for her life.

Chapter Twenty-Eight

Early Sunday morning, while dawn was still a distant glow behind the mountains, Howie and Claire drove to Jack's house in town. Claire insisted on coming. She felt responsible for encouraging Georgie to date Jean-Claude and now couldn't rest until she knew Georgie was safe.

Howie was surprised to see Santo's black State Police SUV in Jack's driveway. He took it as a good sign. Jack had convinced Santo to help find Georgie.

Unfortunately, it wasn't as easy as that. Santo wanted to go through everything again. He was cautious when it came to police business. He needed to be convinced all over again that Jack and Howie were on the right side of what had become an important State Police murder investigation—the Keir Aaronson case, the only official murder. Zia's death was "under review" but still had not been declared a murder.

Jack found it interesting that Keir's murder had been so amateurish. It had been a sloppy job to knock him over the head with a classic blunt instrument, then pretend he had hanged himself from a tree and expect not to be caught. It signified an unprofessional killer.

Santo and Jack were gathered in the big old farm-style kitchen. Emma bustled about in a comfortable old robe making coffee and defrosting croissants. As they sat around the breakfast table, Howie saw that no one had gotten much sleep.

"Okay!" said Santo with forced energy. "We're all here. Jack's been filling me in on Georgie's disappearance. Though I can't say it meets any standard of disappearance I've ever seen. Here's the facts, boys and girls. Georgie went out to dinner with a guy and she went home with him. I'm sorry, Howie, but it happens. She's an adult. Let me break it to you."

"But her date Jean-Claude isn't who he says he is," Howie insisted. "He's a fraud."

"Oh, yeah? And what fraud is he doing?"

"He passed himself off as someone he wasn't and he lied about curating a Rothenstein exhibit in Spain."

"Then bad on him. But there's no law against lying. These days it's done by the best people." Santo looked at his watch. "And I can't officially declare Georgie missing, Howie. Georgie has a right to her privacy."

"People have died, Santo!"

"Let me interrupt," said Jack decisively from his wheelchair. He raised his hand.

"This is a very simple case," he told them. "In fact, two simple cases. Case number one takes place in Albuquerque with Zia, her mother, and the Dweeb coming into her bedroom. Joe Ochoa, the Dweeb, has a lot to protect and so kills Zia, Keir, then tried to kill our client . . . blah, blah, blah!"

"What do you mean, blah, blah, blah?" demanded Santo.

"Listen to me. That's case number one. But this has always been about case number two, Zia's friendship with Uma Rothenstein and her affair with Uma's father. Keir was killed because of somebody's fear that Zia had told Keir a secret. But this secret wasn't about Joe, it's about something Zia had discovered at the Rothenstein house. There's something going on there—I'm still not sure what it is. But that's where we should have been looking. Among all us detectives, it was Georgie who has been on the right track all along!"

Jack was proud of his deductions and looked like he was going to preen.

"That's the problem," Howie said urgently. "Georgie has been on the right track all along. Which is why she's in danger. We need to stop talking and find Georgie, and do it now."

"I agree," said Jack. "Santo, there's no time to waste. Forget hotels and B & Bs. Go to the Rothenstein property. I think you'll find Jean-Claude has been living there. If he was going to take Georgie somewhere, that's my guess where she'd be. There's crime in progress, Santo, so please—you need to find her."

Santo stood up from the kitchen table. "Okay," he said. "I'm going."

"I'll come with you," said Howie.

Santo shook his head. "No, you won't Howie, you'd only be in the way. What you should do is go back to your office and wait to hear from me. For all you know, she's at the office now. Give me a call if she shows up. Meanwhile, try to relax for chrissake. You need to remember Georgie hasn't been gone long."

Relax?

*   *   *

The office was much too quiet without Georgie. For Howie there was a cold emptiness in the very walls. He paced by his desk with restless energy. Claire had stayed behind at the Wilders to help with Jack. Howie would pick her up later, but for now, he felt very much alone.

He hoped Santo had gotten over his doubts and was on the way to the Rothenstein property. It would be interesting to see if Santo took Jack with him. Howie gave it a fifty/fifty chance either way. Jack could be persuasive. Meanwhile, he had his phone ready, waiting for any word about Georgie.

As he paced, an idea came to him, a way he might find Georgie and learn more about her date.

Howie sat at his laptop and focused his thoughts.

First, he went through his photo files until he found a recent picture of Georgie that he liked. It had been taken at a picnic site along the Rio Grande. Georgie was standing sunburned but happy by the river. Howie copied the photograph, cropped it so it was just a headshot, and saved it on his desktop.

He brought up Buzzy's surveillance site on the dark web, hoping the two sets of passwords still worked.

They did.

The site opened on a screen that showed a very unhappy Joe Ochoa propped up on a hospital bed eating breakfast. Joe had been the last surveillance subject.

Howie found the edit page where he changed the subject to Georgina Hadley. Among people in New Mexico, she often introduced herself as Georgina Moon Deer, but Hadley was still her legal name, the one on her passport.

There was a section to fill in as many facts about Georgie as he knew—her height, weight, education, job experience, religion, and more—then clicked the search button optimistically. He hoped Georgie herself would pop into view, but she didn't. A note on the screen in flashing yellow letters said: SUBJECT WHEREABOUTS UNKNOWN.

That dashed the easiest route to Georgie, but he kept looking. There was a time delay option on the software. If he wanted, he could rewind 48 hours, which was more than Howie needed.

He decided to return to 8 o'clock last night.

The screen filled immediately with an image of Georgie walking through the narrow streets of the historic district toward the town Plaza. The camera was somewhere on a rooftop looking down on her. There were many more security camera in San Geronimo than Howie had imagined. The entire downtown was covered, as well as the parks and thoroughfares in and out of town.

Howie watched as Georgie walked purposely toward the El Morocco Café, past groups of tourists and people gathered outside restaurants. She was in the outdoor clothes she usually wore around the campfire, not dressed up. It seemed to Howie that she had a determined expression on her face.

She walked up the steps to the El Morocco and disappeared inside. The view switched to the restaurant lobby where Georgie spent a moment talking with the owner and then was taken by the owner's wife outside to the second-floor deck where there was seating.

At this point, the screen froze. A note appeared again in blinking yellow letters: ON HOLD. SUBJECT BEYOND AVAILABLE CAMERAS.

There was no camera to watch them eat dinner! That seemed almost incredible in this day and age. The second-floor terrace was a small oasis in modern America that was un-surveilled.

Howie set the replay forward at twice it's normal speed, moving quickly through the time Georgie and Jean-Claude were out of sight having dinner. Suddenly they appeared again, walking together from the terrace into the dining room and through the lobby. Howie set the speed back to normal.

Jean-Claude was a good-looking thirtysomething man with a fresh, youthful appearance. He had short hair and he was clean shaven. To Howie, he looked a lot like Gene Kelly in the classic film, *An American in Paris*. Grudgingly, he could see why his daughter would find him attractive.

He watched as Georgie and the man who called himself Jean-Claude left the restaurant and walked diagonally across the Plaza. They were laughing and she was holding his arm. Neither one of them looked entirely sober.

Howie sighed.

From the Plaza, Georgie and the man walked three blocks to the town's municipal parking lots. They got into a car Howie had never seen before, a gray Mercedes station wagon, and drove south out of town. Howie could have followed them if he wanted, but he believed he knew where they were going and he had other questions to pursue.

He backed up the tape until he was able to find a good shot of the man. He froze the tape, framed the man's face, and saved the portrait to his desktop.

Now came the hard part, discovering who this person was. Howie picked up his phone and called a number Buzzy had made him memorize when they said goodbye after his mother's funeral. It was a number Buzzy said would reach him, as he put it, "anytime, whenever, and whatever." Howie wished he had been paying better attention to Buzzy's implied warning of trouble to come.

The number rang three times and then was answered with nearly a minute of static filled silence. Then came four beeps and a sound that was like being inside a cosmic wind tunnel. Howie assumed this was Buzzy's sense of humor. He sensed he was being shuttled along a secure route, from one cyber place to another. Eventually a second phone rang.

Buzzy answered almost immediately. "Howie! How's it going?"

"Not well." Howie got immediately to the issue on his mind. "Georgie's missing and I'm worried about her. She's with a man who lied about his identity. I have a photograph of him and I'm hoping you can help me find out who he really is."

"Georgie's missing? Well, look, I'm not in a secure place right now, but tell me quickly what I can do."

"What do you mean, you're not in a secure place?"

"It's a long story, Howie—but actually, I'm having the time of my life. Here, say hello to Juanita!"

Buzzy wasn't alone. Life on the run seemed to be treating him well so far. A young woman with a sexy voice said, "Hi, Howie!"

"Buzzy, I'm sorry to interrupt. But look, if I text you the photo I have, can you run it through an ID search?"

"I can't use my old Agency program, but yeah, I have other ways. I can do it if you can get it to me fast. I have to be gone from where I am by dawn or they'll find me."

"What do you mean you have to leave? Who's going to find you?"

"It's okay, Howie. It's an alternate reality, that's all. It's like a video game."

"Buzzy, it's *not* a video game! This is real reality, okay? In case you don't know the difference."

"I understand, Howie. You're a little old-fashioned but you'll always be my Big Brother. Now, let me give you another number that you can use to send the photo. Put it on a text."

Howie took a few minutes to put the photo onto a text and send it to the number Buzzy gave him. It was an international number. Uruguay, Howie saw while he was waiting for a reply.

Gimme five minutes, Buzzy texted.

What the fuck are you doing in Uruguay? Howie texted back.

It's just a stop on the relay. I'm not actually there. Now gimme a minute.

Howie waited impatiently. Buzzy texted back less than five minutes later, but it seemed like a long time:

This was easy. You could probably have done it yourself. He's a cop, Interpol, the deputy director of Interpol's art fraud squad. His real name is Daniel Louis Fourier.

Howie was stunned.

Interpol!

Art fraud?

Howie decided he was physically unable to remain pacing in his office another second more. He locked up the building and drove quickly to the Rothenstein hacienda in the foothills south of town.

Chapter Twenty-Nine

For a large sloppy sort of girl, Uma was surprisingly athletic. Moving swiftly, she led the way to a trail that disappeared into the forest. There was a gray light in the east, first dawn. But beneath the trees, the forest floor was dark.

"Hurry!" Uma said. "We need to go faster, Georgie!"

"What's happening?" Georgie called. "Uma, wait up! Tell me!"

Uma stopped abruptly, blocking the trail. Even in the shadows, her face was dark.

"You're a stupid cunt, do you know that?" she said. "You have the hots for Jean-Claude, but you don't even know who he is!"

Georgie had no answer for this because it was true.

"So who is he?"

"Why should I tell you?" Uma taunted. "It doesn't matter anyway because he's dead. Daddy shot him."

Georgie felt as though she'd been punched in the stomach. When she saw Edward alone with his shotgun, she thought Jean-Claude was most likely dead. But it made it real to hear Uma say it out loud.

"Why did your father shoot him?"

"Because he came to ruin our lives. You don't know my father. He's violent."

"Did he kill Zia?"

"Who cares? He's a psycho, okay. Anyway, it's a long story. Now let's go quick. I know a place where we can hide."

***

Uma and Georgie ran steadily single file up the forest path. The trail was a narrow line of brown earth indented in the soft soil that snaked through an overgrown forest of fir and spruce and spongy ground cover. The upper branches of the trees closed off the sky. Chipmunks and birds skittered around in the dappled light of the high branches.

They passed through a sagging gate that had once kept cows in, or maybe out—the wood was rotten and it was a long time ago. From here the trail began to climb quickly toward the mountains.

"Uma, where the hell are we going?"

"You'll see!" she called back.

They gradually slowed from a jog to a walk as the trail climbed steeply out of the trees. After twenty minutes of hard climbing, they reached a clearing where a half-ruined log cabin sat on a rocky meadow. It looked at least a hundred years old, probably more, something a prospector might have built when New Mexico was a Territory. The roof and walls were standing, but the doors and windows were open to nature.

"Come inside," said Uma, walking into the structure.

Georgie hesitated. She wasn't sure the old cabin was safe.

Uma turned. "I'm not gay, you know! Just in case you've been wondering. If you think that's why I asked you here."

"Uma, I've never—"

"It doesn't matter. I don't like men either. I don't like anyone!"

"Uma, life can get better if you let it."

Georgie knew this was pure psycho-babble, which normally she despised. When it came to optimism, she couldn't think right now of anything to say that wasn't a cliché.

"Zia was a slut, you know. She played sex games with Daddy. 'Oh, Eduardo, would you like to draw me naked? Would you like me to take off my clothes?' That's what she called him—Eduardo, for chrissake.

Vomit! But he fell for her big time. Men are such fools for girls like that. Everything was fine before Zia showed up!"

"You were the one who brought Zia here," Georgie reminded her.

"Yes, I brought her here!" she admitted. "It's funny, I see it now. It wasn't just Daddy she wanted, it was her fantasy, it wasn't real."

"A fantasy of the art world?"

"It's bigger than that. Zia used to joke about it. She called it her imaginary life in Paris. She was very funny about it. We used to laugh hilariously making up raunchy stories of what we'd do in Paris the moment we were eighteen, all the men we'd fuck. Artists, mostly. Strong but unconventional men. That's back when we were friends. I didn't know then that she was stalking Daddy."

"Well, I don't know what to say about Zia and your father," Georgie said, deliberately neutral. "But please tell me the truth about Jean-Claude. Was there anything going on between him and Zia?"

Uma tittered. "Hey, I'll tell you the truth, now that we're talking intimate like this. Okay, I just said that to make you jealous. Zia couldn't care less about Jean-Claude. She barely looked at him. Anyway, they only saw each other a few times. There wasn't time for anything to develop."

"Why did you want to make me jealous?"

Uma's lips became tight and nasty. "Oh, I don't know. You're so pretty and smart and everybody likes you. Maybe I wanted to stick pins in you and make you cry!"

Georgie took a long breath and spoke softly. "I'm sorry, Uma. I really am. You should be happier than you are—you have so much, a famous father, a beautiful place to live. There are girls who would do anything to be in your place."

"Oh, vomit!" Uma repeated. It seemed to be her current mantra.

273

Georgie realized she wasn't doing very well with her go-for-it-girl pep talk. But she wanted to encourage the honesty she believed was developing between them.

"I don't understand how Zia ruined your lives?"

"Let's go inside and I'll tell you," said Uma, as she turned and walked inside what remained of the old cabin.

Georgie hesitated. She would have preferred to stay outside. Peering through the ruins of the front door, the interior looked dark and uninviting. The cabin stank of earth and musk and a dead rodent.

Uma was watching Georgie carefully from the shadows. Her eyes reflected the daylight outside which made them appear to glow.

"It's that painting, you know," Uma said. "That's what spoiled everything. Daddy shouldn't have done it."

"*America Girl*? You're talking about the painting of Zia?"

"*America Girl!*" she agreed caustically. "He gives it a fancy title making it seem like it's some great sociological statement. What bullshit! He just wanted to fuck her, that's all. But you see, that painting gave the whole show away. It should never have been painted. Would you like me to tell you an interesting story?" Uma asked. "A story about the past?"

"I'd like that," said Georgie. "In fact, it seems long overdue."

"Then come inside and sit with me."

Georgie knew that she was in a precarious situation. She was 70 percent certain Uma had killed Zia. Make that 60 percent, there were too many variables. She knew she should get away, she was physically stronger than Uma but she was curious to hear her story.

"Are we safe here?"

"For a while," said Uma. "A short while."

***

274

"Twenty-three years ago my parents were living the high life in Paris, but they were broke," Uma began as they sat down in a musty shadow inside the ruins of the cabin. "Stone broke. That's the first thing you need to know about this. They lived a grand bohemian lifestyle but they owed money everywhere. So they committed a crime in order to make the money they needed. What do you think of that?"

Georgie took a moment to answer. "It depends on what the crime is, I suppose. There are bad crimes and innocent ones."

"Edward and Catherine. That's always what I've called them, never Mom and Dad. This was years before I was born, but I've put the story together. They tried to hide it from me at first."

From where Georgie and Uma were sitting, they could see past the collapsed wall and doorway to a slice of the meadow, golden this time of year with weeds and wild grasses warming themselves in the morning sun, a curving hillside that fell to the forest below.

"Go on," Georgie urged gently (she hoped) after Uma had paused for an unusually long time.

"Edward was just getting a reputation, you see. The critics liked him, his sales were climbing, but the money wasn't enough for the way they lived. It was a very cultured crowd they partied with, but you had to keep up. Vacations on Ibiza, sailing to Tahiti on yachts, skiing in Argentina, that sort of thing. I'm sure it was fun—wish *I'd* been there! But it cost a lot of money. Catherine was the one who came up with the answer. She was always way smarter than my father. All they had to do was harness Edward's talent to paint a small number of forgeries. Three to be exact, but they were good. They pretended to be previously unknown canvases by Balthus, the French-Polish artist who had just died at the age of 92. Do you know who Balthus is?"

"Sure," said Georgie. The Balthus paintings Georgie had seen in museums were disturbing, erotic and dreamlike, especially his controversial paintings of pubescent girls, the Thérèse series. But he was a true original, not part of any school, a master, and his work stayed with you a long time. He was really good.

"It would be hard to fake a Balthus," Georgie suggested.

"Not for Edward. You see, Catherine knew Balthus personally. Twenty-three years ago my mother was a sexpot blonde and Balthus was a dirty old man. It's funny, really. Edward had always been in awe of Balthus as an artist and the people who were his friends—Cocteau, Picasso, Salvador Dali, André Gide, even Fellini. He wanted to be in with a high-end crowd like that. But it was my mother who got them an invitation to Rossinière, the Balthus chalet in Switzerland. I bet Catherine hoped he would ask her to model for him—but, ha! She was too old for him even then! But the old man took to Edward and they ended staying a week at the chalet. Edward spent a lot of that time with Balthus in his studio and he saw how he worked. There were dozens of canvases everywhere and Edward studied them intensely. After Balthus died, Catherine knew they could get away with a bit of fraud. When a famous artist dies, there's always a few new paintings that seem to pop up from nowhere. The three that Edward painted were supposed to be part of the Thérèse series that Balthus had been keeping secret because they were pornographic. They were bought for a lot of money by three different collectors, two in Texas and one in Berlin. Are you shocked?"

"Not really, Uma. If your father got away with three forgeries, I'd say it's a victimless crime—except for the suckers who bought a painting simply because of a name. So I don't understand how what happened years ago caused everything that's going on now."

Uma smiled smugly. It was a smile that sent chills down Georgie's spine.

"Yeah, you got it, forgery, who cares? Nothing's real anymore, everything's fake. But you see, they had to kill someone who found out. A carpenter who worked in Edward's studio making crates to transport the paintings, a kid. So now it's a murder they need to conceal. It raises the stakes, don't you think?"

What Georgie thought was that she should have made an exit from this encounter half an hour ago. She stood up intending to get away. But she couldn't help asking one last question.

"Why are you telling me this, Uma?"

"Because you're not leaving here," said a voice from just outside the building. "Pussy wants to play with you, that's all."

Georgie turned to find Uma's mother, Catherine, coming into the ruined cabin through the missing wall. She carried a rifle in her arms.

"Well, well, what fun!" said Catherine.

Chapter Thirty

Howie phoned Santo as he drove toward the Rothenstein estate. He put the call on speaker so he could use both hands on the wheel for the curves of the highway.

"Santo, I'm heading to the Rothenstein place. I think that's where Georgie is. Where are you?"

"We're about to leave. I got hung up with Jack insisting to come along, and me saying no, then saying yes. Have you ever tried saying no to Jack?"

Howie was surprised that Santo hadn't left yet. Even if they left right now, he would arrive at the estate at least fifteen minutes ahead of the police.

"Howie, wait for us at the head of the driveway," Santo said. "I want to feel this out before we barge in. I want us to be in step. You got that?"

"I do. Head of the driveway. Right, I'll try to wait for you there."

"Howie—"

"I got it. See you there. Gotta go. I need to listen to my map app."

"Map ass? What's he talking about?" said a voice in the background. Jack. Howie turned off his phone and kept driving.

It was a beautiful late-summer morning, with a crisp hint of fall, but Howie barely noticed. Once he was clear of town, he drove as fast as he dared. His map app guided him to a two-lane road five miles north of town that led into the foothills. It was an area, once wild, that in recent years had been carved out into twenty acre lots for increasingly expensive homes.

Howie had to put his Outback into second gear for the last climb up a narrow road to the Rothenstein property. At the end of the climb, he came to a plateau with a commanding view of desert to the west, mountains to the east.

"Your destination will be in fifty feet on your right," his phone announced, a woman's voice, congratulatory, as though they had accomplished something together.

He came to a closed gate at the head of a long driveway. Howie stopped by the gate and looked for a way to buzz the house. He could see a fancy complex of adobe buildings at the end of the long drive, the main house and several smaller structures that were gathered on three sides of a meadow.

He decided not to buzz the house after all, thinking he would just hike discreetly onto the property. He slipped through a sliver of space at the side of the gate and was climbing the driveway when he saw something move in the brush on the hillside below one of the smaller buildings. He thought at first it was an animal. It was low to the ground like an animal. But when it moved Howie saw it was a man. He was crawling with great effort toward a stand of fir trees at the far side of the clearing. He was obviously hurt.

Howie jogged up the hillside, climbing overland to the injured man. He was lying on his stomach by a chamisa bush where he appeared to have lost the will to continue any further. He appeared to be breathing. As gently as he could, Howie took the man's left shoulder and rolled him over onto his back. It was Georgie's date, Jean-Claude—whoever he was. He had multiple wounds on his face and right shoulder. He had been sprayed by buckshot and there was a good deal of blood, but he was alive.

Howie knelt on the ground. "Where's Georgie?" he demanded.

The man groaned but didn't answer.

"Tell me. Where's Georgie?" he repeated. "Tell me and I'll get an ambulance."

Jean-Claude rolled his head so that he could see Howie more easily. "They took her," he said.

"They took her where?"

"The woods. There are old mines back there. Old cabins. Fools looking for gold . . . long ago . . ."

Jean-Claude was drifting. Howie shook his good arm to keep his attention.

"Who shot you?"

Jean-Claude smiled as though it were all very sad.

"Was it Edward?"

But he was slipping further away.

"I'm a cop!" he said in barely a whisper. "Interpol."

"Right, I discovered that," Howie told him. "This has something to do with the *America Girl*, doesn't it? The painting?"

"*America Girl!*" repeated the French man, in a voice full of astonishment.

It was the last thing he ever said. Howie watched as he coughed, shivered, and died.

***

He didn't linger by the corpse. He phoned Santo as he was hiking upwards into the forest.

"Santo, where are you now?"

"Ten minutes away, Howie. Stay put."

"There's been a shoot-out here. The French guy is dead. Jean-Claude. I'm on my way to find Georgie."

"Howie, stay where you are!" Jack said loudly from the passenger seat.

"Can't wait," Howie told him.

He stuffed the phone into his pocket and continued up a faint path into the belly of the forest. Howie plunged upward, breathing hard. He had been pushing his body over the past week and he hurt all over, ankles, knees, and back.

It was midday but cool and shaded under the trees. Much of the forest was blocked by centuries of fallen lumber, but the trail itself was clear. There were a number of shoe prints that appeared to be recent. Howie saw at least two prints that looked like they could belong to a woman wearing the sort of hiking shoe that Georgie liked.

He ran until he came to the edge of a clearing, a meadow that was several hundred yards wide. On the far side of the meadow, a sheer granite cliff rose straight upward nearly a thousand feet. This was where the mountains began in earnest.

Howie stood at the edge of the trees watching, looking for movement. It took a few seconds before he saw the ruins of a log cabin on the lower side of the meadow. The fallen timbers of the cabin blended with the brown dry grass.

Movement caught his eye. There was a man on the meadow walking purposely through the tall grass toward the ruins. He was bareheaded, his hair was white. He was an old man but tall and athletic. It was Edward Rothenstein and he had a shotgun slung over his shoulder. He looked like a figure from a rustic 19th century painting. His back was to Howie.

"Catherine!" Edward shouted in a dramatic bellow. "Where the hell are you? I know you're there! Come on out and take your punishment, girl."

***

Georgie jumped at the sound of Edward's voice. She hadn't seen him coming up the meadow. She was on edge anyway, tense with fear that she was trying to control. She didn't want to let it show.

She was sitting in the shade of what remained of the roof. Catherine and Uma were across from her, Catherine with her rifle. Georgie wondered if she could overpower Catherine, get the rifle, and escape. But both mother and daughter were watching her closely. Uma kept giving her sly looks. Looks that said, *now you're in my power!*

"Catherine!" Edward shouted again from outside. "Come on out!"

"Asshole!" Catherine called back. "Come and get me!"

Edward circled the structure until he could see through the missing wall to the women inside. They in turn had a clear view of him.

"Well, what do you know—it's the whole damn cabal!" he said. "What the hell did you do, woman? Are you crazy?"

"If I'm crazy it's because I've lived with you for thirty years!" Catherine answered back.

She turned to Georgie but spoke loudly enough for Edward to hear.

"He's a forger—did Uma tell you? I was the one who introduced him to the old man. Balthasar Klossowski de Rola. Balthus. He was *my* conquest!"

"You just shook your cute little ass at him, that's all!" Edward said.

"At least I *had* a pretty little ass!"

"It was over twenty years ago, Catherine. And you weren't exactly innocent. When the old man died, you were the one who thought up the idea for the three paintings."

"You want to know how it unraveled?" Catherine turned toward Georgie. "The paintings wouldn't have passed if one of the big museums had taken a close look. But they were all in private hands. The fact that they were basically pornographic had increased their price, but it also meant the three owners needed to keep quiet about what they had."

"Woman, keep your mouth shut!"

"Oh, it's too late for that, don't you think?"

Georgie was getting increasingly nervous. Edward had slipped his shotgun from his shoulder and had it cradled in his arms. Catherine had her rifle across her lap, but she too looked ready to fire.

"But you see, here's the serious part," Catherine said to Georgie. "A kid caught on. He was nobody, only a guy whose job it was to make a wooden crate to ship one of the paintings to Texas. He was a carpenter, that's all. But I guess he knew something about art. What was his name, Eddie? Do you even remember?"

"Catherine, this is absurd!"

"He tried to put the bite on Eddie. Blackmail. But then . . . what a comedy! He vanished. Simply disappeared. Poof, he was gone! But *I* know what happened, don't I, Ready Eddie? You killed him."

"*I* did not kill that kid, Catherine," Edward said patiently. "*We* did it together, the two of us. You got him drunk, Catherine. I took it from there."

Catherine smiled knowingly at Georgie.

"It was the Berlin Balthus that was Eddie's undoing," she explained. "The fat-ass millionaire who bought the painting died and his widow tried to sell it. That's when everything unraveled. An expert from the Tate appeared. And soon afterwards, *voila*! We have ourselves the charming Jean-Claude Maurot who convinces Eddie that he's arranging a show at the Guggenheim. My God, Eddie believed it! He was flattered, weren't you, darling? Your silly little ego went through the roof and you didn't suspect he was a goddamn cop who was getting the goods on you. You pathetic idiot! Your career's fading and you thought this exhibit in Bilbao would bring you back!"

"That's not the way I looked at it, Catherine. I felt honored to be considered by a museum of that quality."

"Oh, bullshit! And then there's Zia. Sweet little Zia McFadden! The girlie. She knew too much. She knew all of Eddie's secrets. He was careless and the dear little pussycat had to be silenced. Didn't she, Eddie?"

"*I* didn't kill her!" Edward declared. "I loved that girl!"

"You've never loved anyone but yourself. You're a narcissistic pig, Eddie!"

Georgie wished they would talk more about Jean-Claude. Was he really a cop? Could that be possible?

Georgie turned to Uma, wondering how she was reacting to this drama between her mother and father. Uma had been sitting nearby just a few moments ago, but she was gone. The collapsed side of the cabin had a V-shaped opening to the meadow outside. Georgie thought she might have escaped here.

She had kept quiet up to know, hoping she wouldn't be noticed, but now despite the danger, a question tumbled out.

"If Edward loved Zia, why would he kill her?" she demanded of Catherine. "You were the one who hated that girl. *You* killed her, didn't you?"

Catherine smiled, almost sweetly. "Let's just say that little Zia got what she deserved. Girls who play with fire get burned."

"I was the one who did it!" said a voice, almost merrily, challenging anyone who didn't believe her. It was Uma. She was standing outside on the meadow behind Edward. "All it took was one small push!"

Georgie noticed two things at once. Catherine no longer had the rifle. Uma had it. It was pointed at Edward's back.

"Behind you!" Georgie shouted instinctively.

Edward jumped just as Uma fired. It was a close thing. The bullet missed Edward but Catherine had thrown herself to one side and ironically it put her directly in the line of fire. The bullet tore into her throat.

It happened so quickly it wasn't until later that Georgie was able to sort it out.

Uma stared in horror at what she'd done. Her eyes were literally bulging. "My God, I didn't . . . I didn't mean . . ." She was incoherent, beside herself. But she still had the rifle.

Georgie felt rather than saw a motion to the right of her vision. It was a figure rushing up behind Uma on the meadow.

She didn't recognize who it was at first. But then she saw. It was Howie! With amazement, she watched as Howie flung himself on Uma from behind, tackled her to the ground, and took her gun away. Howie was getting good at this.

Uma was now under control, but in the scuffle, both Georgie and her father lost sight of Edward for a moment too long.

With his crimes exposed, and his flashy life as a famous artist finished, Edward Rothenstein made his exit. He raised the shotgun barrel to his chin and pulled the trigger.

Chapter Thirty-One

Claire extended her stay in New Mexico an additional two weeks. It took nearly an entire day of telephoning her manager in Boston to arrange it. A concert in Amsterdam had to be cancelled which caused difficulties, but Claire was adamant that she had personal matters to attend to and would not change her mind.

The personal matter wouldn't have been easy to explain. Claire was feeling so happy she didn't want to leave. September was usually the most beautiful month in New Mexico, and this year was no exception. The aspen on Howie's land were turning gold and vivid shades of red. With the case wrapped up, he and Claire spent days on the land without ever going to town.

For Howie and Claire, the late summer idyll was filled with small things—weeding the vegetable garden, repairing an old fence, and making a wooden water wheel to set in the stream. Most of all, the days and nights were simply time to be together.

"I always hate leaving you," she told him. "It gets harder every year."

"Then why don't you stay?" he asked mildly.

"Oh, Howie, yes! I want to. And I know it's coming soon . . . but not yet," she added with some regret.

Howie smiled. Over the years he had become accustomed to seeing Claire come and go. He accepted that music came first for her. Her career, her art. There were times when he wished that wasn't so, but her passion for music was also what he loved about her. She was a shy but courageous woman. She went forth into the gladiator ring of the world, guided only by her faith in music and her innocence.

Georgie was inscrutable for many days after the violence on the Rothenstein property. She stayed in town at the office, ostensibly to give Claire and Howie time together, but Howie knew that Jean-Claude's death was hard for her and it was Georgie in fact who needed the time alone. She had spent only one night with Jean-Claude, but she had loved him. Briefly. Before she had found out he was Daniel Louis Fourier. It had come as a revelation that he was an Interpol detective, but if he had lived, she still would have never trusted him again.

Had he loved her? Or was she only an easy conquest? Georgie would never know.

She made a rule for herself: *From now on, watch out for fantasy men who are too good to be true! Ask yourself, is this real?*

Howie didn't know if Georgie was going to stay in New Mexico or return to Britain. He hoped she would stay but he didn't want to press her.

In the second week of September, only days before Claire was to leave, Charles McFadden invited them to a party to celebrate the contract he had just signed with "a major New York publisher" for a book he intended to call *The American Girl*. It was to be the story of his granddaughter, Zia.

For Howie, Zia was a subject to mourn, not celebrate. He was tempted to say no to the invitation. But Charlie became so emotional on the phone that it was difficult to refuse him. "I'm back!" he cried. "They're giving me a huge advance! I knew I could do it!"

"I'll try to stop by," Howie hedged.

"There'll be free eats and booze. And by the way, I have something to give you."

Howie's interest perked. He wondered if this something might be a check for the work he had done. A check would be welcome.

To his surprise, both Claire and Georgie wanted to come. They said it would be interesting. On the way to the party, Georgie turned the car radio to the local NPR station in time for the evening news. There was a new CIA scandal that had grabbed the headlines, a release of more than 7000 pages of classified documents to the *New York Times*. Only fragments had been released to the public so far but there were hints of secret prisons and assassinations, a host of embarrassing revelations. How the Times had got their hands on the documents was open to wide speculation, with accusations flying back and forth. The source was clearly someone with a high clearance but no one knew who it was.

Howie couldn't help the thin smile that came to his lips. He found Georgie studying him from the passenger seat.

"You're grinning, Da. It's Buzzy, isn't it?"

"I'd say there's a pretty good chance of it, wouldn't you?"

"I remember Buzzy as such a sweet kid!" said Claire from the back seat. She and Georgie alternated between the front or the back seats, each one politely insisting the other take the front.

"At least he didn't start World War Three," said Howie. "Yet."

The party was held at the house of a retired banker from Oklahoma, a pleasant man who was on the board of SWAG, the Southwest Writers and Artists Guild who were hosting the event.

Howie, Claire, and Georgie arrived at the party in the early evening when the western desert was ablaze with a spectacular sunset. The house was the usual faux-adobe that retired people with money bought when they moved to New Mexico. The appetizers were likewise generic: guacamole, chips, salsa, cocktail shrimp, a variety of cheese and crackers, and strange little canapés that were difficult to eat. The wine was mid-range but there was plenty of it, white and red, as well as bubbly water for the teetotalers (not many at a book party).

The crowd was polite and elderly. Howie, Georgie, and Claire were the only ones there under the age of sixty. Charlie was at the far end of the living room next to a table that had a display of his last book, published by a small press seven years ago, *Boho Goes Bananas*. He had a drink in his hand and it didn't look like it was his first.

"Moon Deer!" he cried loudly. "Come on over and get some booze, for chrissake!"

Claire didn't particularly like Charlie McFadden. He wasn't her kind of author. There was nothing poetic about him. She saw a friend of hers in the crowd, a woman who played the flute in the San Geronimo Chamber Music Society, and she and Georgie wandered off, leaving Howie to deal with McFadden on his own.

"Come on, let's get out of here, I need to talk to you," Charlie said as soon as Howie had a drink in hand. Howie had debated between the chardonnay and the cabernet sauvignon, but decided on beer. Wine somehow struck him as too literary.

Charlie led the way through a sliding glass door to a garden that was enclosed by an adobe wall.

Charlie lit a cigarette. It was the kind of house where you didn't dare smoke inside. "Okay, so give me the low down," he said. "Tell me what you found out."

"Didn't you get the written report I sent you last week? It's thorough. My assistant wrote it up."

"Your assistant?"

"My daughter."

"Well, yeah, I glanced at it. But it was kinda dry. I like a more blood and guts version. Besides, for the money you charge, I think I deserve a more personal accounting."

Howie shook his head. "For the money you're paying, Charlie, you're lucky to get anything."

"Okay, okay, Moon Deer. I get it. I didn't think you'd be so petty about money. Zia was my granddaughter, this is a very emotional matter for me. I came to you because I was crazy for answers and I thought you'd help!"

"I have helped, Charlie. And it hasn't been easy."

"So tell me, did Zia kill herself?"

"No, I'm sorry. She was pushed."

"Did that bastard Rothenstein do it?"

"No, it was Uma, his daughter. She broke down and confessed after her mother and father died."

"But why? How?"

"The how is the easy part. Zia phoned her that day to say she was confused and she needed to take a good long hike to clear her head. She invited Uma to join her. She said she had some questions she wanted to ask about Edward. At first, Uma said no. She certainly didn't want to answer questions about her father. But her mother convinced her to go, saying they needed to know what Zia was planning. Uma arrived separately at the trailhead, she followed Zia to the falls and gave her a push at the right moment. Then she scratched a short note into the side of the cliff to make it look like a suicide. Have you ever been to Eagle Falls?"

"No, I'm not into outdoorsy stuff. Pacing up and down my kitchen is all the exercise I get."

"The falls are spectacular," Howie told him. "But they're remote and you have to take a six mile hike to get there and back. It's a perfect place to give somebody a fatal push without anyone seeing you."

"But why? Zia and Uma were friends, weren't they?"

"Not really. Zia was beautiful, Uma large and plain. Her jealousy turned to hatred when Zia and her father began an affair. Edward liked young girls, and he fell hard for Zia."

"And that's why she killed her? Jealousy?"

"No, but that's why she agreed to do her mother's bidding."

Howie explained the Rothenstein family secret, the three forged Balthus paintings and the murder of a young carpenter who recognized a forgery and had been silenced.

Charlie shook his head. "Wow! What a trip! What gets me is how people take their dramas so seriously!"

"Well, they do," Howie assured him. "Most people take their dramas very seriously indeed. Edward was so besotted with Zia that he confessed his secret to her, the old crime. No fool like an old fool, as they say. He wanted to unburden himself so they would be as one."

"Obsession!" Charlie said thoughtfully, imagining intense Dostoevskian prose to describe Rothenstein's fixation with his granddaughter. It was a tough subject, but the sort on which a writer could make his mark.

"It was the painting of Zia, *America Girl*, that brought the house down," Howie continued. "The problem didn't have anything to do with the fact that an underage girl took her clothes off. It was the materials, the technique, the brush strokes—to an educated eye with specialized equipment, it showed that the artist who did *America Girl* also did the fake Balthus canvas that came to light in Berlin. It was the same style. Daniel Louis Fourier, the art expert at Interpol, had been investigating the Balthus forgery for well over a year and had been on to Rothenstein from the start. He had done his homework. He knew that Edward had spent time in the Balthus chalet in Switzerland and he came to New Mexico with a cover story to investigate the situation in person. The real Jean-Claude Maurot, who resides in Buenos Aires, had often worked with Interpol in connection with stolen antiques from the Middle East, and they asked him if he would mind if one of their agents assumed his identity for a short time.

"My guess is that Uma enjoyed pushing Zia to her death at Eagle Falls. But Catherine began to worry. Like a lot of amateurs who commit a murder, she didn't have any peace of mind afterwards, worrying about all the different ways she might get caught. For example, what if Zia had confided in her father?"

"Keir?"

"Keir did his best to take care of Zia when she came up here from Albuquerque, though I doubt if Zia confided anything about her affair. But Catherine didn't know that. You can obsess about these things if you've committed murder. You don't sleep at night. And if Zia confided in Keir, she might have confided in you. It doesn't seem likely, thinking about it. But Catherine couldn't be certain."

"Me? Zia never told me a thing about any of this!"

"I wonder why," Howie said, not bothering to keep the disapproval from his voice. "Maybe you never listened."

"Hey, I know I'm not always there for people. But you have to understand what it's like when you're an artist. You have to give everything to your work. You have to be selfish—it comes with the territory. At least I've never killed anyone!"

"Well, I won't keep you from your fans," said Howie. "That's the gist of it, anyway. If you want to know the details, and where the billable hours were spent, read the report. You said you had something to give me?"

Billable hours wasn't a phrase Howie often used but he was hoping a check might magically appear.

He followed Charlie inside the house and over to the table where copies of his memoir were arranged in stacks.

"For you," he said, handing Howie a copy of *Boho Goes Bananas*. "I thought you'd like to read about my early years and all the crazy things I did. Life was good back then, back when people read books and writers were hot. I tell you, Moon Deer, we had girls by the bus load! All we had to do was look profound."

Howie forced a smile.

***

Claire left on a cold rainy mid-September morning, a day full of gloom, to fly first to New York and then London.

They had done this before many times over many years, so they didn't make a big deal about saying goodbye. In the early days, Howie would have driven her to the airport but in recent visits she always rented an SUV that she needed to return in Albuquerque, so they parted in the parking area at the edge of his land.

"I'll be back soon," she whispered in his ear as they hugged. "I love you, Howie. So you'd better stay safe."

"You, too," he said.

They kissed, she got into her car, he watched her drive away.

He was left with an empty feeling deeper than the Grand Canyon.

He had Georgie with him, at least for now. They hadn't discussed her future but he had a feeling she might be leaving soon as well. It was lonely for Howie to imagine his home in the forest without Claire and Georgie.

Georgie had spent last night in town at the office. She said she planned to see a movie with a friend, but Howie knew she had wanted to give him and Claire a final evening by themselves.

After Howie watched Claire drive away, he drove himself into town, feeling at loose ends. He found Georgie in his office in the large rocking chair behind Jack's old desk. She looked bright and young and full of energy. Howie wished he felt that way himself, but he didn't.

He sensed that Georgie was about to deliver the news that she was leaving. He wondered where her next stop would be. Berlin, maybe. Lots of artists and intellectuals there, people her own age. Or some job with an organization like Doctors Without Borders in the Middle East. But not San Geronimo, New Mexico.

He sat down in the client chair opposite her.

"Claire got off all right?" she asked.

"She did," he answered.

"Don't look so glum, Da. She'll be back. She loves you."

"That's what she tells me. I only have to compete with Beethoven, Bach, and Brahms."

"You're very lucky to have her, Da. You know that, don't you?"

Howie sighed. "Yes, I do. And I can live without her for long stretches. I'm self-sufficient. She knows that. But I miss her."

Georgie gave her father a watchful look. "I can understand that. Claire's like a big sister to me and I love her, too. So we can sit here and mourn, if you like. But I thought we might discuss some business."

Here it comes, thought Howie. *She's going, going, gone.*

"Please, Georgie, say anything you like. I promise to listen."

"Well, I think I've found our next case," she continued. "I'm excited about it. It's an interesting situation where I think we can make a real difference."

He raised an eyebrow as he considered her words. It took a minute to fully absorb what she said. *Our next case.*

"It's something my yoga teacher told me about," she continued. "You remember Elke, don't you? Well, she knows a Mexican girl who lives in one of those trailer parks south of town. Most of the people who live there are undocumented so they don't have any recourse with the law. The man who runs the operation is a sleaze by the name of Carlos Montero. Do you know how much they charge for those run down trailers? A thousand dollars a month! Some of those places hardly have any plumbing! And if tenants can't come up with the money on the first of the month, Carlos gives them a few extra weeks in return for the women giving him sex. I say we get the goods on this guy and bust him!"

Howie nodded. "You're right, that's awful. But it would be a difficult situation to set right, Georgie. And we don't have a client."

"We can get statements from the women. Maybe we can even get recordings of Carlos telling girls he won't evict them if they give him sex. This man is disgusting, Da, and we can stop him!"

Howie continued to nod encouragingly. "Georgie, it's wonderful to see you concerned about injustice. I'm proud of you. But we don't have a client and without a client, not only do we not have any money, we don't have legal standing. It would take a good deal of money and time to take on a case like that."

"I bet I can get us a client," said Georgie. "I'll go to the trailer park and talk to these women. They'll be our client, the group of them. We'll fight on their behalf."

"Here's another problem, Georgie. You would need to be careful because a low-life sleaze like Carlos Montero might be a dangerous man to cross."

"Yes, but we can be dangerous too, can't we, Da?"

For a moment, Howie was taken back to the meadow outside the old log cabin, creeping up on Uma Rothenstein who held a rifle in her arms. The adrenalin of that moment was in him still.

"I don't feel very dangerous this morning," he told her. "Now here's the bottom line, I'm afraid. We just finished a case that turned out to be a freebee so now we need a paying client. This office is expensive to run."

"I know that, Da—I'm doing the books. But we can cut down our expenses in all sorts of ways. Do you know how much those bear claws and cappuccinos we have every morning are costing us? I figure we spend almost $100 a week just on that."

"That's true, Georgie. The Dos Flores Café has gotten expensive. But we need coffee to keep us going. I mean, without coffee our world might collapse."

"Da, I can make coffee for us. We don't have to go out for it. And those pastries aren't all that healthy. We can start our days with fruit and yogurt at a fraction of the price. Honestly, I've been thinking about this all morning. We can live simply on the land and hardly spend any money at all. I'll take over the cooking. We don't have to eat salmon and go out to expensive restaurants. I'll make us really good dinners like beans and succotash. We'll save tons of money and we'll be able to take on cases like these women in the trailer park. And Da, you could stand to lose a few pounds."

"Beans and succotash," Howie repeated without much enthusiasm.

"We'll fight for justice!" Georgie declared. "We'll take on slum landlords who demand sex from their tenants. We'll fight for the good!"

Howie took a good look at his daughter. He could barely contain his love for her. She glowed. Her idealism might not survive the test of reality. But she was a warrior.

"And you . . . you'll stay in San Geronimo?"

She laughed. "Of course, I'll stay! Every day with you is an adventure, Da. Will you help me get my New Mexico Private Investigator license?"

"Absolutely! I'll be glad to help. Will you learn to drive a car?"

"I suppose I'll have to," she agreed. "There's so much land here and sky. It's hard to see it all on a bicycle."

Moon Deer and Daughter! Howie's gloom lifted like fog burning off in the sun.

"I feel like we should open a bottle of champagne."

"Da, champagne's not really in the new plan."

"I understand," he told her, walking to the refrigerator in the wet bar where there happened to be a bottle of Moët & Chandon. "But in the spirit of moderation, let's begin tomorrow."

Champagne and a toast at the end of a difficult case was a tradition Jack had begun. Howie believed in tradition. Georgie accepted a glass.

"Here's to the old ways, new ways, and interesting times," he said, clinking glasses. "And to you, Georgie. But perhaps go easy on the succotash. It sounds awful."

"It is," she assured him.

Afterword

This is where I must add a disclaimer that this is a work of fiction and that any similarities to actual places, events, and people are entirely coincidental.

In particular, I want to note that the character Charlie McFadden is a composite of a number of authors I've known, starting with myself, not based on any actual person.

Charlie is a writer who had a movie made from his bestselling novel many years ago, but now has fallen on hard times. This is a subject I know well. My first novel, a coming-of-age story, was published when I was 23 years-old and made into an MGM movie, but three years later I was broke and I couldn't get anything published to save my life. I persevered, as writers must—as everyone must—and I was lucky enough to be given second and third chances. However I know what a difficult profession it is to be an author. Charlie is drawn from many writers I've known—fools, geniuses, drunks, saints, clowns, often just ordinary people. I've made fun of him a bit because writing fiction is like sailing the ocean without a compass and if you don't have a sense of humor you're lost.

In a similar vein, San Geronimo is a community I've made up, along with the surrounding geography. My intention was to create a kind of ultimate northern New Mexico tourist town that is a combination of a number of actual places. However, if you go looking for San Geronimo, you will find it only in these pages.

I would like to apologize to those who read the "coming soon" blurb for "Eagle Falls" at the end of Howie's preceding adventure, "Walking Rain." The novel you have read ended up being quite a different story than the one I presented before I began the actual writing. What can I say? I follow the story telling where it takes me—at least for the first draft. By the fifth and sixth drafts, I try to impose order, sense, and as much magic and suspense as my talent allows.

Last of all, I want to thank Kurt and Erica Mueller of Speaking Volumes, my wonderful publishers who have encouraged me, given me great freedom, and made these books possible.

About the Author

Robert Westbrook is the author of two critically acclaimed mystery series, including *Ancient Enemy,* nominated for a Shamus Award as the Best P.I. Novel of 2002, and *Intimate Lies,* a memoir detailing the relationship between his mother, Hollywood columnist Sheilah Graham and the author F. Scott Fitzgerald, published by HarperCollins in 1995. His first novel, *The Magic Garden of Stanley Sweetheart*, was made into an MGM movie. Robert lives with his wife, Gail, in northern New Mexico. Visit his website: www.robertwestbrook.com

Now Available!

ROBERT WESTBROOK'S
HOWARD MOON DEER MYSTERIES
BOOKS 1 – 9

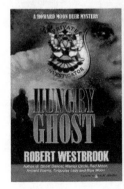  

For more information
visit: www.SpeakingVolumes.us

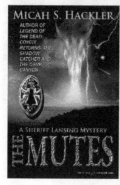

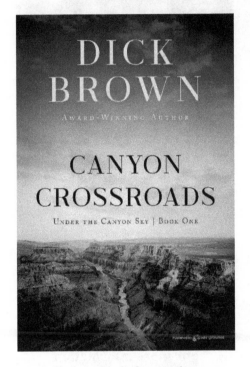

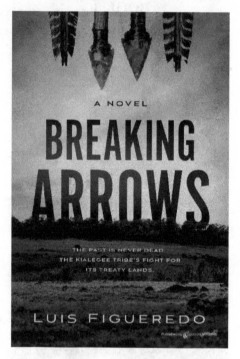